Until

I Don't

T.I. LOWE

Copyright © 2017 T.I. LOWE

All rights reserved.

ISBN-13: 978-1976478390

ISBN-10: 1976478391

DEDICATION

For A.G.

Thank you for sharing your story with me, and allowing me to rejoice in your healing.

OTHER BOOKS BY T.I. LOWE

Lulu's Café
Goodbyes & Second Chances
Bleu Streak Christmas
Bleu Streak Summer
Coming Home Again
Julia's Journey
A Discovery of Hope
The Reversal
Orange Blossom Café
Orange Blossom Bride
Life Unwritten
Until I Do

ACKNOWLEDGMENTS

Thank you to my Lowe, Stevens, and Healy Family for loving me and supporting this dream.

Christy Anderson, thanks so much for putting up with my medical questions. You always have great answers! Love ya!

My beta readers and my author sisters for keeping my ramblings in check.

Thanks Trina Cooke for helping me when I'm stumped on needing a new descriptive word. And thanks Jennifer Strickland for making me laugh when you offer lame ones!

Most importantly, my Heavenly Father for allowing this dream to come true in His time and in His way.

Chapter One

What have I gotten myself into? Again? Limits and boundaries really need to be set, but I'm not so sure on how those babies work. What was I thinking? Was I thinking at all?

"Are you sure we need to do this?" My voice shakes in anxious anticipation. Sweat dews my forehead and stings the corners of my eyes.

"Baby, I can't think of anything I'd rather be doing than having your lovely body in my arms." His exuberant voice presents close to my ear, causing my cheeks to warm further.

This is getting out of hand. I want to flee, but there's no clear path away from the hot water I've gotten myself into, again!

"I'm keeping my boots on," I sternly declare, trying to sound valiant and failing.

He chuckles boisterously. "They're quite sexy. I don't mind."

Oh sugar, as my sister would say. Ugh. Now's not the time to be thinking about her. Mia is going to kill me, if I somehow survive this. She's warned me enough over the years, but do I ever listen? *No*.

I'm way too close to the edge of oblivion. Cognizant of the mess I'm in, my wobbly legs try unsuccessfully to push a step back. This tough guy is not having it—his body an ironclad wall of immovability. I give that step another go, only to push into that resilient wall again. He has enough nerve to laugh at my fruitless attempts. Vulnerability taunts me, leaving me with no option but to submit to my fate.

"Enough now. Let's do this," he shouts, full of authority. His booming voice sends a shot of trepidation to the pit of my stomach and freezes my limbs. He's so close, I can smell his spicy aftershave. Not unpleasant, just uncomfortable. I'm not used to having a man in my personal space. There's no way to escape him or this frightening situation. I'm literally bound to him. Too many limits and boundaries are being blown to smithereens all at once.

My heart leaps up into my throat as I look around once more for a way out of this. Nothing. I can come up with nothing. The idea of this was thrilling at first when the challenge was thrown down. I'm such a sucker for challenges… But now… Now that I'm staring the dare in the face, I'm not so sure. Any appeal of it has vanished right along with my bravado. My inner coward is tsking at me in reprimand for this poor choice—*I told you so, but did you listen? NO!* One of these days I'm going to take a course on how to listen to her. Today it's too late, though. This time, I've allowed it to go too far.

"Stop overthinking it, Neena," the daredevil says with dark amusement lacing his tone. He's practically shouting his tease in my ear. Everything is so loud that the chaos pushes aggressively against me. I wish there was a volume control, but that's not plausible.

He's says I'm overthinking it. This guy I hardly know is practically reading my mind. Swallowing hard, I mumble, "Umm..."

"Just enjoy the ride, sweetheart. I got you... I'll take care of you." He offers these words for reassurance, but I'm not buying it. I should have thought twice about trusting him, but those saucy blue eyes did me in. I bet they are glittering in satisfaction, but I can't turn around to face them.

I feel his body, strong and sturdy, move against the back side of my own fragile and trembling body, and I can do nothing but allow him control. He pushes me forward with such force a scream breaks free from deep within me, but is suddenly stolen as the air is knocked forcefully out of me. The cessation of this nightmare is near, but not coming fast enough. Spots swim in my vision...

The next glimpse of clarity...

I'm soaring! The wind has swooped in and given me wings!

Finally, my lungs regain oxygen, allowing my screams to return. Quickly, screaming turns to triumphant shouting!

"Woohoo!"

"I told you!" Senior Airmen Hawkins yells. "You love it!"

"Yes," I shout back, not sure if he can even hear me above the raucous roar of the wind.

I cannot believe I just willingly jumped out of an airplane! Well, I'm not so sure about the willingly part, but so glad I did now that I'm flying!

Today's task was only supposed to involve me interviewing the parachute team responsible for rescuing three prisoners of war from Iraq. Today is the commemorative jump, celebrating the ten year anniversary of the rescue mission's success. No doubt, the interview was poignant, and I can't wait to share these heroes' story with the world. I can't even imagine soaring in with the cover of night and blindly searching until they invaded the highly guarded enemy camp. Their mission was to not leave empty-handed and they delivered not only the POWs but also two lethal terrorist leaders.

After wrapping the interview, the initial plan was for me to be amongst the spectators on the *ground* here at Shaw Air Force Base, witnessing the soldiers' jump. No part of the plan was for me to witness it in the *air*. Well, there's just something irresistible about a man in uniform... And those darn delicious blue eyes... There was no saying *no* to the handsome

Senior Airman Hawkins when he dared me to jump with them.

I'm tethered to said man at the moment, and if I splat on the ground, it's all on him. But for now, with the ground in faraway plots, I let go of my fears and allow the moment to fly! Arms reaching out to the clouds and the wind whipping through my quickly unraveling braid, I soar!

What a rush!

*****

"I'm going to kill you!" Mia shouts so loud, I have to move the phone away from my ear.

"How did you know it was me?" Might as well give playing dumb a go of it.

"Your wild brown hair and ever-present cowboy boots gave you away." She pauses, breathing heavily into the phone. I can just about bet she's running her hand through her own brown hair. Her hue holds an auburn hint that my lighter hue does not. I like to tease her about it being her feistiness coming out. "The parachute could have malfunctioned... You could have easily died!"

"Now, that's being just a tad dramatic, don't you think?" Tossing my bag in the passenger seat, I load up to begin the not-so-far trek back home to Tennessee. "I didn't splat on the ground. Hawkins took really good care of me." There's no stopping the grin pushing my cheeks way up with the picture of him flashing through my thoughts. Too bad I'm not into dating at the moment. He would definitely make the cut. I pull the paper out of my pocket and read it again. *I dare you to call me.* My new friend slipped that little message into my hand with his phone number scribbled underneath it before he sauntered off into the sunset. Well, it's midday, but the sunset bit seems more romantic than *he walked over to the airplane hangar.*

I switch my phone to Bluetooth mode just in time for my sister's voice to ring out in heavy annoyance through the speakers. I readjust the volume to low—finally a volume I can control. Looking up, my eyes land on my photographer, aka partner in crime, Parker Davidson. He's leaning against his Jeep a few cars down from me, shaking his head in appreciative disapproval. Parker has that boy-next-door kind of look about him—average, lean build with dark hair brushing just past his ears. His mysterious gray eyes are always observing, seeing more than he lets on. He loves an adventure as much as me. We make a pretty good team, even though he wants more than I'm inclined to give.

Parker witnessed the dare gauntlet being thrown down this morning. His refined northern inflection warned me to step away, but did I listen? Nope.

Let's be clear on the fact that I never listen.

I offer him a farewell wave before pulling out of the air force base visitor parking lot and into heavy traffic.

"I turned the webcam feed on just as you said, so I could watch the jump live. Never in that conversation did you mention I would be watching my little sister leap out of an airplane! Have you lost your mind? You could have at least warned me."

"It wasn't part of the original plan. It just sort of happened..." I don't dare say it was a dare. The lecture sure to follow would have her pointing out the fact that I am an award-winning thirty-four-year-old journalist. Not some silly teenage girl trying to impress the hot guy in my class.

I can't help the fact that the dare was presented by a gorgeous guy...

"Are you listening to me?" Mia's voice cuts into my wandering thoughts. Oh boy. She's close to releasing an all-out Mia hissy fit.

"Umm... I'm driving. It's a bit hard listening to you admonish me while I'm trying to concentrate on maneuvering through traffic. It's probably not wise to be on the phone. Downright dangerous really. You've clarified the point of me needing to be more mindful of safety. I'll take your advice into consideration and call you later."

"Neena Cameron—"

I hit the END button, silencing her protest. I'm sure Mia will hunt me down once I'm home to finish her lecture and possibly commit my murder. It's funny how we always tell someone that has done something to scare us, *I'm going to kill you.* Such a silly kneejerk response. Maybe she'll cool down some by then. Or not...

At the stoplight, I summon another contact in my phone through the Bluetooth connection. It's time for a detour ASAP.

His exuberant voice booms through the car sound system after just the first ring. "That was epic, Aunt Neena! Epic!"

"It was epic!" I laugh at Addison's enthusiasm. "How much longer are you and Kaisley in Cleveland?"

"Another two weeks and then it's back to school. Why?"

I guide the BMW to take the off-ramp for the interstate, while answering, "I'm on my way to you. I'd like to do a philanthropic piece about an outreach group for my website, and what better group to highlight than an organization from my home state."

"Liar." He scoffs.

"What?" I ask harshly.

Addison chuckles. "You're just dodging Momma. I talked to her right after the live coverage aired of your skydiving stunt. She's spittin' mad at you."

"Humph." I set the cruise control to not-speeding-too-much. "It won't hurt her to cool off a bit before I get home."

"Ha! You coward!"

"Since when do you talk to your elders this way, young man?" The sun is glaring, so I fish out my sunshades and slide them on to shield my eyes from the harshness.

He snorts like I made a joke. Maybe that's my fault. We pretty much grew up together with me being just over a decade older than him. Hard to believe he's a senior in college this year.

"Okay, okay. Forgive me of my rudeness, old lady. Do you plan on giving us a hand while you hide out here?" He's sounding more and more like his daddy—not sure if that's a good thing or not.

"Of course, I'll help."

"Great, but you can't get on a roof with cowboy boots. You'll slip off."

"Fine. I'll hunt down some sneakers before I get there, which should be before dark."

"Really? That fast?"

"Yes. I'm on the road as we speak, so set me up with someone to interview."

"Yes, ma'am. Love you."

A smile overtakes my face at my nephew's endearment. "I love you more. See ya." Ending the call, I crank up some Jeremy Camp tunes and roll on down the highway.

Chapter Two

A side trip to see my niece and nephew at the Outreach Camp in Cleveland turned out to be a great decision. Kaisley and Addison are just spectacular young adults. Mia and Bode have done an amazing job raising them. They could have spent their summer break from college like most and lazed around home. Not them. Nope. They dedicated themselves to be local missionaries for the summer. There's nothing lackadaisical about those two.

"You just breeze on wherever the wind blows you with no regards to your family, don't you," Mia mutters.

It seems a week hasn't been long enough for her to cool down.

"You and your silly sentences." I laugh, trying to

elicit one from her as well, but fail. "I missed the kids and wanted to spend some time with them. I even helped put on a new roof for this family going through a hard time and snagged a great interview for my website about the organization."

A snort sounds through the speakers of my car as I pass the gates of the community I live in. "Kaisley said the crew leader wouldn't stop flirting with you long enough to get much work done."

My own snort escapes at this. "Alex was just being hospitable and friendly. And I'll have you know we finished the roof a day early."

"Did you give him your number?"

"No!"

"Did he give you his?"

"Maybe." I make a right at the second stop sign while listening to her giggle. I'm antsy with being so close to home that I can barely sit still, so I let Mia tease. Just one more street…

"I miss you. Come over for supper."

"Umm…"

"I'll even try not to bring up the whole stupid jumping out of a plane stunt."

Laughing, I say, "Only if you promise."

"Done."

She's already said enough in the numerous texts and voice messages left on my phone, pointing out how irresponsible and dangerous and blah, blah, blah. Her husband's response to the stunt was much more engaging. I received one text from Bode—*I'm jealous. That was beyond awesome. Way to go, kid.* His big-brotherly encouragement still brings a smile to my face.

"Supper will be ready by six, but you can come on over whenever. I've got the day off. Love you."

"Okay. I need a shower first before heading that way. Love you too."

Ending the call, I finally turn onto my street. This is a fairly new community with plenty of young families. Its youthfulness always sends a satisfying calm over me after returning from a trip. I live for adventure, but there's truly no place like home to kick up your feet and unwind.

My normal calm skitters away as my eyes land on a huge gray Hummer occupying the normally empty spot beside mine. My stone-dressed townhouse shares a wall with another one. It's been vacant since I moved in just after the building was complete, but that looks to be over now. *A new neighbor… Hmm…*

Silencing the engine, I sit momentarily to scan for any sign of life next door. Nothing but the massive SUV points to anything being altered. Maybe someone just needed a park. Brushing off my curiosity, I climb out of the car and hear the familiar sound of a skateboard speeding in my direction.

"Yo, Neena. Looking hot as always."

"Hey, Finn. Not looking bad yourself." I share a grin with my way-too-young-for-me neighbor from down the street. He shoves his hand through his long red curls to push them away from his face. I offer one of the hair ties from around my wrist and he gladly uses it to draw all that hair up into a sloppy topknot.

"Thanks." Twisting the band one last time around the messy do, Finn grouches, "It's about time you got back."

Looking down the street at kids playing, I nod my head in agreement. "Feels good to be home. Hard to believe I've been gone for a month. How's your mom?"

The flirty glint in his eyes tamps down at the mention of his mom. "Much better. I'll be heading back to med school with no worries."

His mom had unexpected surgery at the beginning of the summer, so Finn cancelled the entirety of his summer plans to take care of her.

"You're such a meritorious guy to take care of your mom."

"A what?" He squints his light green eyes at me, causing me to giggle.

"Commendable, praiseworthy, admirable—"

"Oh, I gotcha." He shrugs my compliment off.

"Mom's taken good care of me all my twenty-two years of life. I think it's only fair to give her a summer." He grins, playing off his meritorious quality. "So... You finally got yourself a neighbor." He nods his head in the direction of the massive SUV hogging a good portion of our shared driveway.

We both regard it. "Did I?"

"Yep. Big ole dude, too. I wouldn't want to tangle with him."

It takes a good amount of effort to hold back the laughter wanting to bubble out over Finn's warning that sounds more like a challenge to me. "Okay. I'll keep my distance." *Probably not.*

"From him, yes. From me, no. You still owe me a date, remember?"

Shoot. I was hoping he had finally taken the hint and dropped the idea. "I said once you got older—"

"I am a whole year older now." He spreads his hands, beckoning me to take in his appearance as maybe a sign of maturity. All the view exposes is a tattered Imagine Dragons tour T-shirt and holey jeans.

Finn is adorable as all get-out, but too young. "Finn... I relinquished my date invite to Farah, remember?"

"She's cute, but too shy. I need adventure," he grumbles, sidling closer to me.

Popping the trunk, I dodge his advance by trying to wrestle my suitcase loose from the small space, but he beats me to it and settles the rolling end on the pavement.

"You can work with shy. That would be a challenge. And how cute does Finn and Farah sound together?"

"Maybe I'll go see her, since you are so bent and determined to keep breaking my heart." He fake-pouts, which causes him to look even more endearing.

I offer him a brief side hug, being mindful not to allow it to be too friendly, and turn to head to my door. He hops back on his skateboard and heads in the direction of Farah's house. Relief washes over me, because that little Casanova can be persistent. With *Mission Finn Brushoff* a success, I hurry up the steps to my home sweet home. Before opening my door, I regard the other door to the right, contemplating introducing myself to my new neighbor. A cursory glance down at my wrinkled shirt and coffee stained jeans forces that thought to dissolve quicker than it formed. Maybe after a shower and change of clothes.

Pushing through the door, the familiar, albeit slightly stale, scent of gardenias welcomes me home. It also reminds me that my place needs some life breathed back into it and forgo closing the door to allow some fresh air in.

My favorite feature of this home is my floor to ceiling chalkboard painted wall in the dining room. That paint has to be one of the best inventions. With no walls to obscure the first floor, my eyes easily seek out a glimpse of the beauty marking it—thousands of words I've unearthed over the years. The treasures now keep the wall company. Dropping the bags at the foot of the stairs, I'm compelled to go over and add a word. I select a piece of chalk from a small dish on the table and write the word *draconian* slowly. I'm in love with words—the stranger the better. My word today means severe and strict—not my favorite meaning due to my lack thereof, but the word itself is mysterious and intriguing. Draconian. It's also fun and dramatic to say.

"Draconian," I drawl out to the empty room while placing the chalk back into its rightful place.

Dusting my hands on my jeans, I study the letters dancing together to form a melody of language across the wall. Smiling warmly at them, I turn and head upstairs to take that much-needed shower. Toeing off my boots at the foot of the bed, I notice my phone vibrating in my pocket. I pull it out and see a few missed calls from my editor.

"I love ya, Theo, but you're just going to have to wait," I mumble out loud. Theo is chomping at the bit for my skydiving story, but he can hold his horses for a little while longer. This here girl has to take care of washing several weeks of travel off first.

I toss the phone on the inviting bed and bee-line to the comforts of my shower, which I missed immensely. That's one of the least appealing aspects of traveling—public facilities. Yuck! I like knowing with certainty that I am the only person to ever use this travertine dressed walk-in shower waiting before me now with the double showerheads. I purchased the house while it was being built, so I'm pretty sure...

After a long indulgent shower, I wander back downstairs. The warm August breeze has done its job of sweeping the scent of abandonment out of my home. When I move to close the door the roar of an engine coming to life catches my attention. Sitting in the Hummer is my new neighbor. The dark tint of the windows is stingy with offering me a clear view of him. His large form can barely be made out, but Finn was right. The guy looks like a giant with his head clearly reaching close to the ceiling.

I lift my hand to wave at him. His hand seems uncommitted to returning the gesture, only offering a slight rise of his fingers from the top of the steering wheel where they are resting. With that, he backs the Hummer out and disappears down the street.

"Humph!" It wouldn't have hurt him to step out and introduce himself. I reconsider the hasty thought. *Maybe he was in a hurry...*

Shrugging off his rudeness, I glance down and cringe. *Or maybe I'm the reason.* Who in their right mind would want to meet a lunatic standing by her door in only a T-shirt and her unmentionables? That reminds me of why I came downstairs sans pants in the first place... I think there are some clean jeans in the laundry room. Pushing my damp hair behind my ear, I close the door on my embarrassment and go on a search for some pants.

Supper at Mia's and then a good night's sleep are calling my name.

T.I. LOWE

Chapter Three

My elusive neighbor has been keeping a low profile and that's just not sitting well with me. I've given him well over a week to resurface, but my patience has run out. The only evidence that he actually may live here is the running shoes left by his front door. It's the only clue into who he is, and really, that tells me hardly anything except he sports a size twelve foot and may be into exercise. Yes, I got close enough to check the size. Don't judge. I'm an investigative reporter, so my profession is to blame, not my oddness.

It's time to put an end to the mystery of Mr. Neighbor, so I've brought in the welcome wagon, aka apple pie and ice cream, to help properly introduce myself. The warm aroma of cinnamon and nutmeg sends my mouth to watering. Swallowing down my hunger, I give the door a tentative knock. Mere seconds slide by before the door opens and the view turns impressive.

"Wow," I mutter. My inner voice scolds me on that not being very polite, but wow, just wow! I couldn't help the one syllable word from falling from my mouth when looking way up to this man who is just a few inches shy of giant status.

He runs his hand over his neatly trimmed blond hair and looks at me harshly with hazel eyes. "Wow?" His brute voice booms out, apparently reprimanding me for saying something vile. *I only said wow!*

I decide to overlook his sharp tone and offer my welcome gift like the polite lady I am. "I'm your neighbor, Neena Cameron. I brought you pie."

He regards the pie without taking it as though danger may be lurking in the crust. "Asher Reid," he replies while his brows furrow indecisively. The darker brows contrast his light hair in such an appealing way. "You made me pie?"

My eyes snap back to his and wave the crazy notion of *me* baking off with a flick of my wrist. "Heck no. My oven has a restraining order out against me. However, my sister Mia is in a good relationship with her oven, so she made it for me."

The guy doesn't even crack a hint of a smile at my

joke. I give up on receiving it and try shoving the pie into his hand. He finally accepts it. "It's still warm," he comments.

Oh, wow… That voice is so *warm* and even though there's an edge to his words they are surprisingly alluring…

He clears his throat, pulling me back out of my haze. The look those greenish-gray eyes are delivering undoubtedly conveys the fact that he thinks I'm looney. I won't deny their claim.

Snapping out of my gawking, I answer, "Yes, it's still warm and the ice cream is still cold." I hand over the half gallon of vanilla-slow-churn-gourmet something.

"Apple?" he asks, taking a sniff. He already knows the answer.

"We are nestled in the Tennessee Valley in the midst of apple season. Of course. I picked the apples at an orchard just out of town."

My neighbor of very little words looks none too impressed. All I get is a muttered, "Thanks."

He eases back from the door, so I take that as an invitation and step forward only to meet the door closing purposefully in my face.

What?

I stand my ground by his door for a few moments, thinking the possibility of him coming to some sense and sharing his pie may play out. Another minute passes before I throw my hands in the air in defeat. *It wouldn't have hurt him to share the pie.*

Shaking my head and grumbling out a few sentiments of disappointment under my breath, I go grab my keys and head back out. My sister will share the other pie she made, that is if Bode hasn't devoured all of it yet.

Fifteen minutes later, I'm pulling up to the cabin and wasting no time rushing inside while my stomach growls at me to hurry it up. I find Mia and Bode at the dining table doing exactly what I suspected—eating pie. A quick glance at the pie plate eases my fear.

"Thank goodness," I mutter, plopping down beside Bode. "What's up with the hair, dork? Are you growing a mop?" The temptation to ruffle his dark, shaggy hair is too much, so I reach over and do just that.

Bode swats my hand away and grunts. "You're NL Cameron, award-winning woman of many words, and that's the best insult you could articulate?" He rolls his eyes, unimpressed, before heading to the living room with his substantial plate of pie in tow.

"Don't pick on my husband," Mia sasses as she hands me a piece of pie along with a generous scoop of ice cream.

I scoff. "He looks like a scruffy mountain man." Not really, but I like to give him a hard time. I run my spoon through the steamy apple goodness and on to the ice cream. Delivering the perfect mixture of creamy cool and warm spice to my mouth, the moan slips out as I slowly chew. "Would it hurt him to get a haircut?" I tease some more before indulging in another bite.

Bode grunts from his spot on the couch. Years upon years, this man lived in a shroud of three-piece suits with a clean-shaven face and impeccably neat hair. It's hard to reconcile that man with the burly guy in the ever-present T-shirt and cargo pants who seems to have lost his razor and forgotten the way to the barbershop. His appearance may be different, but I've never seen him nor my sister more happy. And that's what truly matters.

"A sexy mountain man," Mia comments, earning her a smoldering grin from her *mountain man*.

There's no stopping the eye roll nor my dramatic gag. "Whatever. I'm not here to discuss dork's appearance. I just want more pie, please." I offer my sister a sweet smile that is rewarded with seconds.

"You just left here with an entire pie." She nabs a wayward apple and pops it in her mouth.

"I gave it to my new neighbor as a welcome gift. And the rude jerk took it and slammed the door in my face."

"Smart man," Bode says, putting his unwelcomed two cents in from the couch. I don't even know why he retreated to the living room just a few feet away if he's not going to leave me alone.

"Maybe he was busy," Mia offers. "Did you find anything out about him?"

"His name is Asher Reid and he's a giant."

"A giant?" she asks with a mouthful of crust she just swiped off my plate.

"Hey, get your own." I pull my plate out of her reach and take another generous bite. "He's pretty tall and quite built. If I had to guess his profession, it's a tossup between superhero and pro wrestler. There were no tattoos peeking from his T-shirt and he's beyond handsome, so I'm going with superhero. Although the cold-shoulder attitude is making it hard to be sure."

"You're a nut." Mia snickers.

The alarm goes off on my phone, ending fun pie time. I pull it out of my pocket and grimace at the screen as I silence it. "I've got to go." With the last bite shoved in my mouth, I scurry over to the sink and deposit my plate.

"Where are you off to?" Mia asks as she runs some water over the plate.

"I've got that award thing tonight." A text comes

in and of course it's Theo—*You better be there and don't wear those boots.* I glare at the screen, wishing for an escape from the evening ahead. I just want to compose meaningful stories, not receive accolades for them.

"Wait," she summons me to halt. "You're going to change, right?"

I look down at my outfit and then back up to her with drawn eyebrows. "I already did. It's brand-new, too."

"You're not delivering an acceptance speech in jeans and a white blouse. I don't care if they are new. Dad said he's wearing a tux." She gives me that mother hen look. Oh boy.

"So? He can wear whatever he deems fit." I shrug and start for the door, but she grabs hold of my elbow. Bode laughs from his perch while scanning through TV channels.

"So, that means you need to wear a dress."

Before I can protest, Mia starts dragging me upstairs to her bedroom. Bode's laughter bellows out louder from behind us. If there was something in arm's reach, I would throw it at him.

*****

My skin is itchy from the odd material of this

silver evening gown, and my feet scream in protest for the abuse they are having to endure in these outrageous stilettos Mia forced on me. But that's not my only problem. A sea of shiny evening gowns and crisp tuxedos nearly drown me as I push through the crowd. I'm wielding the award like a shield, but it's failing me. The opposite effect is occurring instead, with it acting as a beacon. People are propelling towards me with no end in sight.

"Amazing article on the heroism of our military, Miss Cameron," a gray-headed gentleman comments.

"Thank you, sir," I respond, but keep scooting through the throng of bodies.

"Mr. Cameron, you must be so proud of your daughter," another tuxedo says.

"I'm beyond proud." Dad gently squeezes me on the shoulder, making me pause.

Having Dad as my date doesn't help matters. The New York Times bestselling crime writer brings people our way by the masses.

"Mr. Cameron, your latest book kept me up all night. Wow, sir. I didn't see that twist coming," a younger tux praises.

Dad chuckles. "Then I did my job."

"You most certainly did." The young guy beams.

"And this young lady certainly is doing her job as well," a mature, comforting voice comments. I look over and find a familiar face joining our group. Wisdom glitters in the older lady's eyes. Ruth is my dad's agent. Although she's old as dirt, the woman knows her stuff.

"Ruth, my girl goes beyond the job. This piece on the Special Ops Force certainly shed some light on what our troops really sacrifice."

"You don't have to sell me on it, Richard. That's why she's carrying around that Journalist of the Year Award tonight." Ruth turns her attention towards me and points to the monstrosity in my arms. The weight of it pushes heavy guilt over me. I don't report to receive these things and it feels being awarded tonight diminishes the meaning of the story.

"Thank you." I smile, ready to conclude this and move on.

"Well done, young lady. My offer still stands when you're ready to pen a book." Ruth winks a wrinkly eye before shuffling off into the crowd.

"I didn't realize such extreme branches of the military exist," a dark-gray tuxedo comments.

"We're not supposed to know of their existence," another man replies.

"I think you maintained their confidentiality successfully while celebrating their sacrifice for this and other countries," a woman in black silk says. Her dress looks so much more comfortable than my prickly one.

I have to actively resist the urge to scratch my cleavage while I comment, "That was my goal. The only thing I wanted to expose was their sacrifice. Most of them live like Rambo Monks—no life, no wife, no friends. Total dedication to their job."

As we continue to work the room, my thoughts drift to a more curious place. Somewhere... well, *someone* of whose mystery I've not even scratched the surface. Ugh. Speaking of scratch—I give in and graze my nails aggressively across the skin of my chest while angling away from the crowd. My eyes glaze over with relief. With the itch satisfied for the time being, my thoughts drift back to that particular someone. I'd really like to investigate all things Asher Reid. The man has my interest piqued. I'm used to a man being more friendly, more chatty, more flirty. But the elusive guy seems to not want to be bothered by such formalities as socializing.

"What's next for the legendary NL Cameron?" a young lady in red sequins asks as she approaches us.

"My focus will be the rapidly growing problem of human trafficking in Uganda." The lump in my throat thickens as flashes from the research I've already been gathering slices through my mind. Swallowing it down, I force and fail a smile.

"That's very brave of you," she offers with me

shrugging it off. Those subjected heinously into enduring the cruelty are the brave ones.

Another tuxedo sidles up beside red sequins and says, "I cannot get over how you were able to get right in the middle of the action of a covert mission." He shakes his head with a combination of bafflement and awe.

"It wasn't part of the plan for me to be. It just sort of happened."

Dad snorts. "Neena's shenanigans are never planned. Did you see her recent skydiving stunt that just sort of happened?" His blue eyes sparkle in tease with the lines creasing deeper as he gives in and laughs.

Our little audience laughs at his poking fun at me as well. I don't join in. My emotions are close to getting the better of me, so I excuse myself claiming to need a moment in the ladies room, but head right out of the front door instead.

Once I'm in the car, I secure my chunk of metal in the passenger seat with the seatbelt. Gazing at it with a fragment of resentment, I peel the torture devices off my feet. Why do I feel so disappointed tonight? I can't help but think of those men properly known as ghosts. That elite group doesn't even wear any form of identification—no dog tags and not even tattoos are permitted—so if they are captured by the enemy, nothing is exposed. And if they ever are captured, their captain stoically informed me, they are never returned. They are super soldiers, committing years to special training and then going into missions that have no guarantee of returning them. Each time these men are handed orders, they bravely look martyrdom in the face as if to say, "Bring it on."

I tap the bronze plaque gleaming under the parking lot lights. "You should have been given to those men, not me."

What happened in Afghanistan will forever be a permanent part of my soul. I was brought in after the initial mission was complete and was supposed to interview soldiers on their daily lives, only all hades broke loose right before my eyes. One minute I'm sitting under a thicket of spindly trees with this guy called Barge, then the next thing I knew orders were being shouted and I was pulled into a bunker while the world sounded to be crashing down around me.

Images play in a looping reel as I stare blankly at the windshield—men running in one accord and then disappearing into military vehicles to take out the opposition, me being left in darkness for a little longer than a day, reemerging after the threat was taken out, men slumped on their cots to mourn the loss of the very guy I was interviewing...

Sniffing the sorrow back, I crank the car and ask it

to autopilot me home. Within twenty minutes, I've managed to collect myself back together. I pull into my familiar driveway with the unfamiliar Hummer taking up more than its fair share of space. Once the engine is silenced, I gather my discarded shoes and the fancy award and make my way up the porch. My foot lands on a creaky plank. As it moans out, Asher's door flies open with force, causing me to drop the heavy plaque on my bare foot in surprise.

"Ow!" The jolt of pain bursts from the top of my foot and races to the pit of my stomach. Hopping around in hopes of dancing the pain away, I grumble, "You scared me!"

"I heard a noise." With four words delivered from his deep dark voice, my focus is stolen from the pain and it recedes back a few notches to a more tolerable level. Never has the sound of someone's voice affected me in such a way that my brain turns to mush and my insides warm like melted honey.

How peculiar...

Annoyed, I plop down with the frilly dress gathering in disarray. If I were alone, the darn thing would be peeled off and in a heap on the floor by now, but I'm not. Instead, I ignore the itchy thing and try to inspect my foot, but it's hard to tell if it's going to fall off in the dark. I glance up and really wish the porchlight was on, and not so I could see my foot...

The faint light from his house shows off a glimpse of the fact that Asher is shirtless in only a pair of night pants. Oh my! He crouches down beside me and I'm immediately engulfed in the clean masculine scent surrounding him.

"I don't tolerate suspicious noises." His tone tells me that he doesn't tolerate much of anything.

"Good to know. I'll avoid that board from now on." I massage the throb away while trying not to sniff him. His bare chest is so close, I can feel the heat of his skin. He must sense my unruly thoughts, because he stands up in a flash and backs away.

"So you're okay?" he asks as he reestablishes his post by the door.

I stand up to test the achy foot and find it passable. "I'll survive—" Before I get the *ive* out of survive, Asher has disappeared back into his house with the door shutting firmly behind him.

How rude!

This man has just royally ticked me off. I limp over to his front window and tap it vigorously with my knuckles. The curtain pulls back instantly, producing the rude jerk.

"What?" he says loud enough so I can hear him through the windowpane.

I press my nose to it, causing him to lean away like my nearness is enough to repulse him. "I forgive you for scaring me and for not being a gentleman and helping this damsel in distress into my house." I motion towards myself, making it clear that I am the damsel in distress.

The cold look he offers to go along with my sarcasm expresses nothing but annoyance. The curtain floats back in place and then all of the lights downstairs blink off. Well, I guess he's done with this mostly one-sided conversation. Giving up, I blindly gather my belongings that are now scattered along the porch and limp inside my own dark home.

I'm over the challenge of Asher Reid. He can keep to his grumpy self for all I care.

An icepack and pint of chocolate gelato will help me feel better. Good thing I keep a stock of both in the freezer at all times for such emergencies. The word wall grabs hold of my attention before I make it to the fridge. Detouring, I hobble over and scribble *churlish* as homage to Asher Reid. Nothing describes that man better than a word meaning rude, funny how that was my word for the day. There's a deep drawl in his tone, making it evident he is in fact southern, so I know good and darn well his mother taught him some manners. Somewhere along the way, he clearly lost them.

Sticking my tongue out at the word, I toss the chalk back into the bowl and redirect back to my original path leading to the icepack and gelato.

Chapter Four

August snuck away and took a majority of September right along with it. The air is dressing in a crisper edge and the leaves are beginning to try on their fall colors. Outside in the thick of it is where any sane person living in these glorious mountains should be. I sure could think of something better to do than being cooped up inside than what I'm currently stuck doing.

"Wouldn't you rather we go grab a bite to eat? I'm starving." My stomach grumbles its agreement. I run my hand over it to try soothing the ache.

Mia has roped me into accompanying her to the gym again. Luckily, tonight the aerobics demon... I mean *instructor*, had an emergency and had to cancel the step class. Now I'm strolling casually along at a lazy three on the treadmill, while Mia is jogging at a speed of six with her dark ponytail swinging merrily along with her steady pace.

"You're the one to get me hooked on working out. Come on, bump it up a little." She reaches over without my permission and dials the speed up to a five. I compromise by only bumping it back down to a three.

The words are on the tip of my tongue to tempt my sister with her favorite take-out pizza, but are instantly forgotten when I notice Asher Reid sauntering in.

"Look! That guy is my new neighbor."

"That's Asher? Oh sugar. You weren't exaggerating. He is *hot*."

"Tell me about it, but there's nothing sweet about him. He's a freight train of *hot* masculinity until he opens his mouth. Certifiable jerk." I scowl over at him, even though his back is turned to me and doesn't catch it.

Or maybe he does because his shoulders stiffen all of a sudden. He angles so his back isn't to the room while waiting on the counter girl to retrieve him a towel. I notice she's chatting away and taking her sweet time, but he's paying her absolutely no attention. *You're wasting your time on that one, honey.*

The few brief moments I've seen him in the past

few weeks, he seems to take it as his personal mission to ignore me or bark a word or two in disdain. He has taken it personally for some reason that I never lock my door and sometimes leave it open altogether. I can't help it, I like fresh air. Last week, he tore into me about this little habit. Our porch has become the meeting place for these little disputes.

"Are you insane to just leave it open as a free-for-all?" That's the longest sentence he has muttered to me since we've met.

"We live in a gated community. *Hello!*" I tried brushing past him, but he kept on about it.

"You're delusional to believe a mere gate can protect you."

He stormed off after that. Maybe I am a bit naïve, but never has anything happened in my community since I moved in... Well, if you don't count the time I came home from a trip to find Finn on my couch. The poor guy was in need of a time-out after his dad passed away last year. Besides, I like the idea of people feeling like I am an open door—yes, pun intended.

Asher hasn't barked at me about the door any more, but I keep finding it inconveniently locked now. I should get me a cane and wave it at him in a threatening manner and demand him to stay away from *my* door!

Both of us girls stare in his direction as if picking up a towel from the desk is the most intriguing action ever performed by man. Simple black track pants and a sleeveless T-shirt have never looked so complicated and intimidating. The man has substantial guns and carries them with ease. With the ever-changing hue of his eyes and neatly cropped blond hair, he would make for one fine superhero. That is if he could learn the skill of smiling or at least smirking. That perfectly sculpted jaw of his seems to be molded in such a fashion as to not allow a kind facial expression.

"Have you found out if he's a superhero for sure?" Mia asks, seemingly reading my mind.

"No. Definitely not a superhero. However, with the clues I've unearthed, I'm leaning towards a military man."

"Yeah? How so?"

"Considering the fact that I've interviewed enough soldiers to pick up on similar mannerisms, he's pretty easy to peg as one. He keeps a precise schedule, constantly on guard with taking in his surroundings... Look at him now. The man is aware of everything going on in this room. Those eyes never settle long in one spot. I bet he already knows I'm here. And talking about his eyes, those babies are a mysterious shade of camouflage."

"How fitting."

"Yep. *Ooh.* Here he comes now."

"He walks like a soldier, too." Mia says with a slightly tilted head in his direction.

She's right. The man's posture is always ramrod straight and his steps are stealth and reminiscent of a predator.

The possible GI Joe walks past our line of treadmills, so I wave and say, "Hey, Asher."

His eyes meet mine briefly before sliding back away. He keeps to his path over to the free weights, acting like I didn't just speak to him.

"See what I mean? He's so rude." I let out an exasperated huff.

"Maybe he doesn't like to be bothered when he works out," Mia offers like it's her place to defend his actions. I'm half-tempted to reach over and bump her speed up even more.

"No. He's rude. I have evidence."

She chuckles. "Do tell."

"Take yesterday for example. My newspaper never arrived, so I *borrowed* his. I just wanted a quick glance at my article and had all intentions on returning it, but he came storming up the steps from a run and went to barking at me to stay away from his door and property. Really!"

"You got caught swiping his paper?" She laughs so hard, she finally has to slow her treadmill. Taking a few breaths, she continues, "He sounds like a private person who likes to keep his private space *private*."

My hand slams down on the STOP button. "Why are you defending him?"

"Don't get so tetchy. I'm just trying to be your sounding board."

"Well, you suck at it." I storm off the machine, trying not to think too deeply as to why I'm so upset. *This is just an excuse to get out of exercising... Yes, that's it!*

"Where are you going?" Mia calls out as I round the corner, closing in on freedom.

"Pizza and ice cream," I grouch out and work on doing just that.

By the time I arrive home with my piping-hot supreme pizza, night has settled in on a cool breeze. I toss the empty pint of caramel ice cream that was an appetizer on the way home into the outside garbage bin before settling into the rocking chair on my side of the porch. The heavenly aromas of tomato sauce and herbs release as I peel the lid back on the pizza box. *Oh yeah.*

I enjoy the first slice of cheesy goodness in peace, but nearly become queasy when the monster SUV barrels up beside my car. Too late to retreat inside, I sit my ground and refuse to let him intimidate me. I keep my eyes glued to the neighbor's house across the street while forcing a nonchalant bite. The sound of the driver's door shutting and then his deliberate steps onto the porch and then the sound of his house door unlocking and opening cause me to recoil with aggravation. Would it kill him to mutter *something*?

"Not even a hello?" I grumble, not realizing he caught it.

"I don't do chitchat," he says as the door closes behind him.

Well, I wanted him to mutter *something* and he delivered. Good grief. I gather my pizza box and call this day done.

*****

Two nights of restless sleep have accompanied me since the gym bust... I mean visit. Not even the pattering of rain last night quelled my irritation. I don't know why on earth this man is getting under my skin so severely. Never have I allowed one to do this before. Taking a sip of my coffee, I scan over my wall of words. *Asher* is now added to the bottom right-hand corner—tucked there in the sea of unique words. How bizarre is it that the man's name actually means *happy one*. Yep, that is odd enough to be included on my wall.

The buzzing of my phone pulls me out of my

stupor. Glancing down, I read—*Need you in the office today*. I text Theo back—*That's my plan*. My office is located downtown and I stick to the routine of popping in at least once or twice a week. Mostly, I freelance my articles across the nation to numerous affiliates, but Theo gave me my first break in journalism and I believe in loyalty. He'd took my under his wing before I completed college and showed me the ropes at the local paper. Even with my history of illness, he took a chance on me. Fresh in remission from cancer doesn't normally produce much stability, but Theo overlooked it. For that, I'm thankful and that's why he is still my editor/boss.

A quick glance out of the window finds the clouds are still lingering, but the rain has alleviated to just a fine mist. I grab the umbrella to be on the safe side, along with my computer bag and travel mug of coffee. The juggling act while fishing my keys out is unsuccessful, and I lose the umbrella and keys to the ground by my car. After retrieving them, I absently climb in the car and come undone from finding a massive man crammed in the reclined passenger seat.

A scream rips from me, causing a sleeping bear to awaken on a gasp. Asher Reid's eyes shoot open as he bangs his head on the ceiling of my car.

"What are you doing?" I ask on a gasp.

He rubs his head while trying to unfold himself

out the car. The show would probably be comical if I wasn't so shocked. I climb back out as well and watch him over the top of the car.

"I locked my phone and keys in the Hummer last night," he groans out while stretching. He's wearing a black chef's jacket, something I've not seen him in before.

"Are you a chef?"

He straightens his coat and adjusts his pants. "My restaurant opened last night. Guess too much excitement caused me to not pay attention when I got home. I'd have slept on the porch, but the rain was coming in sideways." He points to my car. "Since you never lock anything…"

"You could have knocked last night." I motion to my door, noticing I didn't get it shut all the way.

Asher eyes it with clear irritation. "I um… I really need to use your bathroom." He adjusts his pants uncomfortably again.

"Sure." Before I say anything else, he takes off in a clipped pace, so I follow behind him. "It's probably a mirror set-up of your home. Guest bathroom is just off to the right," I call behind him as he disappears. I cringe with thinking how long he may have been holding it, and me screaming probably didn't help matters.

I head over to the coffee pot, where some is left in

the pot, and retrieve the last cup for him. He reappears moments later and actually accepts the mug when I hold it out to him.

"Strong and black. It's the only way I serve coffee. Hope that's okay?"

"Took you for one of those froufrou coffee chicks who only drink lattes," he mumbles before taking a sip. A raspy moan escapes him in approval.

A smile eases over my lips with hearing such a rugged guy use a word like *froufrou*. He strung together thirteen words as well—a new conversation record for us.

I bat his notion off with the flick of my wrist. "Latte is not real coffee." My eyes ease over to the clock, knowing Theo is expecting me. Looking back at Asher, I regard his chef's coat again. "I didn't realize you were a chef. And did you say you have a restaurant?" How would I realize, really? He shares nothing of himself.

"We opened last night." That's all he offers and it only tempts me to question him more, but time won't allow it right now.

"Do you need to use my phone?" I motion towards the landline sitting in the dock on the counter.

He nods as if just realizing that's something he needs to do. I think he needs some more sleep, no matter how attractive he is all rumpled.

"Please," his groggy voice rings out. He seems to fill the entire space with the robust timbre of that one word.

"Okay. Just make yourself at home." I regather my stuff and head for the door.

"No. Wait. I'll wait outside."

"You may need the bathroom before you get into your house." I nod to the coffee cup.

Running his free hand through his slightly disheveled blond locks, he regards the cup in his hand. "Good point. You sure?"

"Absolutely. Mi casa es su casa." With no more time left to chitchat, no matter how badly I want to do just that, I leave the very private, but slowly opening up, neighbor in mi casa and head to work.

The day meanders on by with Theo going over a few article prospects and discussing some edits I disagree with completely. Ultimately, I win that small battle. Parker joins us somewhere along the way to discuss a few ideas of his own. And then sometime in there, we end up in the conference room with a few other staff members. All the while, my mind keeps skipping back to Asher. Never has someone intrigued me as this man has. Could it be the elusive bit drawing my curiosity? Probably. It does present a tempting challenge.

"Earth to Neena." Parker shoves into my shoulder with his own.

I look over to see him watching me. Glancing around the small conference table, more eyes are trained on me.

"What?"

"How's the investigation going with Uganda?" Theo asks.

"Oh..." I shuffle through a few papers in front of me, seeing nothing in particular. "I'm still gathering leads on a few sources. This one is proving to be tricky."

"Maybe it's a sign you need to stay out of this one," Theo says protectively.

My back automatically straightens in defiance. "The only sign is that this is going to be a challenge I'm prepared to face."

"I won't allow you going in blind." Theo crosses his arms. A faint blush is barely noticeable on his dark skin. His daddy instincts are clearly on display.

"Theo, you know I won't let anything happen to our girl." Parker rests his arm around my shoulder, staking a claim to which he has no right.

I wiggle his arm loose and defiantly scoot my chair farther away. "I'm a *grown* girl and can take care of myself."

"We'll discuss it further once you collect some

more information." Theo shuts the conversation down and moves to less pressing topics until I accompany him back to his office.

After a few hours of Theo tapping an impatient fist to his desk, he gives up on grasping my attention and frees me from the office around four. I head straight home and discover Asher's SUV gone, which is evidence he procured his keys. I go to shove my door open, but only bang my shoulder when it doesn't budge. Of course, he locked it. Holding my frustration in check, I fish out my keys and free the lock. The first thing to catch my attention is the sparkly clean kitchen with the over-filled garbage bag missing. The next thing I notice is the sleek black business card placed by a sheet of paper that holds five precisely handwritten words—all blocked and bold.

THANKS. DINNER IS ON ME.

"Humph." I pick up the business card for I'm guessing his restaurant. Charlie Mike is in a gray masculine font. I know that from somewhere, but can't place it. Intrigued, I type it in the search engine on my phone. As soon as the meaning pops up, it resurfaces in my memory as well; leaving no doubt that Asher Reid is a GI Joe. Charlie Mike is a military code meaning *complete the mission*. Goose bumps rush along my skin with the realization that the mystery of this man goes very deep and my instincts are insistent for me to solve it.

"What mission are you completing, Asher?" I ask out loud while gathering my bag to go find out... Probably not, but I am hungry. At least that could be solved and quite possibly some snooping.

I head out to the address printed on the card, which leads me to the upper class section of town. As soon as the valet takes my keys I'm rethinking my choice of not changing first. A cursory glance at my blouse and jeans finds no stains. I try smoothing a few sneaky wrinkles as I head through the heavy metal door of Charlie Mike. The newness of excitement is evident with the waiting lounge overflowing with chatty patrons. The place has an industrial vibe with polished concrete floors and dark wood accented with metal work. Very masculine.

A friendly hostess beckons me to the hostess stand with a welcoming smile. My attention is quickly snatched by the stand she's leaning against. It's made from a hefty wood with metal rivets securing each side. The most enthralling feature to the stand is the five medallions dressing the top edge, each representing a branch in the military. I run my fingers over each in reverent awe—Army, Navy, Marine Corps, Coast Guard, and Air Force. I glance around and take in more subtle hints of the military signets almost hidden throughout the restaurant. What I would give to have free reign to unearth each concealed treasure. Whoever decorated this place really did a tasteful job.

"Do you have a reservation?" the chipper young lady asks, bringing my focus back to her.

"I may... My name is Neena Cameron."

She looks at me curiously before scanning her thin computer screen. A few seconds pass before a smile relights her face. "Ah yes. Mr. Reid has you listed as his special guest for this evening. Would you prefer a table on the patio or inside?"

With the packed-out house, I'm surprised I even have a choice. Thinking some fresh air would be nice after spending the day cooped up in the office, the patio sounds most appealing. "Patio, please."

With no hesitation, the hostess retrieves a menu and escorts me outside. The patio was most definitely the correct choice. The wood-planked deck is under a canopy of maple and oak trees and overlooks the river. The sound of the water gliding by is an instant salve and my shoulders relax on their own accord. I'm seated at one of the only two available tables. Looking around, I take in the people chattering away while contently eating and make note to bring Mia back sometime soon.

Moments after the hostess seats me, a waiter

scurries out with a frosty glass of iced water and a basket of mini cheese biscuits.

"Good evening, Miss Cameron. I'm Richie and I'll be serving you tonight."

"Nice to meet you." I smile warmly at the young guy.

"Chef Reid sends his regards. As you can tell, we're quite busy tonight, but he said to indulge in your choice of fare on the house."

I pop a warm biscuit in my mouth and moan as the flaky treat practically melts. You just can't go wrong with butter, cheese, and garlic. "I could make a meal off of these babies." I point to the basket, eliciting a laugh from Richie. "Just keep them coming."

"Yes, ma'am. Me too, but I would recommend sampling more than that."

"What do you recommend?"

"All of it." He nods confidently.

"You've not tried everything on this menu." I scoff, finally opening the leather folder to take a peek at the bounty of selections.

"Actually, all of the employees have sampled everything the restaurant serves. The chef and his team treated us last week to a feast before the soft opening. He wanted us to know what we were serving."

"I'm impressed. Tell me what was the first thing you reordered since the feast." This should give me a better reference as to what to order myself.

"The SOS. It's outrageously good." He laughs when my nose wrinkles in disagreement.

"Honey, I've had the distinct *privilege* of sampling that dish at a military base just last year. No thanks." I shake my head and begin looking over the menu for a better choice.

"The chef took the traditional dried chipped beef in thick white gravy and turned it on its head."

I shake my head again, still not sold on it. The dish I had was way too thick and salty. "No thanks."

"Seriously. Ours is made with sirloin tips, baby portabella mushrooms, rosemary, and a light garlic cream sauce. It's also served over thick slices of toasted sourdough bread." He swipes my menu before I can make a selection.

"Hey," I scold.

"SOS it is. You'll thank me," he says over his shoulder as he hurries off.

And boy do I ever. I practically lick my plate clean. I'm in love with Asher's SOS! The tender meat was like butter and the sauce was surprisingly light. Halfway through the meal, I stop shoveling the scrumptious fare in long enough to shoot a text to my food critic friend, advising him to check this place out. He actually texts back that it's already on his list. I guess being gone months at a time lately have put me in the dark about the local happenings. Either way, I'm glad Luka will be coming around to spotlight this superb restaurant.

The waiter hands over a warm apple crisp served in a mini cast iron skillet for dessert, with the comment that the chef especially prepared it for me. The apple reference didn't get past me either. By the time the caramelized goodness is scraped clean, I can hardly breathe from being so full. This is the best meal I've had in ages, by far. Asher Reid may not be on my friendliest list, but he most certainly blows every restaurant out of the water with his culinary skills.

If I could just get him to work on those social skills...

Chapter Five

Sleeping in my car and the kind gesture of treating me to a meal did little in regards to warming Asher Reid up to a friendship. That sucker has been avoiding me even more now and is back to his "I don't" phrases. Never have I heard someone use that negative phrase so much in all my life.
Would you like to join me for coffee?
I don't care to.
Have you met our neighbor, Finn?
I don't socialize.
Would you like to share my leftover pizza and watch the game?
I don't do leftovers.
Hands thrown up in the air in defeat, I've given up. The man is a *don't* downer.
Brushing that frustration off, I try to take a few calming breaths as I drive through my neighborhood after work.

I overdid some article bookings and the deadlines all landed on today, so Theo and I worked on edits until both our sets of eyes crossed. This day has worn me out so badly I *don't* even notice Asher getting out of his vehicle at the same time as me tonight. We meet up on the porch, but I *don't* bother with any form of greeting. Ugh, his *don't* habit is rubbing off on me.

As he brushes past me, I can't help but greedily inhale the succulent scent he's wearing.

He stiffens and glowers down at me. "Did you just smell me?"

My shoulders lift in a defensive shrug as my stomach lets out a mean gurgle. "I can't help it. You smell like a five star meal and I'm starving. I've been too busy at work to eat today."

He huffs and actually *asks* a question. "What kind of job doesn't allow you time to eat?"

"I'm a journalist with too many deadlines this week, which equates to very little food and sleep until it's done."

Asher shoves his door open and I think my tired eyes are playing tricks on me, because I could have sworn he just motioned me to follow him. I blink away the curious idea and feel my exhausted body sway.

"Come on. I'll cook you something."

Now my ears have gone on the fritz. "What?" I mumble, confused.

He seems to be losing his patience when his hand meets the small of my back and not-so-gently ushers me inside his house. As I suspected, it is a mirror setup from mine—open space, kitchen off to the left back and dining room beside it with the living room upfront. But there are some opposites of our spaces. His walls are neutral beige with hardly any wall art, where mine are a vibrant shade of plum with the lively word wall. My space is a bit messy with papers and books precariously strewn about where his is incredibly orderly and spotless.

Taking in as much as possible, I follow him to the kitchen where he points at a leather bar stool. He leaves me there and heads to the fridge. As if he were a magician, Asher makes a shrimp stir fry quickly appear before me in no time. I'm in awe of his skills and actually keep my mouth shut for a change, which I'm sure he appreciates.

This GI Joe/Master Chef presents the steaming dish and it looks like delicious art—plump pink shrimp surrounded by a medley of vibrantly colored veggies. With my mouth watering severely and my stomach growling, I tuck into the meal like a starved woman. A touch of warm spice and a note of citrus awaken my taste buds, causing them to do a happy dance. All I can do is shovel it in and embarrassingly moan. I catch myself mid-moan and look up to find Asher watching me with his unreadable expression firmly holding his features in check.

"This is amazing," I compliment, earning a grunt from him. I'm just noticing he doesn't have a plate of his own. "You're not eating?"

"Already ate at the restaurant."

"How on earth can you be this excellent of a chef and not be as big as the side of the house?" I hold my arms out motioning at my gut region. The man is big in muscular stature, but there is no fat to be found.

"Regular gym visits, so it all works out in the wash," he says as he unbuttons his chef coat. He tosses it on the counter before turning towards the fridge, giving me an unobscured view of his wide shoulders stretching the plain white tee to its limits and on down to his nicely formed backside in a pair of low-riding jeans.

My eyes are fixated on his rear like it's my mission to inspect when a growl sounds from the giant. Looking up I find the grouch is donning his other expression—the glare—over his shoulder.

"Do you mind?" He snaps this out like me checking him out is repulsive.

Do I mind? Yes. Yes I do.

I demand my unwilling self to drop the fork and then force my legs to make a swift exit.

As I reach the door, he barks out, "You didn't finish your food. I'd rather you not waste it."

That sharp tone is just too much tonight. I've reached my limit and glare right back. "And I'd rather you not be such a jerk all the time, but I'm guessing neither one of us is going to be getting what we want."

With that, I make my exit and dramatically slam his door and follow suit with my own door once I enter through it. Stomping to the fridge for a bottle of water, I'm quite surprised when I hear my door bang open. I whirl around as Mr. Grouch storms in with the plate of food. He deposits it on my counter and heads right back out, but not before he takes a second to flip the lock on the doorknob. I stomp over and finish the job and click the deadbolt into place as well.

Turning my attention back to the plate, I grab it up and escort it to the garbage bin. But before I can toss it, my hand betrays me by picking up the fork and delivering another shrimp to my mouth. Yes, I eat the blame food, and I'm mad as fire about it, too. That man makes my blood boil!

*****

Repentance for my inappropriate anger and *thoughts*—if I'm going to be honest—about my frustratingly handsome neighbor is overdue. Rising early this morning, I forgo jeans and put on a lace dress along with my boots for services. This here girl is in dire need of some church time. After taking the time to plait my hair in a loose side-braid, I call the primping complete, gather my Bible and head out to properly welcome this fine fall Sunday.

The devil must have the same plans as me, because I'll be darned if he hasn't delivered Asher coming up the steps from a run at the exact same time I'm about to go down them. My eyes commence to sinning right away without my permission as they peruse his well-defined calves and thick thighs on full display with the help of his running shorts.

I snap out of the ogling before he calls me out on it. And it's been duly noted he will. Never one to suppress my manners, no matter if they are forced, I graciously say, "Good morning, Asher."

He stops to stretch his nice long, lean legs. "Morning."

Oh boy. And there goes that deep voice playing crazy with me. It's such a deep, authoritative timbre. It deliberately beckons a response right out of my body—stomach fluttering and eyes glazing.

Get behind me, SATAN!

I glance over my shoulder, but I'm not sure if that devil listened. My mind says get the lead out, but my legs refuse to budge. Before I can pull it together that voice summons me.

"A dress?"

Blinking out of my haze, I notice Asher studying my outfit. "I like to wear a dress to church." I smooth my hand over the soft lace

His eyebrow rises slightly, indicating a change in expression—intrigued or impressed maybe? He straightens from the stretch and leans against the porch post, looking like he may stay a while. Really?

"What church?" Oh, so that is his *curious* look.

"Valley Church," I answer, adjusting my Bible and bag to my other arm.

He balks... I think. "One of those new age social gatherings pretending to be church?"

"Not even close. People are so hung up on labels these days, so our church decided not to have one. No titles so all will feel welcome. We may be considered nondenominational, but doubt it none that we are all about our Father's business." I tick a list off on my fingers. "Teaching the Bible front to back, explaining what Jesus did so we could all be free, loving and ministering to people, and praising our Savior."

Asher throws his hands up at my onslaught. "Didn't mean to offend you."

"You joke around about my church and I'll be taking offense." A few seconds of quiet pass between us before I ask, "What about you? What church do you attend?"

"I was raised in a Baptist church, but I haven't had a home church in a long time. Just popping into places, but nothing has fit."

"You're welcome to come join Valley."

He motions to his sweat-clad outfit—exactly what I don't need my attention drawn towards. "Maybe another time."

"Worship service doesn't start for another hour. You have plenty of time to get ready."

His eyebrow moves back up again. "Why are you going so early then?"

I glance at my nonexistent watch. "They hold a dating game for all of the singles before church. They serve cookies, too."

I watch that eyebrow elevate a little farther up.

"I'm just kidding." I roar in laughter, but he keeps giving me a blank stare. He actually took me serious!

"You're not remotely funny." Him saying that makes me laugh even harder.

Toning it down, I say, "I meet the youth group at the coffee shop most Sundays before church." I fish the bulletin out of my Bible from last week and hand it over. "The address is on the front. You should join us for worship service." I would invite him to ride with me, but that would certainly be a big fat no. A girl can take only so much rejection, so I leave the ball in his brooding court.

"I may."

Satisfied, because that's all I know I'm going to get, I wave and head out.

The hour at the coffee shop zooms by, and as I settle in the pew at church, I can't help but scan the congregation. I don't know if it's the coffee or the anticipation of Asher showing up, but I'm one antsy woman today.

"Get still already," Bode grouches, nudging me in the side with his elbow.

For good measure, I wiggle some more. It's what he gets for sitting between Mia and me. He said it was to keep us quiet, but I know he did it just to annoy me.

"Shh!" I scold, using his shoulder for leverage to scan the crowded sanctuary. I've been doing this for the past ten minutes and I'm ready to give up as the opening song begins. Glancing one last time, I'm pretty shocked to find my giant tucked on the back pew. The astonishment is even more pronounced at finding him actually singing along.

Oh… That's not good… Now my fluttering belly just turned all warm and gooey like heated honey on a hot biscuit.

Chapter Six

Fall is my absolute favorite season—sorry winter, spring and summer, but it's the truth. The landscape exudes warmth in rich yellows, vivacious oranges, and deep reds. All of these lovely hues have decorated my community beautifully. It's exquisite, but the absolute best part of this neighborhood is that it's brimming with lots of little rascals. So tonight, with the splendor of the season strutting around and lots of kiddies to accompany it, Halloween is sure to be a great time.

"You sure I won't tear the dress?" I ask my friend Jane who works with me at the paper.

"You won't. I know my newspaper design." She chuckles while straightening the hem of my Word Witch dress.

"You most certainly do. The layout of last week's paper was well thought-out."

"Why thank you, my dear." Her smile of pride is unmistakable.

We've spent the last week working on my get-up for tonight along with the newspaper-covered witch's hat. Theo griped at us a few times to do some actual work, but all in all he left us alone with the project. We took a plain black dress and sewed row after row of newspaper strips in a tiered fashion. It's pretty darn cute.

"Okay, my friend. I'm off to have myself some fun." I grab up the dress and hat and make for the door. Stepping into the hall, I bump into Parker.

"Hey, darling," he says, reaching out and brushing a wisp of hair behind my ear.

He's always looked for excuses to touch me over the years—nothing inappropriate, just deliberate as if to remind me he's a part of my life. I need no reminding. Parker is such a phenomenal guy and would make a great catch, but the evidence that he's not to be my catch is found in those small touches— no feelings are provoked from them other than familiar comfort. I'm beginning to think that maybe a catch for me is not in God's plans for my life. It's probably for the best, anyway.

"Hey, hot stuff. What's up?" My tone is playful

with hopes of keeping the conversation light.

"Meeting with the boss on some photos." He produces a flash drive from his pants pocket as evidence. "You heading out?"

"Yep. It's closing in on trick-or-treating time." I barely refrain from bouncing up and down in my giddiness.

"If you want some adult fun, come by the costume party at my loft later on tonight," he says, leaning closer with his gray eyes twinkling in tease. "My vampire costume will go perfectly with your witch."

There's no doubting the man will make one sinfully tempting vampire. The image of him dressed in black with all that lush, dark hair styled back flashes before my eyes.

"That sounds past my bedtime," I sass. He knows I won't go, so why does he even bother?

"One of these days, you may just surprise yourself, Neena Cameron, and finally give me a chance."

My eyes focus on his fitted button-down shirt to evade his gaze as the tension in the hallway escalates to stifling. This is not our normal, and it's starting to really tick me off. My hand itches to slap him out of whatever un-normal he's picked up lately.

Jane exits and comes to a halt when she spots us.

Perfect timing!

"Jane, has Parker invited you to his costume party?" I ask exuberantly, hoping the tone isn't too forced or fake.

"No—"

"Tell her about it, Parker." I brush past him and make for a hasty departure, but not before catching his heavy sigh. I don't look back, just keep propelling forward and away from the situation.

Once I've arrived home, I set up in the living room and get to work immediately. I toss the word stickers I printed at work on the floor by the black wicker basket and box of full-sized candy bars that Mia picked up for me from the wholesale store yesterday. Plopping down beside the bounty, I take to placing a sticker on each treat before tossing it into the basket.

Truth—I'm considered the weird word woman of the neighborhood, but I don't mind. It's actually a compliment in my opinion.

After filling the basket to the rim, I wiggle into the dress. My anticipation for the evening builds as the rustling of the layers settle around my body. *This is going to be so much fun.* Shoving into my boots and hat, I grab up the basket and set up shop on my side of the porch. The entire front of both adjoining townhouses is entwined in orange and white twinkle lights. I hurry to plug them in and then light the bounty of jack-o-lanterns I carved a few days ago. Asher hasn't said a word—not that I expected him to—about the decorations. It pleased me to find a few colorfully odd gourds tucked in with the pumpkins. That's another clue to this strong silent man—he's not as frigid as he makes out to be.

By the time I've managed to light a few fat candles along the railing, a flood of little ninjas, princesses, and an assortment of beyond-the-dead characters have begun their procession towards the house. They pounce on the candy bars immediately.

"Convivial?" the little princess reads the sticker on her Milky Way, pronouncing it wrong. "What's that mean?"

"Kuh-n-viv-ee-uh-l. Say it again." I wait for the whole group to repeat it, with only a few getting it right this round. "It means friendly, fun."

"That's neat," says a cute pirate.

Asher comes up as I'm handing out my words and candy, carrying a box and looking so distinguished in his black chef's coat. I take a moment to study the signet on his lapel as each character plunders my basket for their favorites. This is the closest I've come to being able to study the unique embroidery. It's an odd mix of all the branches of the military. I wonder if it was specially designed for the restaurant.

"I like your costume, mister," says a mini chef in a white coat and a poufy chef hat.

"Yours is pretty impressive, too. Here," Asher says, handing over a ginormous caramel popcorn ball that's bigger than my fist.

He's surrounded at once by a mob of characters with arms reaching way up in eagerness. He doesn't scowl at them as he does me sometimes, just the blank stare that gives nothing away.

"Y'all got the bestest stuff," lisps a gray zombie.

"Sorry it's not brains," I say.

"What?" The little zombie pales a bit more with his eyes widening to full capacity. Guess he's not been thoroughly informed about the role he is modeled after tonight.

"Nothing. It's best not to listen to her." Asher motions for them to get on with their night, and they listen.

"I'll let that snide remark go, if you so kindly hand over one of those popcorn balls."

He takes a step closer to my rocking chair. "How about a trade?" He holds out the popcorn ball, so I take it and hold up my basket for him to select his poison. Of course, he would pick the one candy bar everyone else avoids. He studies the label. "Fluky?"

"Yes, it's another word for odd. I thought it was

most fitting for that particular candy bar."

"What's wrong with a Zero?"

"Fluky," I mumble while peeling the plastic wrap off my homemade treat.

He rummages around in my basket some more. "You put words on all of them?"

"Yes. It's my thing." I shrug before attacking the salty-sweet goodness.

Another motley crew begins the path up to our porch, so Asher takes up his post in his rocking chair. I pause long enough in devouring my snack to offer my treats.

"Fatuous?" a little gremlin says curiously.

"It means all that candy is going to make you fat."

I do a double-take towards the other end of the porch, not believing my ears. Asher Reid just cracked a joke! His face doesn't reveal it, but that tone he just used was no doubt fatuous. Must be the spirit of Halloween getting into him.

"Don't listen to him. It means silly, which is exactly what the Top Chef over there is being." I roll my eyes and twist my mouth in a goofy manner.

The children giggle as they grab treats and scurry away. We both tuck into our treats as another group heads up. I see nothing but glitter in this group of girls—fairies, princesses, a ballerina, a go-go dancer. There's no pausing in my eating this round, so I point and grunt towards my basket.

Once we're left alone again, he says, "So I'm guessing you're a word witch."

I tap a sticky finger to the tip of my nose and point in his direction. Licking the caramel from said sticky fingers, I comment, "You made those popcorn balls, didn't you?"

"Yeah." He pops the rest of the fluky candy bar into his mouth.

We both rock in our chairs in a comfortable silence until my treat vanishes. The only evidence it ever existed is from the few errant kernels stuck between my teeth. My eyes ease back in his direction and regard the box with longing.

"Can I have another one?" I ask, batting my eyelashes in a quick flutter. His lips twitch, almost betraying him by smiling. He pushes it away with a large huff. Too late. I caught him, but decide not to call him out on it. He knows he finds me cute. I did catch him eyeing my boots and those babies are all kinds of cute. I pick my chair up and scoot it over to him and then go back to retrieve my basket, eyeing his delicious box of treats with pouty lips all the while.

"Take one before you get too fatuous," he scolds, causing me to giggle.

The man is on a roll tonight! Hot dog!

I grab one up and slowly eat it this time, savoring every morsel. He seems to be in an uncharacteristically social mood for a change, so the notion to press my luck is too tempting.

With hopes of easing him into a lengthier conversation, I keep my eyes trained on the candle flames dancing from the light breeze in front of me, while I say, "You're a soldier."

"How do you know that?" The edge is back in his voice—not what I was going for.

"Honey, everything about you tells it."

"What are you talking about?"

"Why do you drive a Hummer?" I long to look at him, but focus my eyes on the massive SUV instead.

"It's what I'm used to driving."

A chilly breeze picks up and brings in the scent of the small bonfire next door. Inhaling the smoky aroma, I steal a quick glance at my company. His eyes are trained on the hulk of vehicle parked in front of us.

My hand flicks towards it. "When I look at the Hummer, all I see is the impenetrable force of intimidation. Much like its owner."

He grunts at my assessment.

"Charlie Mike is a symbolic homage to your military roots, isn't it?"

He doesn't answer, but looks over at me with

slightly raised eyebrows. I return my gaze to the busy street with the caravan of costumes parading by. A little tiger waves as he skips by.

"Also, the more I think about it, the more I realize you didn't mind me checking your backside out that night. It was more because your back was turned to me and it made you feel vulnerable—something a soldier never settles for being."

Out of the corner of my eye, I catch him rubbing his neck. Guess he doesn't care for my assessment being so spot on. I've covered a lot of military stories over the years, which means my soldier character study has been an extensive education.

Our conversation is interrupted by a superhero and pumpkin. The caped hero bounces up the steps while the toddler pumpkin waddles up behind him. Momma is at the end of the driveway, instructing the superhero to wait-up in an insistent tone he seems to be ignoring.

"Trick or treat," superhero bellows.

"Twick or tweet," tiny pumpkin repeats.

We divvy out our treats with Asher reiterating to the superhero to look out for his little brother. Such a fatherly gesture, and it causes my heart to twinge.

Once we're alone again, I continue the mostly one-sided conversation. "What puzzle piece I don't see fitting with you is how you go from GI Joe to Top

Chef?"

"What's with the twenty questions?" he mutters, annoyance edging his tone.

Only two questions have been asked, but I decide not to point that out. "I'm a journalist. I can't help but ask questions. It's what I do."

A lone vampire magically appears and quietly swipes a popcorn ball and Almond Joy before vanishing back into the dark with us barely noticing.

Silence overtakes us, so I'm guessing Asher has shut me down. I'm about to scoot back to my side of the porch when he speaks in a lower tone than normal.

"Wounded while on a mission. We'd already had plans to open a restaurant after retiring. That just got pushed upon faster when an AK47 slapped me in the gut and I could only finish out my time in the mess hall."

I've actually seen the damage an AK47 inflicts firsthand while visiting a veterans hospital. It wasn't a pretty sight. The popcorn balls begin churning in my stomach with those memories. "If your wound was that extensive, shouldn't you have been sent home?"

He releases a gruff sigh, evidence I'm pushing it too far.

It's on the tip of my tongue to ask who *we* are

with the restaurant plans, but he's off the hook when a group of fairies flutter up the steps. After they receive their treats and fly away, Asher clears his throat, seemingly building the valor to speak. I wait patiently.

"I refused to leave my battalion. We started the tour together, and we took an oath to complete it together."

This confession settles between us for a while. The merry sounds of young laughter echo from around the neighborhood as our rockers keep with their slow dance, while I consider the information he just shared.

"How did you end up here to open a restaurant?"

"I attended Le Cordon Bleu in Atlanta as a promise to my buddies from my unit. My captain is from these parts. He suggested I open my restaurant here. It's a great location."

"What about your family?"

"They're in Georgia, so I see them more now than I have in the past eighteen years."

"So you served our country for eighteen years?" This should put him in his mid-thirties, same as me, if my math is correct.

He lets out that gruff sigh again. "You ask too many questions."

"I'm curious." My shoulder lifts in an I-can't-help-it shrug.

He grunts at this. "I consider that a character flaw."

His harsh tone is clearly warning me. I disregard it, though.

Another group of hodgepodge costumes comes and goes, but my focus isn't on them. This dedicated soldier has seized it completely.

After they scurry away, I say, "You're welcome to ask me questions, too. It's how you get to know your friends."

"I *don't* do new friendships. I'm good with minding my own business, too," he says, successfully shutting me up.

If that's not my cue to move back the other side of the porch, then I don't know what is. I gather my chair and half-empty basket and scoot back to my side.

Not one more word is shared between us with my eyes stinging with indignation for the remainder of the trick-or-treating time. Not even a *goodnight* is exchanged after all of the treats have been divvied out. He simply picks up his box and vanishes into his house, leaving me on the porch alone and fuming.

And that's just not sitting well with me. At. All.

One step forward, two steps back. Twirl and repeat. This complicated dance routine with Asher

Reid is beginning to exhaust me.

Chapter Seven

Storming into the newspaper building, I head straight into Theo's office without permission. He looks up from his computer with raised eyebrows.

"Knock much?" he grumbles, pulling his reading glasses off.

"Send me somewhere." My voice sounds exasperated to my own ears. It's truly how I feel at the moment. I don't like this aggravation infuriating me, so I need to flee from it.

"Already? You've only been home for not even two full months."

"I know, but I'm antsy. I need a story to focus on." I point towards the door, so there's no mistaking that the story needs to be out yonder somewhere. Not here.

Theo shakes his head and exhales heavily. "Uganda isn't planned out enough yet. That's going to take at least a few more months. There's no way I'm sending you into that situation blind."

"I'm well aware of that, but you have to have something else that needs covering in the meantime." I cross my arms and plop down in the chair across from his desk.

"I have one, but it's not pretty."

"Where?"

That's all I really want to know. I need a break from the growing tension between Asher and me. He's taken to totally ignoring me again since Halloween. I've tried to make nice, not being able to resist righting my pushy wrong with him. I even went to his restaurant for a late lunch with Mia yesterday. When I asked the waitress to get him to come out, she replied a bit embarrassingly that he said no. No niceties at all to soften his rejection. Just flat out *no*.

Theo clears his throat, drawing my attention back to him. "Deep in Texas."

"Great. I'll go. Should we phone Parker?" I ask, already pulling up the airline app on my phone.

"Don't you want know what you're covering first?"

I shrug. "Deep Texas. What is it, some festival?"

"Like I would consider sending NL Cameron to something as trivial as a festival. Neena, it'll be you covering a high-profile case."

"Okay." I shrug again, not getting his reluctance.

"I'll need you to cover a heinous hate crime. One that will disgracefully make the history books."

Theo has my attention now, so I lay the phone in my lap and *pay* attention. "Details."

He slides his glasses back on and begins clicking a few passes on his keyboard before scanning the computer monitor. "Young black man by the name of Jacob Washington. Executed by being dragged behind a truck by a group of white extremists."

My stomach flip-flops.

"Why are such hate crimes still on the loose? Such mess shouldn't be prevalent in our world today. This is the twenty-first century for crying out loud!" My pulse is hammering away. "What psychotic reason did they claim to have for doing this to the poor guy?"

"It was told that one of the extremists' daughters was caught having sex with him."

I shake my head, tears stinging my eyes. I can only imagine what he had to endure. "Society is so busy playing judge for others that they can't see past their self-righteous bull. Jesus loved everyone. Why can't we be the same way?" I pound the armrests with my fists, punctuating each word. "We are all sinners! And the girl? What was her punishment?"

"See. This is why you need to stay here. I don't think you can handle it. You go into these situations with your whole heart and end up battered emotionally. I saw it last year when you returned from Afghanistan. Neena, I was worried." His dark eyes do carry quite a weight in them.

"No. This isn't about me being a baby about witnessing life happen. Yes, it can get heavy laden, but I get over it. There's no way I can't go to Texas and you know it. It would be remiss to ignore this injustice. This needs the proper light shed on it. I'm going."

"I shouldn't have said a word about this, but now that I have you need the rest of the story before you head out with guns blazing."

I flick my wrist in his direction. "Then get on with it, so I can round up Parker."

"Another group took justice in their own hands. Found out where the extremists were meeting and burned three of the members alive while making the rest of them watch at gun point."

"What?" Oh, now it's just too much. "So this is white verses black hate crime?"

"Pretty much," he says softly, trying to lessen the blow.

Shaking my head, I just don't see how people can be as narrow-minded as this. I look up and study Theo, and the only thing I see is a man I admire for being so committed to reporting truth and justice. He is well accomplished and big-hearted, my friend and mentor. He and I are cut from the same cloth even though our skin tones do not match. People who choose to look no further than shallow exterior are shallow themselves. No matter how much those prejudice, hate-filled fools need a slap upside the head, no one wins when violence is fought with violence. More blood being shed doesn't justify the blood already spilt.

I've not even left the state yet, and my story is already writing itself.

"Neena," Theo says, drawing me out of my thoughts again.

My mind has already traveled to that courtroom in Texas. Blinking my attention back to the present, I ask, "Yes?"

"Riots have already been brewing for the last few months. With this trial, insiders are predicting it to hit a crescendo."

"With two crimes to be tried, I'm guessing one has already taken place. So the trial beginning next week is for whom exactly?" I pick my phone up and text Parker to pack his bags and grab his camera.

"The remaining members who murdered Washington were tried and convicted last month. Two got life in prison and the driver got the death penalty. Of course, his lawyer is appealing it. The trial starting next week is for the friends of Washington who burned the three extremists."

Theo looks as tired as I feel after taking on the weight of such an atrocity in mere minutes. I have a feeling the upcoming trial is going to add to it significantly.

*****

With the plane yet to touch Texas soil, an unsettling apprehension has already clamped me on the back of the neck. Looking out of the window, I notice the clouds parting to give a peek to the state below us.

"Do you have that odd feeling that is usually our traveling companion when we head into a warzone?" I ask Parker, not liking the peculiar feeling. Out of the corner of my eye, I catch him fiddling with his camera lens.

He releases a deep sigh, his tell for being anxious. "Yeah."

"But we are only meandering a few states away from home." I shake my head.

"Yes, but racism is a vulgar war happening right here in our homeland."

"Sadly, you're correct. Why do people allow such hate to fester in their hearts? Seriously, it's poisonous and destructive."

The pinging sounds and then the warning light flashes for us replace our seatbelts as it's announced we are preparing to land.

"Just promise you won't leave my side."

Snapping the lock in place, I glance over at Parker and find his gray eyes assessing me. "Of course."

"Neena," he says, forming my name into a warning.

"Promise."

*****

Each day we head to the courthouse three counties away from where the actual crimes took place, Parker makes me promise again to not leave his side. There's no hesitation to keep this promise either. As predicted, the streets are a menagerie of picketers shouting their views, harsh words escalating to physical brawls between bystanders, and news crews dotting throughout the chaos. The tension outside the courtroom has stretched to such a severity that a county-wide curfew has been issued. My thought on the matter is this should have been put in place before dozens of arrests and emergency room visits mounted.

Today, the verdict is to be delivered. A jury of twelve peers from many ethnical backgrounds has been deliberating since yesterday, giving away evidence of the decision not being made so easily. A vast amount of police are armed and ready to combat the reaction of the crowd when it finally erupts. Not if, but when that dam breaks, those men and women in uniform will be needed.

The cacophony of chants and roars entwine in a maddening chorus as Parker and I move through the throngs of people. My eyes nervously scan the crowd, reading the signs and studying the owners. Lines are clearly set in the groups—blacks, whites, and even a few mixed groups. No matter what the hue of skin, each face holds the same anxious grimace. A conclusion to this storm is clearly needed in this community. They need to move on, but also to learn from this atrocious crime. One can only hope they do just that.

Even though it's November, the humid heat of this southern state seems to be ignoring that fact. My sweaty fingers feel slippery, causing my promise to stay by Parker's side to prove a little difficult. I have to actively tamp down this unnerving anxiety as my hand keeps fumbling to keep a grip on the hem of Parker's shirt. He leads us through the thick of it, stopping every now and then to capture an image with his camera or to remind me to hold on to him. We keep scooting along until we finally meet the edge of the congestion. Parker comes to a halt again and begins snapping more pictures with his camera angled downwards toward the sidewalk. I ease around his tall figure to see what he's found. Not a what, but a who—an elderly black lady on her knees praying. Once she lifts her head and opens her eyes, I kneel beside her.

"Hi, I'm Neena."

"Martha," she says, her voice frail with age and grief.

We pause in the moment to regard each other, while the mass of protestors curse and shout at one another. Their anger bounces off of us and returns to the chants and cries across the street. Her milky brown eyes seem to look past my blue shields. Wisdom is richly evident in her features and I would love to pull her out of this chaos and beg her to enlighten me.

"Did you lose a loved one in *this*?" Words have fled from me, and I cannot find one to accurately describe this nightmare.

She nods her head, understanding me anyway. "I have, child. Yes, I have."

"Did you lose Washington or one of the men who pursued vengeance for him?"

She shakes her head somberly. "No. I lost my brother back during the fifties in *this*."

"Oh." Same nightmare, but a previous chapter in time.

The need to nudge her any further dissipates, knowing she'll share more if given the freedom. I wipe my sweaty palm on my jeans before reaching out and gently taking hold of her tiny hand. She in turn grasps mine.

We watch the angst of the large group anxiously ebb and flow around us as she speaks. "My brother's only crime was being a young black man who chose to walk down the wrong road on his way home."

My stomach starts to burn with her words. So much unnecessary hurt being inflicted continuously throughout history… It leaves me absolutely baffled. The sounds of her weeping draw me back to her.

"They beat him before dragging him down to the river where they drowned him."

I say nothing. Really, what can I say to make it any better? Not one word comes to mind that would deliver an ounce of comfort. A dispute catches our attention off to the left. We watch as two men shove each other while they spit words of hate in the other's direction. A cop breaks it up and the crowd seems to settle back down a bit.

"May I pray with you, Martha?"

She nods. "Yes, child. I'd like that very much."

Grasping hold of her other hand, I bow my head and begin to silently pray.

Please, Lord. I come to you with a heavy heart. Please dear God, please heal Martha's heart as well as each one here. Please clear away the confusion and help all to focus on understanding and healing. Help our nation realize they need your love so that they can love. Heal us from the festering boils of hate. Please...

Firecrackers explode around us, interrupting my prayer and jolting my eyes back open. Dreadful understanding pinches me all at once, but before I can react, Parker has launched himself as a barrier on top of me. Screams, muffled by his body, shrill out as more gun shots fire. The tension has finally hit a perilous crescendo as Theo had predicted.

Time warps in and out for an undetermined stretch as pandemonium breaks out in a rage so malicious it seems unreal. Crushed under Parker's weight, panic convulses through my body as I listen to screams ringing out, bodies slapping against pavement and each other, and gut-wrenching wailing.

"I've got you. You're okay," he yells.

"Everyone is to evacuate the streets. I repeat, evacuate!" A voice booms from nearby speakers.

Parker yanks me up and spins me away from something he obviously wants us to avoid. Before I can protest and go see for myself, red splatters glistening in the sun and dripping down his shirt catch my attention.

Grabbing on to him, I yell frantically, "Parker, you're hurt! Help! Someone help us!" I look around, but everyone is running around in pure insanity.

"No. Not me. Hurry!" He starts dragging me away. I turn in time to see someone dragging Martha to her feet and away unharmed, thankful she's okay.

I scan back to where we were kneeling and freeze. There, only mere feet from our previous sidewalk perch, lies a body void of life with blood pooling underneath him. Hoarse screams rip from my lips.

"We've got to get out of here, Neena!" Parker yells over the roar of the chaotic crowd. Bodies shove into mine as they fight for an escape. I hear him, but cannot move away from what I see. Losing his patience, Parker grabs me up and starts carrying me through the masses. The reality of knowing someone lost their life within reaching distance to my living one overwhelms me. Defeated, I bury my face in the crook of Parker's neck and continue to scream.

"Shh... Calm down," he repeats as he jogs through the crowd.

I don't look to see where he's headed. The jostling of our bodies tells me he's working on getting us the heck out of here as fast as possible and far away from the madness. I feel like I've gone mad myself. The screaming won't stop even though it's already drained my voice to only a meager shriek.

Slowing his stride, Parker speaks with somebody and then the next recollection I have is him setting me down in the back of a news van. Time lapses and somehow we end up back at the hotel. We say no words, but there's a silent understanding we won't be parting ways. He grabs up my stuff from my room and hurries us to his, securing each lock behind us as if that can keep the reality of what just transpired away from us. *I wish it could.*

Shock has me frozen except for the slight tremble vibrating my body. I watch as he peels off his bloody shirt, using it to wipe some from his forearm before throwing it in the trash bin. Relief washes over me when no wound is evident on his torso. He walks me to the bed, sitting me down on the edge, and kneeling before me.

His glassy eyes meet mine. "I've got to shower. You'll be okay?"

I nod my head, but he seems to be uncomfortable leaving me in the room by myself. He shakes his head and sighs deeply. There's blood drying in his thick dark hair, so I understand his urgency for wanting it off, knowing it belonged to a man no longer living.

"Go ahead," I squeak out, resisting the urge to wipe the smear of blood off his cheek.

"I'll hurry," he reassures me before rushing into the bathroom.

Sitting here in the quiet hotel room, I listen to Parker lose his bravado. He probably thinks the shower drowns him out, but the sobs reach me as I release my own tears. They fall heavily down my face as the crying from the bathroom echoes throughout the space. He obviously witnessed that man being murdered.

Questions loop in and out of my disjointed thoughts without any answers presenting themselves as I sit frozen on the edge of the bed.

What happened?
Who?
How?
Why?
Why God?
Why?

Finally the sobs subside as the shower shuts off. A few more minutes pass before Parker scoots out with a towel secured around his waist. Averting his swollen eyes, he picks up my bag, grasps my hand, and leads me into the bathroom. Without saying a word, he sets the bag down and shuts the door after exiting, leaving me to wash my part of the nightmare off.

Glancing down, I notice only a few speckles of red have made it to my clothing, but I toss the shirt and pants in the trash anyway. After turning the shower on, I climb in and scrub with Parker's soap until my skin is bright pink and stinging.

"Neena, you okay in there?" Parker's hoarse voice reaches through the door.

"Yes," I say, but only a rasp sounds.

I pull on a pair of sweatpants and a T-shirt and hurry back out of the bathroom. Seeing Parker in one piece again with his own sweats and tee on, I lose it and launch into his arms. He holds me until his own grief weakens him. I feel him guide me over to the bed where we lie down and allow the shock and hurt of the day to clamp down on us. Eventually the tears subside and exhaust me to the point of nothingness.

Later... I'm not sure how much later... Night has darkened the room, yet I can barely open my swollen eyes. My head pounds and it's clear if I don't seek some relief for it, I'm going to be sick. Parker lies beside me, arms wrapped securely around me. Rolling over, I find him still out. I hate to wake him, but the nausea is closing in on me with the pounding in my temples.

"Parker," I try saying, but still have no voice. I nudge him.

His eyes open in panic and he jolts up to a sitting position. "You okay?" he croaks out.

I cradle my head and squeak out a silent no.

He climbs out of the bed and somehow produces a bottle of aspirin and water. Grateful, I accept it and pop the lid off in haste, wanting to rid myself of this massive headache.

"We should try to eat something, and then maybe try to figure out what happened today." He looks at me wearily.

I slowly nod my head before washing down the pills with a large gulp of water. The realization of just how parched I am shows up with the first sip, so I chug the entire bottle.

More foggy time passes with a pizza showing up at the door. We both pick at a slice, not really having an appetite. My phone pings from my bag again. I've ignored it for the past few hours, so I reluctantly fish it out and cringe. Mia must have seen the news. I show the screen to Parker.

"Here. Let me call her for you." He holds his hand out for the phone, so I gladly hand it over. He presses the CALL button and immediate yelling sounds from the other end. "She's fine. We're both fine. We're back at the hotel eating pizza." He pauses to look at me skeptically. "She can't talk." Another pause with more yelling sounding through phone. "Mia, calm down. She's got laryngitis." She yells him quiet. "Fine." He holds the phone out, but I shake my head. He shoves it in my hand anyway.

I place the phone to my ear and say nothing, just sigh loudly.

"You take off to get in the midst of a violent storm brewing down south and don't even take the time to tell me. Neena, you cannot do that without telling anyone. Four people were shot today outside of the courthouse... *You* could have been shot today. I didn't even know if you were or not for the last few hours! So help me, if you don't stop pulling these stunts, I'm going to strap you down and beat some sense into you." She halts the yelling and starts sniffling. "I can't lose you. Please come home." Her voice wobbles.

My throat thickens and guilt clamps down on me for putting my sister through this worry. "Okay," I rasp out and hand the phone back to Parker.

He listens, nodding his head in agreement. "As soon as I get off the phone with you, I'm calling the airline to book the first available flight home." He pauses to listen. "I promise, Mia. I'll have her home as quickly as possible. Okay. Bye." Hitting the END button, he hands my phone over and fishes out his own.

He looks so tired with his disheveled hair and bloodshot eyes. I feel guilty for him having to bear the weight of this situation, but there's nothing I can do about it. With no voice and very little sanity, I'm of no use. Pacing around the room, he begins the task of getting us back home and out of this nightmare. All I can do is lie on the bed and pray we get there soon.

Chapter Eight

Twenty-four hours is all I allow myself to fall apart before taking on the excruciating task of pulling myself back together again. The story will go cold if I wait much longer, and I won't allow our time in Texas to be in vain. Parker made good on his promise to Mia and delivered me within hours directly to her door. I gave in and allowed my breakdown to unravel before her, wishing I hadn't. She all but suggested I go to the hospital to be treated for shock. So this morning I woke up in my niece's bed, pulled on my breezy façade, and made my normal kooky Neena exit—annoying Bode by stealing his breakfast and leaving in my pajamas. I made it to my sweet secure home before breaking again.

Sipping some herbal tea in hopes of recovering

my voice, I scan over the notes on the trial. It's painful to read over the summaries of the courthouse shooting, but what happened will have to be included in the story. It wouldn't be fair to the victims to not cover it, no matter how painful. I set my cup down and send Parker a text.

Me – *We need to get to work.*

Parker – *Agreed. Tonight?*

Me – *Yes. Don't come empty-handed.*

Parker – *Chinese it is.*

Me – *Hurry.*

We are both pretending to be okay. Maybe if we pretend long enough, it will morph into the truth. It's something we've perfected over the years together from working on difficult stories. I place the phone on the counter and go back to sipping the tea while I wait on Parker to arrive.

Later, the sound of the jeep engine pulling up has me at the door in a flash. I stand by the open door and watch him retrieve the take-out bag and his messenger bag from the passenger seat. A throat being cleared catches my attention. Glancing over, I notice Asher rocking in his chair silently with his eyes fixed on me. It's the first time I've seen him in almost three weeks, and I hate how my heart picks up its pace. Why can't that happen when I see Parker? Oh how much easier my life would be if that would happen. On paper, it makes perfect sense, but try explaining that to my curious heart.

I give a slight wave, but nothing more, before heading out to help Parker. I bound down the steps barefooted towards him.

"Hey, darling," he says, wrapping me in a one-armed hug. His familiar cologne engulfs me as I snuggle into his side. Again, my heart only responds with a comforting rhythm that always accompanies my time with my friend—no sparks and no butterflies flutter about.

I say nothing for obvious reason. Instead, I secure the savory smelling food in my arms and head back toward the house.

"Hey, man. I'm Parker," I hear him say politely from behind me as I reach my front door.

Turning around to see if Asher acknowledges him, I'm surprised to find them shaking hands like civil humans. *Why can't the big jerk be courteous to me?*

"Asher," he replies coolly as ever, leering a few inches above Parker. It's quite menacing.

"Nice to meet you," Parker says in a slightly strained voice, backing away from my neighbor.

The food is calling my name, so I leave them and head to the kitchen. I'm digging out the bounty of selections, but halt in doing so when I catch the scowl on Parker's face as he joins me. He closes the door with unnecessary force and stalks into the kitchen.

"What?" I squeak out.

"Is there something going on with you and that guy?" His tone is thick with accusation.

I snort at the absurd idea. "If you define relationship as war, then yes. The man loathes me." The words are barely audible, but he looks like he understood me.

"By the force of his grip on my hand, I beg to differ." Parker flexes his hand several times before showing me the evidence.

Blinking a few times in disbelief, I grab up his red, swelling hand and inspect it. "That jerk!" I rasp before marching back to the porch where the jerk in question is back in his rocking chair.

"That was uncalled for," I whisper-yell, pointing in Parker's direction. He joins us on the porch, trying to pull me back inside. I yank out of his grip and glare at Asher with all my might.

Asher halts his rocking. "Are you sick?" he asks with actual concern lacing his words. *That's certainly something new.*

"In the head," Parker mutters, our inside joke. It's always our kneejerk response over the years.

With no mood for joking around, I pop him in the gut.

"She's got laryngitis, which can be a blessing if

you think about it," Parker continues to joke, sounding like his normal self. For that I'm grateful, especially after the nightmare we've just endured, so I decide not to pop him again.

Asher grunts a response, his hazel eyes never leaving me.

"You had no right to do that to my friend's hand. Apologize." The words only come out in breaths, but I think he gets his error.

Breaking our stare-down, Asher glances behind me at Parker. "Sorry, man." He apologizes instead of grunting, which totally surprises me.

I give him a stern look and point my finger at him in warning before pulling Parker back inside with me, hoping to leave the giant on the porch to think about what he just did. The man makes no sense to me whatsoever. I fish out an icepack from the freezer and hand it over to Parker.

"He clearly has a thing for you, Neena."

"No." I adamantly shake my head.

"Yes, he does. When a man tries breaking another man's hand during a handshake, it's his way of staking a claim. What's with you? Does your attraction radar not work at all?" He glares at me in bafflement as he adjusts the icepack over the top of his hand.

Ignoring him seems to be the best idea, so I do

just that and pile two plates full with shrimp lo mein, fried rice, and sweet and sour chicken.

"Fine." He sighs deeply. "Just keep ignoring it, but one day you're going to find yourself wishing you hadn't."

We leave that particular matter in the kitchen and settle on the coach in the living room. Tucking into our food wholeheartedly, my thoughts drift to the story that needs to be submitted by midnight.

"The verdict," I whisper between bites.

"Yeah. They got life in prison." He shovels in the last bite of noodles, places his empty plate on the coffee table, licks his fingers, and retrieves his messenger bag. "I've got a few pictures in mind for the story." He pulls out his laptop and brings the images up. There is one of the crowded courthouse steps, filled with grimacing faces and signs held high. The other image is of me and Martha, heads bowed in prayer.

I point my chopsticks at it. "Not that one. You know I never use photos of myself," I rasp.

"Your face isn't showing. I really think it's the most moving image I captured." His brows pucker as he studies it. I understand his reaction. It's because there are other images he captured that infamous day that are now being held as key evidence in another case.

I cannot even begin to imagine him actually watching the murder through his beloved camera lens. It hurts my heart to know that he will have that burden to forever bear, and knowing he took no thought for his own life as he tried and succeeded in protecting mine. Thank goodness, an officer took the gunman down before he spotted Parker. I know beyond a shadow of a doubt, my friend would have been the next target.

Giving in, I whisper, "Fine, but not for the local story."

"Done. I'll only send it along with the Time article."

I nod my head in agreement. Pulling my laptop before me, we begin piecing the story together. It's mostly me writing and Parker keeping me company while I do so. Normally I would send him on his way after the meal and picture approval, but I genuinely want him near tonight.

At a quarter till midnight, I load the story along with the photos Parker downloaded and hit SEND. With the story out of my hands now, I place the laptop on the table and lean my head on the back of the couch, watching him finish up some photo edits for another article.

"Done," I whisper on a yawn.

"Finally." He sighs while powering down his

own laptop. "Christmas is only a few weeks away, so I think I'm going to head home to Connecticut for a while. It's time for a break, so don't go chasing after any stories until the first of the year." He leans over to place the computer in his bag.

"You're due a break."

"You as well, darling. I'm set to fly out Friday, but before I go..." He releases a deep breath, instantly causing unease to creep over me. "There's something... I think if I don't act on this now, I'll never get another chance at it."

"What?" I'm not so sure I want the answer.

He turns to face me on the couch and rests his hand on the side of my neck. His thumb caresses my cheek as his stormy eyes gauge me. "I think you should allow me a kiss—"

"You're my friend... I just don't think that's a good idea," I rasp out nervously. I try to pull away from him, but he gently refuses.

"Please, Neena. I've tried subtly for years to get your attention. After what happened this week, I've been thinking about chances I've cowardly not taken. Please..."

"I just don't feel that way for you." My eyes sting all of a sudden with disappointment in my own statement and worry hits me in the stomach. I don't want to hurt him or endanger our friendship. I can't lose him.

"You won't know if you never allow us a chance. Just one kiss." Parker leans forward, pausing close enough to my lips that the lingering scent of sweet fortune cookie on his breath reaches me. It is most definitely a tempting invitation.

Taking an unsteady gulp of air, I give in and allow him this one moment. After everything we've endured, it seems almost criminal not to attempt it, so I lean the rest of the way and meet his warm mouth.

The kiss… the one that opens your soul and shows the exhilarating possibilities life kept hidden until that very moment of connection. As flesh caresses flesh, a bond forms in the two hearts, altering the rhythm permanently. So much so, one heart will never properly be the same without the other.

The kiss that awakens princesses and magically creates princes…

That's what I want with this kiss…

But it's not to be.

Parker weaves his hands through my hair and presses me closer to him, giving it all he has. I allow the kiss to linger with hopes the spark is taking its sweet time igniting. He is one exceptionally skilled kisser and my heart does pick up its pace, but the connection just isn't there. It only confirms what I've known all along. Parker will never be more to me than my dear friend and that's more than enough for me. I just wish it were enough for him.

Sensing my withdrawal, he slowly releases my lips and presses his forehead to mine. No words are exchanged as we collect ourselves.

"Can't blame me for trying." His voice sounds hoarse all of a sudden.

My eyes shut, not wanting to see the hurt in his. "You know I love you, just not like that—"

"I know." He sits back, finally giving me some much needed space, and scrubs his face with his hands.

We won't be able to survive this awkwardness, so I decide to try teasing him. "Don't tell me my jerk of a neighbor spurred this jealous caveman claim tonight." I nudge him in the side.

He shakes his head. "No, Neena. I already planned on it. It's why I'm heading out of town. I knew you'd turn me down, and I'd need some space while I licked my wounds." He gives me a sad smile.

"I'm so sorry," I whisper.

"Don't be. You've made it clear over the years. I just thought that maybe if you'd kiss me, you would finally see the possibility of us."

"We're still a team, though, right?"

"Always." He checks his watch. "I'd better go." He leans over and gives me hug, lessening the tension a little more.

That's Parker for you, never wanting someone unhappy.

After collecting his belongings, he's out the door quickly, fleeing my rejection. I let him go, knowing I've let him down as much as myself. Fake is something I am adamantly against, so there's no way I could do this without being in it wholeheartedly.

Alone again, I glance over my word wall. The need to add a word about regret seems to be calling me. After flipping through one of my thesauruses for a few beats, I pick up a piece of chalk and scribble the word *woebegone*, for that's exactly how I feel. I'm completely beset by woe for not being able to love Parker the way he desires and, more importantly, deserves.

Leaving the words and regret in the dining area, I head back to the sink and begin loading our plates and glasses in the dishwasher. I try keeping my mind busy as to not linger on the last several days.

Tomorrow… What to do tomorrow?

Before I can come up with an answer, a knock sounds at the door. I look around the room before heading over to answer it, wondering what Parker forgot, but find nothing left behind. I open the door and find Asher standing before me instead. His big imposing form, clad in track pants and a hoodie, fills the doorway. A thermos in his hand.

"It's for your throat," he says, thrusting the thermos forward.

I cautiously accept it. "What is it?" I squeak out.

"This and that." He shrugs, but I keep eyeing him warily. "Basically apple cider, vinegar, ginger, and honey."

My gaze slides from the thermos and then back to him. "I'm supposed to drink it?" That idea isn't very appealing.

"Sip it."

"Thanks." I go to close the door, but he takes a step inside, shocking me.

He runs his hand through his blond hair. "I'm sorry... For tonight... For everything. I don't know how to do this." He motions between us, causing goose bumps to blaze rapidly along my skin.

It strikes me odd how my body instantly reacts to this man. Is this what it means by having chemistry with someone? I haven't a clue. Never have I had a reaction to anyone like this in my life. It makes me downright mad, to be honest. Why can't these feelings happen with Parker? Life sure would be easier. Staring at this brooding package before me, it screams complicated.

Asher takes another step forward, eliciting a shiver from my traitorous body. He takes this as me being cold, so he reaches back and shuts the door. How peculiar is it that he is willingly standing in my house with me.

"What is *this*?" I whisper, motioning between us just as he did.

"I don't know." His gaze carries that ever-present blank stare. Did the military teach him that? It gives away nothing, and I'll be darned if it doesn't make me want to go on a search to decipher him.

We stand before each other, having a staring standoff. I've been through too much in the last few days to even begin *this* with him tonight. I shake my head and point to the door. "I'm tired."

Truly I am, in more than one way.

He nods. "Drink some of that before you go to bed. It's better warm, so heat up a cup in the morning and then another around lunch." One thing is clear about this mysterious man, he's used to giving orders and having them obeyed without any lip. He must be ranked considerably high, but I won't be asking him to confirm my assessment. I'm too circumspect of the battle that will surely follow if I go there again.

I nod my head in agreement and hold up the thermos. "Thanks. Good night."

Asher seems reluctant to be dismissed. Good. He needs some of his own attitude medicine. I know he's trying, but I can't even think about that after the emotional rollercoaster of a night I've already had with Parker.

When he continues to just stand there, I ease around him to open the door and usher him outside. The man then takes the slowest steps back to his side of the duplex until turning to look at me when he reaches his door.

Shaking the confusion and frustration off and begging the slight breeze to carry it away into the night, I close the door on those feelings and Asher with hopes both leave me be for a while. Too much to process...

Chapter Nine

Have you ever sat before a puzzle, totally perplexed by it, but determined not to let it be victorious over you in the battle of wits? Frustration begs you to swipe the puzzle in one fell swoop, scatter it into oblivion, wipe your hands of it, and carry on as though you never met up with the obstacle in the first place. Only your stubborn nature rebels and refuses to let the darn infuriating thing get the best of you. It's like intentionally banging your head against the wall over and over and over again. Senseless. Absolutely senseless.

Asher Reid is my infuriating puzzle. Never have I encountered such a person. The man downright baffles me. A few weeks have passed since the caveman confrontation between him and Parker—I'm still scratching my head over that one. My brooding neighbor has taken the hint that I needed space or has simply regressed back to his nonexistent social behavior, so I've not seen him. He's fairly skilled at making himself scarce.

Either way, I'm grateful, because the space has been much needed. It always takes me a little bit of alone time to move past a detrimental story like the one from Texas. I become a hermit in my little home and get lost in some mindless task to help decompress. I've focused on my Christmas decorations and have pretty much lived in pajamas nonstop. Mia keeps threatening to come over and un-hermit me, but I've asked her for this time and she's graciously granted it.

The man may have left me alone lately, but the baffling part of the Asher puzzle is the meals being delivered to my door each Monday and Wednesday evening. Like clockwork, at six on the dot, a delicious bounty of food has shown up from Charlie Mike. I've tried paying the delivery guy, but he refuses each time.

I'm staring him down now as he hands over two carry-out containers while I try shoving a fifty in his free hand. Of course, he bats it away like it's the nastiest thing.

"Take the money, Duane!" I lunge for him again

and he dances out of reach again.

"I'm under strict orders not to accept any money from you." He places his free hand behind his back to avoid taking the money.

"Not even a tip? Surely, I can tip you for your trouble. Come on, man. Take my money!" I noticed while I've been ranting, he's having a hard time not staring at my fuzzy hair, which hasn't seen a brush in days.

"No, ma'am. I'm being paid just fine to do this." Dune's eyes flick up to my hair as he pushes the containers closer.

"Something wrong with my hair, Duane?"

"No ma'am," he stutters out, eyes wide and cheeks turning red. "Please, Neena, please take the food and stop giving me a hard time."

I give in and accept them. "Tell your stubborn boss I said thanks."

Delivery Duane steals one more quick look at my head and is probably thinking his boss is off his rocker to tangle with this here wild woman. Let him think what he wants. It's sort of amusing, and I really like amusing.

"Yes, ma'am," he mumbles, scurrying away before I can cram the fifty into his jacket pocket.

Asher and I have been doing this tango for a few weeks now, and it still makes no sense to me. The man seems repulsed by me, but is now feeding me. *Really? Why?*

As soon as I crack the lid open, revealing a lush steak and fire roasted root vegetables, all the questions of his behavior vanish amongst the robust aroma. The gorgeous food has been arranged with much thought. It looks like art on display in this black container. My curiosity has me opening the other container before sampling the main course and I'm rewarded by more edible beauty. Not one but two pumpkin tartlets are nestled in the box. Oh yeah! The spices perfume the air and warm my senses and I'm forced to take a bite. The flaky crust and the custard pumpkin filling blend together seamlessly and melt in my mouth.

One small sample bite turns into a second larger taste and then another until my dessert has vanished. I regard the second tartlet, but move back to the steak before it gets cold. Mmm... The steak is so tender that a mere fork does a perfect job of serving me a bite with no need of a knife. Buttery and spicy and perfect...

After half of the meal has disappeared, I plop down at the dining table and search for another word for *perfect*. Certainly, I've used my quota of it during these last few weeks' worth of perfect meals. Asher's creations deserve something more creative than that. I pop a baby carrot and mini red potato in my mouth as I scan the thick thesaurus that is permanently at home on this table.

Perfect.

Flawless.

Impeccable.

Superb.

Adept.

Ambrosial.

Paradisiacal.

I drop my fork and swipe a piece of chalk from the bowl and scribble the word *paradisiacal* on the wall close to Asher's name. Surely this man's food is heavenly and deserving of such a unique word as paradisiacal. He even made that sore throat conglomeration surprisingly tasty.

"Paradisiacal," I say to the empty room, trying the word on for size and finding it most fitting.

Much to my displeasure, the food is gone way too quickly. I mourn this fact as I toss the empty containers in the trash and go back to crafting my ornaments for the tree. I pull Jeremy Camp's Christmas tunes up on my iPod, crank up the volume, and settle onto the floor. Surrounded by the needed materials next to the fresh fir tree that was delivered this morning, I set in to finish them. I came across this chalkboard spray paint a while back, so I got the wild hair to spray clear glass balls and now I'm putting my Neena touch to each one. Two dozen down. Two more dozen to go.

The exterior decorations have already been placed in their rightful spots outside, but were mysteriously repositioned, I'm guessing by Asher. I don't fancy myself a by-the-book kind of gal, so the strings of lights and wreaths may not have been hung properly by my neighbor's standards. I went to retrieve my mail after dark one day last week, because I forgot during the day, and found the lights and wreaths rehung with precise placement. I can guarantee the man used a measuring tape. Never have my decorations been so neat and orderly as they are now.

Obviously, Asher *don't* put up with such—yes that should be *doesn't*, but then I couldn't be sarcastic over his ugly word with proper English. While I'm on the subject—proper English is so overrated. Just let your words free. So be it, if they don't come out in just the right rule book order. Wouldn't it be just the most boring conversation if we all spoke exactly the same? No fun is what it would be, I tell ya. And isn't *ya* much more happy than *you*? I could go on and on, but I ain't. Yep. Did it again.

Daylight peeks in the window as I hang the last ornament on the tree. Another all-nighter is in the books. While I gaze at the twinkling tree, my hand tries to thread through my hair, but gets tangled in the snares of knots. Maybe it's time for a shower and a long winter's nap...

I head towards the stairs but come to a halt from the knock at the door. A cursory glance at my wrinkled pajamas that are now speckled in red and silver glitter glue causes me to cringe. Maybe I can tiptoe by the door, so I give it a go.

"I already saw you through the window." His voice booms from outside.

Asher calling me out only spurs me to go on to bed, but before I even take two steps up the stairs the door creaks open.

"When are you going to learn to lock your blame door?" he grouches out.

Whirling around, I settle a hand on my hip and glare at him. "Leave and I'll give it a go right now."

He slowly takes in my unkempt look with that blank stare of his, making me wonder what he really thinks of me. I doubt I'll ever find out the answer to that. Maybe I really don't want to know, anyway.

"Your voice is back."

"Yep."

"I just wanted to wish you a Merry Christmas before I head home."

Wow. That is actually a kind gesture. I notice the

huge duffle bag resting at his boot-clad feet. My eyes coast up along his long legs covered in worn denim and the button-down shirt peeking out from underneath his olive-green fatigue jacket. It's an authentic soldier's coat, but holds no clue about his military status.

Breaking the trance this man seems to put me in, I look around the living room until my thoughts clear. "Oh. I'm glad you stopped by." I hop down the steps and head over to the Christmas tree. "I've got you a gift."

"A word tree?"

I turn around and find GI Joe considerably close behind me. So close, the crisp earthy fragrance that follows him around engulfs me. His scent is oddly inviting, a total contradiction of himself. Before I do something foolish like sniff him, I turn my attention back toward my masterpiece—Christmas bulbs gleaming from the glittery words decorated on each one, all meaning Jesus. I love how the strings of white lights catch on the words and cause them to twinkle. *Messiah, Gift, Savior, Redeemer, Emmanuel, Liberator, Christ, Deliverer, Jehovah, Bridegroom, Cornerstone.*

"Only the most beautiful words in existence," I declare.

He steps around me and studies the words and then looks back at me with a slightly elevated brow. I think he may just be impressed by my tree. I know I am. This is what a Christmas tree should represent. Society forgets all too easily or ignores the true meaning altogether, and that is just so sad.

Before he can speak, or more likely not, I hand over his gift.

He frowns down at the red and gold wrapped box in his hands. "I didn't get you anything."

"I didn't expect you to, but you have been giving me culinary gifts for the last few weeks."

Asher glances up and then back to the gift without acknowledging his act of kindness I've been happily receiving lately. Opening it and then lifting the crazy contraption out of the box, he eyes me with a hint of confusion in his hazel gaze.

I take the headband out of his hand. "Bend down, so I can place this on your head." He does, and I place it on his head before folding the mirrors out to the side.

"What is this?" Asher looks like a mean mac truck with huge rearview mirrors and a deep scowl on his face.

"It's for you to wear the next time you cook for me. This way you can keep an eye on me while I check you out the entire time. Turn around."

Once his back is to me, I begin making goofy faces with him watching me through the mirrors. I look like a wild woman with ratty pajamas and tangled hair, and it's astonishing that he's not rolling on the floor in a fit of laughter. All I get is that inscrutable look, making it impossible to read him. The man has that expression totally mastered.

"You're a strange woman."

"Why thank you." I grin, watching him turn around while pulling the contraption off his head. "You can also wear it in the kitchen at the restaurant. I don't know how you can stand not seeing behind you there."

He glances to the tree then back to me. "I have mirrors over the stoves and grills," he admits, flooring me completely. "They're a pain to keep clean, though."

His eyes hold just a smidgen of a twinkle, giving away the only evidence he's amused at the moment. I wish he would give me the gift of a smile, but I won't overstep and ask that of him.

"Here. Let me toss the wrapping for you." I pull the balled up paper out of his hand, being mindful not to linger with my touch, and place it in the trash bin.

"So... You have plans for Christmas, right?"

I wonder if he's worried I'll be alone.

"Actually, I do. I'll be celebrating with my family at my sister's tomorrow."

Sure, Mia and her crowd would welcome me tonight. I just get tired of feeling like the third wheel. They deserve to have their private family celebration. My usual plans are to hang out with Parker and some of our mutual friends. Beings that I ran him off all the way to Connecticut after our epic kiss-fail, I've made my solitude bed and plan on hibernating in it later.

"What about tonight? It's Christmas Eve."

I try chewing some dried glitter glue off of my thumb nail, not wanting to sound like a total loser for not having plans. All I want to do is crawl into bed and sleep through it. Exhaustion is weighing down on me at the moment. Loneliness won't leave me the heck alone either.

"Umm…" Standing before this man, I feel right pathetic and ashamed that this is how I plan on spending this blessed night—alone and feeling sorry for myself.

This needs remedying.

"Neena—"

"Do you have to go just yet?" I sputter this out quickly as a plan materializes.

Asher checks his watch. "Why?"

"I may have gotten myself into some serious trouble."

His dark brows pinch together. "I don't do trouble."

"But I could really use your help. I'm way in over my head." I lean close and whisper, "I may accidentally kill someone if you don't agree to help me."

Alarm flashes in his eyes as they widen. He shared a new emotion! Now I want to break out into a happy dance, but I abstain. Victory!

He braces his hands on his lean hips as a thick sigh rushes out from between his lips. "What is it?"

Ooh… Those three words sound more like a threat than a question. This is just too much fun.

"I promised to bake some treats for the Youth's Christmas party tonight. Me in a kitchen with unsuspecting ingredients…" I shiver dramatically.

Asher rolls his eyes. A new emotion and eye rolling! What a treat!

"What I actually promised the youth is that I wouldn't bake them anything ever again. Some of them punks are under the delusional notion that my cookies made them sick last year. I considered them gooey, while others declared them raw. Either way, I did not force-feed anyone. Those belly aches are all on them." I nod my head adamantly on that fact and cross my arms.

"You need cookies?"

"Or whatever you have time to bake up for me." I offer him a pleasantly pleading smile.

"I'll run to the store." He places his duffle bag by the stairs and heads to the door, but pauses. "Do you think you could at least brush your hair before I get back?" His brows are puckered, but I know he's teasing and that right there completely makes my day.

The man just proved he can cut a joke, even if he has no skillset on cutting a smile. With patience, I'm beginning to suspect even that can be possible. Asher is most definitely one ruggedly handsome man, but the guarantee of a smile transforming him into pure beauty has me optimistic.

"I'll do you one even better, sir. I'll wash *and* put on a clean outfit, too." I wink and he glares.

"Get on it," he orders before shutting the door.

I groom as promised and do the dish. Yep, just one coffee cup and I'm done. And I'm done in more than one way. I make the mistake of sitting on the couch and that's all she wrote.

*****

Heavenly spices of cinnamon and something else warm mingle with sugar and vanilla in my dreams. It smells so good that it pulls me right out of my slumber. I drag my eyes open and find a plate piled high with beautiful, fat cookies being held before me by Master Chef himself. Blinking, I look around and see the kitchen counter holding another bountiful tray of cookies. It's evident that those yummy smelling treats were baked here, but the kitchen is already cleaned spotless.

"How did you do all this with me sleeping through it?" A yawn muffles my words.

"I know how to be quiet."

"Like a ghost," I mutter with amazement. Sitting up, I swipe a giant cookie off the plate and take a monster bite. Oh my... An oatmeal cookie loaded with white and dark chocolate, pecans, and coconut. "These are the best cookies ever," I say around a mouthful of the warm treat. "I'm guessing this is the proper way to bake a gooey cookie." I cram the remainder in my mouth on a moan. "Paradisiacal."

"Come again?"

"It means heavenly. Asher, your culinary skills are beyond heavenly."

Asher grunts his thanks and sets the plate down before pulling his coat on. I don't want him to leave but have no right to keep him from his family. Disappointment overtakes me as I watch him prepare to leave.

"Hurry up and get your boots and coat on so we can get these treats delivered," he orders full of authority.

"No... I'll deliver them. You need to get on the road. It's got to be getting late." I glance at the clock and see that I've slept for a solid three hours. "I'm so sorry for sleeping on you."

"It's still early afternoon. I've got time." Mr. Bossy snaps his fingers. "Now let's get going."

Before I can wrap my mind around the idea that this man is willingly spending time with me, on Christmas Eve no less, we are out the door heading to the youth center in his massive SUV. I glance at him, not used to his slightly longer hair. It's still incredibly neat, just not so buzzed close. The new style lends a softness to all of his sharp edges

"I like your hair this way," I comment.

He takes one hand off the steering wheel and runs it through the top of his hair. "Blame it on my weekend waitress. She talked me into it."

"Oh," I say quietly, sounding jealous. I look out the window, feeling embarrassed by my ill-placed emotion.

He clears his throat, and if I knew him better, I'd swear he was covering a chuckle. I don't dare look to confirm my suspicions, not wanting him to see more of my embarrassment.

"Lynnette is a hair stylist, too. She cuts my hair," he clarifies.

"Oh," I say again, feeling even more foolish.

There is a satisfaction that he took the initiative to clarify their non-relationship, though.

"How's your boyfriend? Parker is it?" Asher gives me a sidelong glance.

Well now. He just gave away too much in that question. We seem to be on the same page, and I'm itching to turn it.

"Yes, his name is Parker, but he's not my boyfriend. We work together."

He grunts and seems to be done with chitchat, because the rest of the drive is done in silence. I'm good with that, though. I like the idea of not having to work on filling every moment with words. Sometimes that's just fine by me, and this is most certainly one of those times.

We arrive at the center in no time, and the kids reel us into their holiday shenanigans. Asher is polite but standoffish during the hour we spend with them. He basically mans the refreshment table, organizing platters with precision. It's quite cute. Every time a kid grabs up a treat from a tray, he rearranges it back to uniformity.

Even though I participate in all of the silly games, my attention continuously slides back to Asher. Kids keep stopping to talk to him and he actually responds to them, showing that he really can be social if the notion strikes him. Still, no smile ever presents itself on his handsome face.

The music eventually gets cranked up and the kids go to town with their dancing. I'm good with the Cupid Shuffle, the Cha-Cha Slide, and the old-school Electric Slide, but the Wobble and the Nae Nae throws this not-too-old girl for a loop. So while they break those dances down as only the nimble youth can, I break out some of my day's moves—the Roger Rabbit, the Tootsie Roll, and something I think we used to call the Running Man.

"Neena, what are you doing? That's not the Wobble!" Ginny, one of the youth, hollers over the music.

"You wobble it and I'll roll it!" I yell back, trying to be as goofy as ever.

The next song, "Watch Me," cranks up, so I bust out some of my moves again.

"You're supposed to be doing the Nae Nae, Neena!" Seth laughs out. He's Mr. Cool when it comes to the dance floor.

"I'm doing the Nee Nee. That's close enough!" I look over at Emily, a pixie of a girl, and laugh at the weird leg move she's performing.

"Emily, what on earth is that called?" I ask, busting out my Butterfly.

"It's called the Stanky Leg." She laughs.

"Stanky Leg? Seriously? That looks more like the

Achy Leg!" Everyone bursts into a fit of giggles, so I consider my goofing off job done. I think this is why they allow me around in the first place.

"Neena, you're such a nut," Pastor Chase yells over the loud, booming music.

"Takes one to know one!" I point over at him. He quickly shuffles back into the sidelines of the dancing before I make him show these kids the Macarena as I did last year.

Each time I steal a glance at Asher while we carry on with the wild dancing, I discover him watching me. A few times he gets caught biting his lip, giving away to the fact he's refraining from laughing. That little gesture just makes my night, and spurs me on to act up even more.

Time flies by and finds us back at the house all too soon for my likings, I stand by the door and watch Asher gather his bag so he can hit the road.

"Asher, this has been one of my favorite Christmas Eves. Thank you for spending it with me."

He grunts his normal reply while eyeing his bag, evidence he's had enough of me.

I join him by the door and chance placing my hand on his. "You've already given me so much for Christmas, but could I ask you for just one more thing?"

"Anything," he says quietly.

This response stuns us both still. He obviously didn't think that through.

"Can I have a hug before you go?"

He doesn't agree or disagree, just keeps his predominantly green gaze glued to mine.

"It would mean a lot," I whisper.

Still no response, so I take that as my go-ahead and gently wrap my arms around his waist. I rest my head over his heart and listen to the steady beat of it. I might as well be hugging a board with how stiff he is, but I don't let go.

Asher doesn't hold me back, but he does whisper, "Merry Christmas, Neena."

He leaves quickly without another word and all I can do is smile.

I heard a wise woman once say that our lives are much like seasons—ever-changing with some seasons being pleasant and renewing, some harsh and detrimental, while others veer more towards adventurous excitement.

I felt a shift tonight in my life's season with adventurous excitement on the horizon. If hope was a specific season, it would begin to bloom in this moment.

Chapter Ten

The lights wrapped around the porch railing twinkle in hope for the New Year ahead, and I couldn't be more excited to begin one. My fingers feel like ice cubes, but midnight is nearing, so I keep fastening the vinyl tags to the strand of lights. Before the last tag is secured, Asher's monster headlights light up the entire porch, nearly blinding me.

Shielding my eyes, I grouch out as he opens his door, "Does such a colossal vehicle really necessitate high beams?" Everything goes back to a soft darkness all of a sudden, but leaves my poor eyes unfocused and feeling like I've just spent the last hour staring directly into the sun.

He says nothing—big shocker—just strolls up to the porch and studies the tags. I know he wants to ask. It's obvious in his glances between reading them.

"These are my resolutions for the year," I answer his unspoken question.

"Isn't that supposed to be private?"

"Not mine. It's easier to stick to something when you put it out there." I keep adding the tags as he keeps reading.

"Make Asher smile?" he reads out loud, forming it into a question.

"Oh yes. And I won't stop until I succeed." I narrow my eyes and point sternly, hoping to mark that one off this list right now, but all I get is a blank look in return.

He reads another one as I continue working. *"Uganda."*

"That's a tricky trip I've been working on. So far, I keep plowing into walls, but I'm resolved to make it happen."

"Those walls are your indicators that Uganda isn't a place you need to be," Mr. Bossy Pants says with enough authority that I'm sure could make the toughest guy pee his pants. But I'm not much on being bullied to back down on what really matters, and Uganda matters.

"I hear ya, soldier," I say, brushing off his order.

Asher halts when he finally makes it over to his side of the porch and points to the tags floating in the wind. "Are these my resolutions?"

"Yes. I thought I'd help you out."

"I don't do resolutions."

"Of course you *don't*. That's why I did it for you." I add another tag before quoting Psalm 139:23-24. "'Search me, O God, and know my heart; test me and know my anxious thoughts. See if there is any offensive way in me, and lead me in the way everlasting.' We all have parts that need to be improved upon. What better time to focus on that than on New Year's Eve."

"*Stop using the word don't... Be nice to Neena... Become Neena's friend... Smile at least once a day...*" Asher keeps reading out loud as he moves along the string of lights.

There's no holding the smile back, knowing he's probably annoyed by my resolution declarations. It's clearly on display in his irritated tone.

"I'm about to head over to the Valley Apple Orchard. It's where our church rings in the New Year. Would you like to join me?" I glance over at him and admire the view, handsome as always, in his fatigue jacket and dark jeans. He even pulls off looking tough while wearing a gray beanie hat.

"I don't care to," he mumbles while regarding the tags on his side of the porch that seems to offend him.

A pinch of regret jolts through me. Maybe I

misjudged and should have kept to my side of the porch on this one. I decide to take them down once he's out of sight.

"Well, Happy New Year. Good night." I offer a quick wave and a smile that goes nowhere near my eyes before going inside to gather my bag and keys.

After waiting a good ten minutes, I grab a pair of scissors and head back outside to take care of my blunder. A fluttering of white pieces of paper catch my eye in the sea of blue vinyl tags as soon as my feet land on the porch. Curious, I step to the rail on my side and read the new additions.

Learn to lock the door.
Buy decent groceries at least once a week.
Learn to cook.

There's no holding back the giggle as I read them. Asher has a sense of humor and can be a good sport. Too bad he doesn't openly share these qualities. More papers catch my attention on his side, melting my heart that he added his own resolutions. With no need for the scissors, I drop them in the rocking chair and sneak over to read his additions.

Don't hold back and learn to let go.
Don't be rude to my neighbor.
Remember but don't regret.
Don't give up.

Of course, each one would hold that ugly word.

His resolutions give away more about his character than anything else in these past several months. Obviously, life has hurt him. Beyond a shadow of a doubt, I know God put this man in my life with a purpose, so I resolve this very night to not give up until that purpose is revealed.

*****

Time has carried on with a breeze of unrushed care. Those words couldn't be any less true for me. My patience is teetering on a dismal incline and I'm close to bursting with anticipation. Perched by the large front window with a cup of coffee in hand, I keep studying the languid snowflakes as they arrive on a slow angle. Every so often a substantial one whirls by in a tease, looking like an angel feather escaping straight from heaven. I want it all here and now, but the precipitation is in no hurry to gather enough for a good bout of snow shenanigans. A quick glance at the uniform waiting by the door—gloves, scarf, toboggan hat, undercoat, thick overcoat—indicates I'm ready for the fun waiting to be had.

Unfortunately, my usual fun partners are all out of town. Parker hasn't made it back yet even though the New Year started over two days ago. Mia and Bode hauled tail on a cruise with the kids, a total opposite of the weather spectrum, leaving me high and dry as well. Finn is off gallivanting in some serious snow in Utah. Yes, jealousy is a wicked friend keeping me company on this late morning.

"Come on, snow! Get the lead out!" I shout at it through the frosted window. The Hummer is blocking my little car, so the gray monster has a white blanket over it now. The weather has shut down most of the town, so that explains why my neighbor is still home. I press my nose to the glass and glimpse next door. The lights are on, but that doesn't mean I'd be welcome.

Restless, I finish the cup of coffee and wander over to the dining table to work on a local article about Charlie Mike. I'm not a restaurant reviewer like my friend Luka, but I feel well-versed with the menu beings that my meal delivery is still happening. The least I can do is offer a nice write-up for the paper and my website.

That only kills an hour of my time, leaving me hungry and cranky since the snow still has yet to mound enough for proper play. I devour a peanut butter and jelly sandwich, pretending it's something scrumptious from Asher's kitchen. That ticks hardly any time off the snow timeclock.

With nothing better to do, I begin a cheesy romance my sister insisted I read. Mia is a romantic. I am not. Halfway through, I'm laughing when it's evident tears are supposed to be the reaction. That does it for me and whether only a few inches or a few feet have accumulated, I'm going for it. I glance out the window, super stoked to find a small mountain of snow glittering in the late afternoon light. It's perfect and fluffy and begging to be tousled.

Donning my snow uniform, I push into the snow boots and march next door. Serious snow playing has to have a partner. Unfortunately, my option is highly unlikely to agree. I stand tall and push my shoulders back in preparation. Giving the door a firm knock with my gloved knuckles, I wait only seconds before it slides open. Asher just stares at me, so I return the favor. Jeans and a cream-colored cable knit sweat never looked so domineering.

Crossing his arms, he says in that always deep authoritative tone, "Nice cap."

That voice beckons a response right out of me, belly flipping and eyes glazing over. Good grief. This is embarrassing. Clearing the swoon away on a quick cough, I reply, "I'm in the know on where to find these babies. I could hook you up." My head bobs, causing the fuzzy, hot-pink ball on top of the toboggan hat to bounce around.

"I don't wear children's apparel. I'm good." His lip twitches, giving away his amusement. I am so on to him and that lip twitch!

"Fine. Go put on your boring old man cap and come play in the snow with me."

"Do I look like I'd play in snow?" He's one strong tower of a man, looking none playful.

I shrug and lie, "Sure."

"I don't."

"Err! You need to take that ugly word and permanently delete it from your vocabulary bank."

His brow knits together. "What word?"

"*Don't*." I mimic his deep moody tone in what I think is a perfect impression. "I *don't* smile. I *don't* do polite conversations. I *don't* pick my nose."

This earns me another lip twitch. I'm just going to go ahead and catalog that as a smile.

I huff, sending a cloud to fill the air between us. "Fine. Stay on the porch sulking for all I care. I'll just enjoy this beautiful snow without you." Turning on my heels, I hurry down the steps.

The satisfying crunch of my boots sinking into the lush snow does wonders for my mood. Something about the languid flakes whirling around while being emerged in the vast white bounty of icy beauty just lifts my spirits. Giddiness takes over as I begin working on my first snowball.

"What are you doing?" he grumbles from his post on the porch.

Without stopping my task, I say, "Building a snowman. Throw a coat on and come help me."

"I don't build snowmen."

I look up with a glare and point my gloved finger at him. "There's that ugly word again. I can't believe you would use such vulgar language in front of a lady." I bat my eyelashes and clutch my chest in offense before bending back down and continuing to roll the ball around to collect more snow.

"You're not packing it enough."

The nerve of him!

"Look, buddy, if you're not gonna help then I suggest you keep your comments to yourself." Pausing, I glance up. "Better yet, why don't you just mosey your brooding behind back inside."

He says nothing, just leans on the porch railing and keeps watching me.

A side of the large snowball shears off, so I try angling my body to hide it while trying to pack more snow into the void. Does he have to always be right? After all three balls are properly rolled and packed, I'm struck with another problem. I can't stack them! Every time I try lifting the medium sized ball, chunks fall off.

A loud grumble sounds from behind me before feet begin pounding down the steps. I almost hope his brawny-self slips and he busts his grouchy butt.

"Move over," Asher orders while buttoning his thick gray coat.

I do as he says and watch on as he stacks the snowballs with little effort to form a five-foot-tall snowman. I pull off the extra scarf and hand it over to Asher to wrap around our snowman's neck while fishing out the black buttons and carrot to form our new friend's face. I'm careful to form the mouth in a wide grin with hopes he will be a good example to my moody snow partner. I'm beyond thrilled as we study over our handiwork with clouds of our breaths puffing out into the night. It's magical to be in the midst of a soft snowstorm, and oddly romantic to be enveloped in it with such a handsome man. Mia's romance novel has my imagination running amuck. No way would Asher Reid ever have a romantic bone in his sulking body, but the notion to test this theory overrides my better judgement.

"Dance with me," I say. I'm obviously a glutton for punishment.

Looking at me curiously, he shakes his head. "I don't dance."

"Fine," I grumble, taking a step away from him.

A tune sings through my thoughts as I begin swaying. My feet slip and slide on the frozen ground while I hum along. The solitude dance continues while the snow sprinkles down around me. The little icy gems keep colliding softly with my frozen cheeks. Twirling around in my best ballerina impression, I accidentally bump into that solid mysterious wall known as Asher Reid.

He lets out a grunt, reaching out to steady me on my feet. Holding me close, he regards me in a contemplative way. After a long sigh, Asher totally floors me by wrapping his arms around me and leading us in a slow dance around our front yard. He escorts me in slippery circles, never easing up his firm grip on my waist. I give in to my romantic notions and lean my head against his chest, pretending we are a happy couple suspended inside our own magical snow globe.

A deep groan vibrates through his chest, and it's the first one elicited from him that isn't due to aggravation—more on the lines on contentment. Releasing my own sigh of comfort, I melt deeper into his arms. Even out in the frigid Tennessee night, warmth rebels and begins as a small alluring beam in the midst of my chest, blossoming out in bursts of optimism. Each time he reaches up to brush my slightly damp hair away from my face, an ache of sweetness so tangible I can taste it on the tip of my tongue warms me further.

Asher tries ending the dance after a while, but I whisper a soft, "Please." He understands and gives in to my plea, pulling me closer and circling us in the yard. He surprises me further when he begins humming his own song of choice. Minding it none, I allow this surprisingly gentle giant to lead our dance at his pace, knowing this is quite an extravagant gift I'm receiving from him. Never have I felt so safe and adored as I do right now in this colossal man's securing arms. Spinning me around and around, he breaks my train of thoughts, beckoning an elated giggle from me.

"Who are you?" I ask breathlessly with the cold air tickling my throat.

"Asher Reid," he replies, dipping me grandly.

"I thought I heard you mutter mere moments ago, 'I don't dance.'"

"You did. I said I don't dance, not that I didn't know how."

He most certainly knows how and then some. Oh my.

"Just think… months upon months have been absolutely wasted. All this time we could have been dancing instead of glaring!" I say dramatically, pulling a halfhearted glare from him.

The tease slips away as he watches me intensely with the gold whirling out from the green in his iris. He blinks, releasing me from them as he scans the details of my features. Not being able to take the scrutiny any longer, I bury my face in the warmth of his coat. I move my hips in sync with his, not wanting to try figuring out what that particular look could possibly mean. Moments of contentment later, tiny pelts of unwelcomed ice begin popping my back, completely ruining the mood.

On instinct, Asher unfastens his coat and shields me under it while ushering us up the porch and away from the sleet.

"No!" I holler out.

"What?" he asks crisply when we reach my door.

"That stinking ice is going to ruin the snow!" I stomp my foot like a child and yank my cap off in a flourish, pulling another lip twitch from my neighbor. His little gesture halts my fit, causing me to pull my glove off and slowly run the tip of my finger over his bottom lip. "I can't wait for this gift."

"What are you talking about?" He takes a step back, effectively removing my touch.

"When you finally allow me a smile. I just know it's going to be one spectacular sight."

He grunts, taking another step away from me. I do not like the distance after the closeness we just shared in the snowy yard. It leaves a void.

"Good night, Neena." He keeps taking steps backwards until he reaches his door.

"It truly has been, Asher. Thank you." I grin

widely with happiness.

He stares, holding that blank expression with precision until the neighborhood lights unexpectedly blink off.

"You've got to be kidding me! The ice just began." I stomp again.

I see the outline of his large form draw closer in the pitch-black. Leaning down, his breath hits the side of my face, automatically making me turn towards it. My own breath hitches, thinking he is about to brush a kiss along my lips.

Instead, the door opens behind me, and he gently pushes me inside. The now familiar sound of him sliding the lock into place on the doorknob pings right before he closes me into my dark home, leaving me alone and flustered. I have to lean against the locked door and take several calming breaths, trying to rid myself of the exhilaration evoked from him showing me another side tonight. It feels like we've added a few new steps to our two-step dance tonight and I really like the possibility of the change up.

A shiver trembles throughout my body, bringing me back to the reality of standing in the dark with cold damp clothes chilling me to the bone. Shuffling through the shadowy space, I begin plucking the wet layers of clothes off and continue until I'm upstairs in my room.

After stumping a few toes and knocking into a few furniture pieces, I reprimand myself for not preparing for the weather. The reports warned, but did I listen? Nope. I believe it's been established that that is a character flaw of mine. Instead of wasting the evening with reading that cheesy romance, I should have been stockpiling flashlights and candles and... oh stink! I forgot firewood. If Bode were in town, I would have had a nice stack on my porch. Instead, my brother-in-law is probably lounging on a beach sweating while I stand in the dark shivering. Yep. He's to blame. Not me.

As a few frigid hours pass, that's what I keep telling myself while hunkered down underneath two thick quilts, still shivering. I inventory my layers of clothing and wonder if another item can be added.

Underclothes.

Tank top.

Thermal top.

Hoodie.

Long johns.

Thick sweatpants.

Three pairs of socks.

A knit cap.

Gloves.

Nope. Another item is impossible. Argh. All of this and the tip of my nose is an ice cube. I'm downright chilled to the bone and nothing but a cozy fire or a long hot bath is going to be able to cure it. Sadly, neither one is an option in this lifeless house. I could kick myself for not preparing.

Silly girl, romance novels and snowmen distracted you and look what it got ya!

Curious, I ease over to the door, open it, and lean out to peek at Asher's side. Not surprising, a warm glow dances from his front window. I can almost feel the warmth of it. Before I register my own reactions, I'm standing by his door and knocking on it with my knuckles.

Now in sweats and thick socks, Asher looks down at me as he stands by the open door. It's unnerving how he chooses not to speak. Ever. *Just stare and make the girl squirm!*

"I'm freezing," I say through chattering teeth.

Still saying nothing, he widens the door and allows me entrance into his warm domain. He doesn't have to silently offer it twice. I scurry in and plant myself in front of his fireplace.

"Just let me get the chill off my bones and I'll head back home," I stutter out, almost convulsing.

"Why don't you have a fire going?"

There's no need to turn around to face his scowl to know it's there, so I keep my focus on the wild flames licking the sides of the fat wood logs. "I forgot to round up some firewood."

"You've been sitting next door in the freezing cold for the last couple of hours?" he asks on a growl.

"It didn't get cold right away." I peel the gloves off and nearly stick my frozen fingers in the fire. It stings at first as the heat melts the chill away. My front unthaws eventually, so I turn to get the backside of me back up to temperature.

Asher sits down on his massive leather couch, watching me. I'm about to pull my gloves back on when he pats the cushion beside him, inviting me to stay awhile. I gladly take him up on his offer, not wanting to reenter the icebox next door just yet. His quiet kindness presents more as he covers me with a warm, thick quilt, tucking it firmly around me.

"You're welcome to stay until the electricity comes back on."

"Thank you, Asher." I snuggle into his large side instead of keeping to my side of the couch and melt even more when I feel his arm wrap around my shoulders. He rubs his hand up and down, working some more heat into my cold limb. This gesture feels too familiar to have never lived it with him, but I decide to just enjoy it without overthinking matters.

We watch the flames dance around in the fireplace as if it's the most captivating show ever while time lapses in silence until I open my mouth and chance ruining the night.

"Tell me something."

He stiffens beside me. "Tell you what?"

"Anything. I know you were in the military—"

"I don't want to talk about that."

His tone leaves no room for that topic, so I pick something safer and easier. "Tell me about a recipe you created. Or how about a recipe you totally botched in culinary school. Now that would be fun to hear."

"Why do you think I would ever botch one?" Asher challenges, making me grin.

"Honey, as close as you are to perfect, we both know you can never achieve perfection in this life." I lean away slightly and eye him, trying my best to pull something out of him.

I don't know if it's the fire dancing in his eyes or maybe a memory of something amusing, but I'm close to begging him to share it with me when he clears his throat.

"I made a dumb rookie mistake my first week at school."

This gets my attention, so I tuck my feet underneath me and demand, "Tell me!"

He rubs his hand through his slightly tousled hair, giving off the illusion of casualness. "My first pastry assignment was a chocolate torte. It came out beautiful. The best looking one out of all the class. I was a bit smug about it until we tasted it. I used salt instead of sugar."

"No way!" I laugh on a gasp.

"Yep. You should have seen my instructor's face when she took a bite. It was horrible." He scrunches his perfectly straight nose, almost looking cute in a boyish way.

"See! No one is perfect." I slap my blanketed knee in amusement.

"I always double-check the container labels ever since then. The next blunder was using bittersweet chocolate instead of milk. Big difference."

And this is the key to Asher Reid opening up—food and his love of creating recipes. After confessing his chocolate blunders and how he steers clear of that dessert theme, he launches into telling me some menu ideas. His dedication to his restaurant's success is clearly evident as he speaks for the next hour or so on that topic alone. All this time, I could have been bathed in his conversations if only I directed my questions to the subject of food. Who knew!

His deep nuance is a lullaby and without thought or warning, I doze off while he explains a brisket dish he wants to add as a spring special.

*****

Layers of heavy fabric become stifling and choke me awake. Sweat dampens my skin, but I'm too tired to do anything but kick off the quilt and doze back off...

Reawakening in a pant, I frantically begin peeling the socks off. Once I've kicked out of them, I yank the hoodie off along with the thermal shirt and other shirt, leaving only the tank top. Cool air hits my skin, but the heat is still overbearing. Without opening my eyes, I shimmy out of the layers of pants all the way down to my boy shorts. How on earth did I ever manage getting all of these layers on in the first place? I'm about to die of a heatstroke from my own doings.

A throat clears as I reach for the hem of the tank top. *Oh shoot... I'm not in my house.* Glancing around, I find Asher on the floor by the fireplace stretched out in a sleeping bag.

"I'm hot," I moan out breathlessly, trying to explain myself. From the heated look on his face, I'd say that was an epic fail.

He groans and flings an arm over his eyes.

Embarrassed, I bolt off the couch and start collecting the massive amount of clothes I just stripped off right before this man, unbeknownst to me.

Way to go, Neena, giving your neighbor a private strip

show!

"I'll head home."

"No. Stay," Asher orders.

"I'm plenty warm. I'll be fine." Too warm, in more than one way at the moment.

He sits up and watches me hop around and gather pieces of discarded clothing, but embarrassment keep my eyes directed firmly to the floor. With the flames dancing around the room in hues of amber, the space feels too intimate and the need to escape quickly beckons.

"Neena, stay."

"I can't."

"Why not?"

The tension is already mounting rapidly in the glowing den and pushes me toward the door. "Because I want nothing more than to join you inside that sleeping bag," I confess, glancing over my shoulder to where he remains by the fireplace.

He lies back down on the sleeping bag and lets out a growl that sounds almost painful.

I take that as my cue to flee and hurry across the frozen porch barefooted. Entering my icy house is exactly what I need to cool down my bizarre libido. Still sweating, I plop down on the cool couch and shake my head. Never have I felt so strongly connected to a person, nor attracted for that matter.

That little confession probably just erased all the progress I made with Asher tonight. With slumped shoulders, I begin to redress to cover up how exposed I made everything just now.

Way to go, Neena!

Chapter Eleven

The damage has been done and Asher has withdrawn back away from me again, just as suspected. The snow eventually melted after a few days, taking away all the evidence of our newfound connection with it. The meals still show up on Monday and Wednesday, but no Asher can be found as weeks have slipped by.

Well, I've had enough of that, so today after a meeting at the office, I've dragged Parker to Charlie Mike for lunch. Yes, I'm using my friend to help fish the elusive chef out.

"You're using me, but I'm hungry so I'll let you just this once." Parker calls me out, always reading me like I'm an open book.

"Why do you say that?" I feign innocence as the hostess seats us near the back of the busy restaurant.

"It's already been made perfectly clear the guy doesn't care for me, but I'm willing to bet he cares about you."

I snort out a humorless laugh. "The guy doesn't care for anyone. Don't make yourself out to be special and set apart."

Parker picks up the menu, studying it a little too intently.

I take a sip of water to buy a few seconds before fishing for details. "Tell me about her."

He glances. "How do you know?"

"She has to be someone special to make you stay in Connecticut for over a month. Plus, I overheard you telling Theo about moving back after our Uganda trip."

"Neena..." Parker trails off, running his hand through his dark hair.

"I'm happy for you, but I'm hurt you've not told me," I interject and sniff back said hurt. "I thought our friendship meant more than that."

"It does... You do... Her name is Danielle. She's a friend from way back. We went out and reconnected while I was home."

"Wow. It must be pretty serious for you to up and resign."

He finally sets the menu down and meets my eyes. "I think so, but it's also time for a change. After

Texas..." His words choke off as his brow furrows. What he witnessed has impacted my friend greatly. I push my selfishness aside and focus on what he evidently needs—me being a supportive friend.

Offering a genuine smile, I say, "Congratulations on Danielle. I'm truly elated for you, but it's going to be boring around here without you helping me keep Theo riled up." I'm really going to miss the guy, but will support him in this decision.

The waitress sidles up to our table, her eyes drawn to my handsome lunch companion. Parker offers her a polite smile before going back to perusing the menu.

"We will both have the lunch special and sweet tea," I answer for the both of us.

Parker plops the menu down. "What she said, I guess," he says with a smirk.

The waitress gathers the menus, but before she scurries away, I place my hand on her arm.

"Also, could you tell the chef I have a complaint I need to discuss with him personally?"

She eyes me and visibly pales. "I'll make anything I wronged right. I need this job. Did I keep you waiting too long? I—"

"No, sweetie. You've been perfect. No complaint on you. My complaint is strictly the chef's fault, I assure you."

She nods frantically, seemingly not believing me, and hurries off.

"Way to give the poor girl a panic attack, darling. What are you up to, anyway?"

"I'm just trying to get the big oaf's attention."

He snorts. "By causing a scene in the guy's restaurant? Not cool, my friend."

"I have no intentions of causing a scene."

"Liar," Parker mutters under his breath just as Asher stomps up to the table.

"What?" Asher hisses through gritted teeth, crossing his arms with nostrils flaring.

"Oh, hi, Asher. You remember Parker." I wave towards my slightly blushing friend.

Both guys grunt and grumble their responses. No friendliness can be found between them.

"What's your complaint?" Asher's camouflage eyes darken with anger.

I tap my chin, drawing out the moment. "My complaint is that I'm in dire need of a chocolate torte and would really appreciate it if you left the salt out this time."

Asher's arms unlace and land by his side. His relief is evident with finding no real complaint. The man takes this place deftly serious. Boy, does he need to loosen up.

"I don't have time for this."

"Ha! Now you're using obscene words again!" I whisper yell. "I'm quite offended by your naughty mouth."

His lip twitches as he rolls his much calmer eyes. Without another word or grunt, he storms off.

Parker kicks me playfully underneath the table. "Neena Cameron, you're being a little brat."

"It's his fault." I point in the direction Asher disappeared. "The man runs hot and cold, and it's driving me absolutely crazy."

"I knew it! I knew it on the stinking porch that night!"

"What are you yammering on about?"

"You and your neighbor. I'm not blind."

Guilt pushes my eyes towards the napkin in my lap. "I didn't mean for it to happen."

Parker gently entwines our fingers resting on the table. "I'm just glad you're actually acknowledging it." He squeezes my hand, summoning my gaze back to his. "I want you to be happy. You, my friend, have too much greatness to not be sharing it with someone special to you." His eyes hold so much kindness, it pulls a genuine smile to my lips.

"Thank you."

"He's one lucky son of a gun."

I scoff. "One *stubborn* son of a gun is more like it."

He releases my hand as a much calmer waitress

places the basket of mini biscuits and glasses of tea on the table.

After she leaves us again, Parker whispers grace, and we both devour a biscuit.

"From what you've told me, I'm guessing the guy is probably from a hardcore military background. Give him some slack on the whole social etiquette protocol. You know from experience, soldiers sometimes have a hard time fitting back into civilian society."

"True," I agree. Leave it to Parker to be the voice of reason, pointing out a detail I've been too stubborn to see myself. I'm going to miss that balance he offers my off-kilter-ness as well. I push the uncomfortable thought away for now. He's here and we will enjoy the moment.

Our generous bowls of catfish stew served with fat squares of jalapeno cornbread arrive, so we leave the conversation and dig into the delicious fare.

"So good," Parker moans around a mouthful of cornbread.

All I offer is a nod and keep shoveling the stew in. The rich broth is over the top.

Surprisingly, mini chocolate tortes arrive just as we finish scraping our bowls clean.

We stare in awe at the beautiful pastry shell with a decadently dark-chocolate filling. Both are garnished with a snowflake made from thin pastry dough and a delicate sprinkling of powdered sugar.

The snow dance comes to mind, producing a smile before I'm able to stop it. Seeing that little symbol on top melts my heart yet annoys me at the same moment.

"See what I mean." I point my spoon to the dish. "He runs hot and cold."

Parker moans with a substantial mouthful of the torte. "I don't care how the man runs as long as he keeps serving up this amazing stuff. How are you not pudgy from eating here all the time?"

He's right. The torte is to die for—a buttery crust superbly complimenting the delicious dark chocolate. It's flawless with no hint of salt to be found.

"I don't eat here all the time," I say, but Parker gives me a look, demanding the truth. "Well, only about four times a week. There's three whole days I live off of coffee and cereal," I defend, beckoning a chuckle from him. He's got chocolate sticking to his teeth, producing my own laugh to join his.

"Just be glad you've been blessed with an unusually generous metabolism."

I take another considerable bite, feeling very blessed indeed.

After parting ways with Parker, I head over to Mia's office and discover it quite busy with little patients scurrying all around. I move up to the receptionist desk and find a familiar comfort in the form of Mrs. Janice. This adorable lady has been a permanent fixture at Sunshine Valley Pediatrics since Mia and I were babies. I love that she now works alongside my awesome Nurse Practitioner sister.

"Hello, young lady," I say with as much sunshine as I can. "I'm here to escort my sis to the hair salon. Our girl's getting old and seems to not be able to get that gray washed out of her hair without me."

Mrs. Janice looks up from her computer. "Hey, sugar. Mia had a slight emergency with a patient. She said to tell you to wait in her office."

Fish swimming across the giant flat screen TV in the waiting area catch my eye. "I think I'll just sit out here and see if they find Nemo again."

"Okay. I'll let her know."

The soft chair in the corner is my favorite and luckily it's vacant, so I plop down and focus on the animated movie along with a few others. The ocean sea with vibrant blues and brightly colored sea creatures lures me in until a child whimpering draws me back.

"Mommy, I really gotta go," a little girl whines out.

I look over and find the toddler trying to pull her mom out of her chair while the lady clings to a little guy in her arms.

"The restroom is right there, Maddie. Go ahead." The mom's tired eyes plead with the little girl while patting her on the arm encouragingly.

Tears stream down the young girl's flushed face. "But I need you. Please."

"I can't leave Hunter. He's sick. Please, baby. Be a big girl for me and go ahead. I'll be right here."

"No!" Her little face crumbles and her tears begin to shed earnestly. The poor mom looks like she's close to breaking as well.

"I can take you, Maddie," I offer. "I'm Mrs. Mia's sister," I add for both their peace of mind.

"No! I want my mommy to take me." The aggressive dance she's doing gives away the severity of her need for the restroom.

I direct my attention back to the mom. "I can hold your little guy while you take her. Mrs. Janice will vouch for me."

"Neena is a good girl, honey," Mrs. Janice reiterates.

The wary mom glances at her then back to me while the little girl continues to have her meltdown. Instead of waiting for her reply, I get up and go sit beside her on the small couch and open my arms toward the little boy who can be no more than two. He slowly climbs onto my lap and snuggles close to my chest, causing my heart to pinch painfully.

"Thank you," the mom says before hurrying her daughter into the restroom.

I look down and find Hunter's glassy eyes staring up at me. From the elevated heat his tiny body is emitting, I'd say a high fever is raging war with some foreign bug inside him.

"I'm Neena," I say softly. "You're not feeling so good, huh?"

He slowly nods his head, the movement almost nonexistent. I lightly dust my fingers along his blond curls.

"We will get Mrs. Mia to fix you right up, okay? She's the best."

He watches me blankly until his eyes drift shut. My heart melts further when he snuggles closer to me. I give in and nestle my face in his soft locks, inhaling the sweaty scent of him mixed with hints of baby lotion. And that right there does me in. I should have known better, but the longing has already taken root, producing hot tears that blur my vision. It's a longing that has been avoided and ignored over the years, seemingly the only way to survive it at times.

See, God. Look at me. I could totally rock as a momma. See, God. I could have handled it.

I sniff back my selfishness. Ovarian cancer may have stolen my ability to conceive, but my life was spared in the battle. With that reminder, my selfish thoughts drift away, and I refocus on the sick child in my arms. This moment is a gift God just graciously laid in my lap, literally. I can offer my heavenly Father's compassion to this tiny guy.

"Please, God, heal Hunter of whatever sickness has gotten ahold of him. Please grant this fever to break. And bless him and his momma some peaceful rest, for they are weary. Thank you for allowing me the opportunity to share your love. Amen," I whisper while listening to the little guy snore. My body begins swaying gently on its own accord with hopes of soothing him.

"Hunter," Mia's nurse, Renee, calls from the exam entrance. She spots me and waves with a confused expression skirting her face. "Oh. Hey, Neena."

"Hey. His mom is in the restroom with his sister," I explain.

Renee goes over to the door and talks through it with the momma. She turns back to me and beckons me to follow her. "She said you can take him back, if you don't mind."

"Not at all." I gather Hunter closer while I slowly stand and carry him to the exam room where Mia is already waiting.

"Hunter, you've met my little sister, Neena?"

He barely responds as she starts the exam by

taking his temperature. She tsks. "One-o-three. That's a little high, buddy. Renee, will you go see if his mom has given him anything for the fever? If not, let's get some Tylenol in him."

"Sure thing," Renee agrees, rushing out of the room.

"Is he going to be okay?" I ask, watching her swab his tiny nose with a long Q-tip.

The mom shuffles in with the little girl in tow, both looking as worried as I feel, with long drawn expressions. Mia pulls Hunter out of my arms and gently lays him down on the exam table. She asks the mom various questions while administering the medicine. Renee comes back with the test results, confirming he has the flu. Poor kid.

In the end, Mia has to cancel our hair appointments so she can accompany them next door to the hospital after finding the little guy dehydrated and in need of fluids. I stick around until they head out with him, hoping to lend some comfort and support. With nothing better to do, I head back to the office to bug Theo and help him find me a close assignment. After receiving word from Mia that they let Hunter go home after the fever broke, I head to my own home, feeling relief that he's going to be all right.

It's been one long day and I'm feeling quite drained by it.

Chapter Twelve

The world drifts by in a haze of ambiguity. I'm still a part of it, I think, but cannot grasp ahold of anything. My body feels like lead and is on a steady simmer that is so uncomfortable. I'd give anything to be able to push it off. Every inch hurts in a peculiar ache... Mia's concerned face flickers in glimpses during this purgatory.

It's time for medicine...

Let's get some fluids in you...

I'm being tended to, but am unable to acknowledge any of it. Whatever has grabbed ahold of me has captured my thoughts and speech with both being jumbled and obscured. A dreadful, fitful sleep keeps meeting up with me, but it offers no relief.

*****

A new day dawns after who knows how many have snuck by unnoticed, finding the debilitating fever finally gone. I blink open my pasty eyes, but have to close them with the odd image they produce. Giving them a good rub, I reopen them and still find Asher sitting across from me.

"What are you doing here?" I croak out, trying to right myself on the couch. He's beside me in a flash, helping to steady my weak body in a sitting position. A sigh slips out as my tender bones shift, relieving the ache in my back. *I wonder how long I've been stuck on this couch.*

"You were sick. I've helped Mia take care of you," he speaks, bringing my attention back.

"Why?" I can't help but ask.

He gives away nothing in his features as always. "You were sick."

Obviously, the man doesn't get that I want to know the *why* behind his presence. The excuse of me being sick isn't substantial enough, but I quickly give up on getting an in-depth answer and just stare at him. Besides a slight shadow underneath each of his eyes and the stubble on his chin, he looks normal. But these two indicators give away the fact that he's probably been here the entire time. *The man never has stubble.*

"Mia?" I mumble, looking around the room, but not finding her.

"Work."

"What about your work?" I ask, licking my chapped lips.

"Our other chef has it covered."

"Why?" I ask again while running a feeble hand unsuccessfully through my rat's nest. The motion stirs the air and delivers a sickly scent to my nose. Gross...

"You had the flu," he answers, still not explaining why he's here.

Slowly, I rise from the couch, only to fall back down from the massive wave of vertigo slamming into me. Asher's arm catches me and doesn't let go. I can't help but worry he can smell me, so I try wiggling out of his grasp, but he's not having it.

"I need to shower." My head lobs against the back of the couch and my eyes drift shut.

"You need some fluids first."

He releases me and then the sound of the fridge opening and closing barely registers as sleep slowly creeps over me.

Seconds, minutes, hours? I'm not sure how long, but eventually my eyes reopen. Asher hands me a lemon Gatorade. My mouth feels like the Mojave

Desert, so I gladly start chugging it. Half of the bottle is gone in a flash.

"Whoa," Asher says, pulling the bottle out of my grasp.

"But I'm so thirsty."

"Yeah, but it'll make you sick if you drink it too fast."

Several minutes tick by before he hands it back to me. My stomach is already churning the liquid in protest, so I take his advice and slowly sip the remaining contents of the bottle. After another lethargic stretch of time, I try standing again. Before I can protest, the man has me cradled in his arms and is carrying me upstairs. I'm too weak to fuss about it, anyway.

Asher walks us into my bedroom and on into the attached bath before sitting me down on the vanity chair. He then turns the shower on as I can do nothing but watch with my head whirling.

"Asher."

He raises a hand into the stream and tests the temperature of the water. "Yeah?"

"You can't stay in here while I shower."

He glances over his shoulder. "What if you get dizzy and faint?"

"You can't."

Asher scans the room. "Sit tight for a sec," he says

before sprinting from the room.

While waiting, I make the mistake of looking in the mirror and cringe. Staring back at me is a corpse with sickly pale skin, dark circles, and knotted hair that's oddly limp and greasy. I look away from the vile image due to it wreaking havoc on my self-esteem. I'm sure after Asher gets me settled, he's going to avoid me like the plague.

I'm beginning to think he came to his wits and made a run for it, but he finally returns with a plastic chair, placing it inside the steamy shower stall. I'm too worn out to ask where it came from, but I'm guessing Mr. Recluse had to break his 'I don't talk to my neighbors' clause to acquire it.

"I'll be right outside the door." He turns to leave me as I notice he's gotten half of his thermal shirt wet along with one leg of his track pants.

"Why?" I ask again.

"In case you need me."

"No... Why have you done all of this?" I motion at nothing.

"You were sick," he repeats before shutting the door, but that still doesn't answer my question.

That man can be so frustrating.

Slowly standing, I manage to undress and get into the shower before collapsing into the chair. Thank goodness Asher thought to do that or I would have been in a mess. I spend most of my shower hunkered down on that chair. Two shampooing rounds leave my arms feeling like wet noodles. The odd weakness of my body won't alleviate. That flu bug sure was vicious. As I scrub the soapy sponge over my body, I can't help but feel sorry for little Hunter if this is what he endured as well.

After shutting the shower off and toweling dry, I scoot the vanity chair to the sink and begin the task of washing death out of my mouth. Two rounds with the toothbrush and mouthwash, the job is done, but it's left me wiped completely out.

"You okay in there?" Asher's deep, muffled voice carries through the closed door.

I stare down at the hairbrush in my lap, trying to gather the strength to use it.

"Yeah." The word comes out feebly.

"You decent?"

I tighten the towel wrapped around me. "I guess."

The door opens and his imposing form steps inside the small space. Gone is the wet thermal shirt, only leaving him in a fitted white undershirt. Thank goodness he left the pants on. Even in my puny state, the man's presence still quickens my heart. It's doubtful that this is something I'll ever be allowed to act on, but I'm pretty sure I'm in love with him.

"Do you need some help?" he asks, surprising me yet again.

"Do you have a beautician with you or a pair of scissors?" I point to my wet, matted hair.

Asher strides over and claims the brush from my lap. I'm too tired and too stunned to stop him. For the next longest spell, this hulk of a man patiently takes on the task of detangling my long hair in a gentleness I would have never believed possible from him.

Tears well up in my eyes, evoked from the compassion he's so graciously given me.

His eyes meet mine in the mirror as he stills his hand. "Am I hurting you?"

"No." I sniffle the word out.

"Are you hurting somewhere?" He assesses me, eyes skimming over my body thoroughly.

Shaking my head, I mumble through tears, "No. Just... Thank you for this."

He grunts his reply and goes back to gently brushing out my hair.

While we are at it, the man has the most alluring grunt. Not like a pig grunt, but a deep-chest rumble that has to make more than just this girl weak in the knees. Okay, now I love his grunt? I may be in trouble...

Afterwards, Asher carries me to the bed, sits me down on the edge, and allows me to direct him in retrieving a fresh set of pajamas. Giving me privacy, he waits in the hall while I dress. As soon as I open the door, he gently sweeps me back in his arms and deposits me downstairs in a cushiony wingback chair. Talk about feeling like a princess.

"I've made some soup. It just needs to be warmed." Without pause, he does just that.

Watching him move around my kitchen with purpose, I'm unable to suppress the flow of my silent tears. Asher effectively ignores them as he presents me with a steamy cup of chicken noodle soup.

"I don't think I can eat." I eye the food warily.

"Humor me," he says, sitting beside me in the matching teal chair beside me.

The desire to mouth off on the fact that for the last several months I've been trying to do just that is squelched by the softness in his stare. Those same eyes that have kept a steely shield before me, drop their guard unexpectedly now. It's a look of pleading, and so it talks me right into picking up the spoon. I take a tentative taste of the warm broth. The flavor isn't enough to overwhelm my puny taste buds, but enough to intrigue them, making it easy on my system to slowly eat it.

Once the cup is empty, Asher places another Gatorade in my hand.

"Thank you," I say, offering him a weak smile.

Of course, he offers the usual grunt before going to work on my living room while I can only sit and watch on. He efficiently scrubs all the surfaces with precision and smothers my couch with disinfectant spray. The cleaning continues on to the kitchen with him only pausing long enough to tend to me, whether it's something to drink or carrying me to the bathroom. After being fortified with the soup and lots of liquid, I could easily walk, albeit slowly, but the boss won't allow it.

As I continue to regard him moving about my space in an almost ownership manner, another layer unfolds of this guarded man. One thing's for certain, Asher Reid likes to take care of people and is quite good at it—even if he *don't* care to admit it verbally.

Chapter Thirteen

By my calendar that hangs slightly askew on the wall, February has arrived with as little patience as me to move forward. My corpse was raised from the flu grave just over a week ago. It's been slow moving, but beings that I've spent the entire Saturday morning at Mia's house helping her eat her humongous heart-shaped box of chocolates from Bode, I'm feeling more energized than I have in quite a while.

"How many more of those things are you making?" she asks, licking caramel from her thumb.

"Just a few more," I mumble, trying to steady my sugar-induced jittery hand as I write the word, *compassionate* on a pink heart-shaped sticky note.

"Does Asher even know he is your Valentine?"

My shoulders shrug with indifference.

"Regardless, I'm claiming him as such this year."

"Neena," she warns quietly.

Looking up from my sea of pink hearts scattered all over her dining table, I ask, "What?"

"I'm more than thrilled you've finally shown interest in a guy. Seriously, I was worried joining a convent was next on your list, but what if he doesn't feel the same way?"

"Asher nor you can convince me of that. He has feelings for me or he would have never taken care of me while I was sick." I drop my metallic silver marker and eye her sternly. "And speaking of which, did he say anything to you?"

"He actually found you sick and called me. Said you didn't know how to lock or shut a door." Mia chuckles, but then sobers. "Asher found your phone and called, and I'm glad he did. I'm impressed by how attentive he was to you, but I really feel that it's a character trait of his. He didn't engage in any small talk with me, just did whatever I asked. It was almost like he was putting up with the both of us out of duty."

My silly hearts seem a bit misplaced with her putting it that way. "Thanks for ruining my Valentine's Day," I grouch, collecting all of my foolishness.

"I didn't mean to do that. Neena—"

"Forget it." After gathering my mess, I stalk to the door but backtrack. "I'm taking the chocolate and you're not stopping me." I glare, tucking the half-empty box under my arm and stomping out.

Before I make it out of her driveway, the past taps me on the shoulder.

Cancer showed up when I was only seventeen.

Seventeen!

That age is just on the cusp of great sweetheart moments, but I was robbed. Not many Valentines were kind to me in the romance department during my early adult years. Operations, treatments, and recovery took a lot of my time and a lot of my self-esteem. I've never much romanced the notion of finding someone to be my Valentine, beings that I felt stripped of my femininity for so long. Cancer put me behind with school, so college wasn't complete early as the norm, and then years of establishing myself as a hardworking, respectable journalist kept me busy from having to worry about a social life.

After all of these years, some big brooding brute dares to show up and puts a desire in me to want something I felt unworthy of having—love, a relationship, a life partner…

"Stupid girl," I mumble on a repeat all the way home. My phone keeps going off, and I keep ignoring it, knowing it's Mia. Parking in the deserted driveway, I text her an apology. *I know you are just concerned for me. Sorry I acted out, but I'm keeping the chocolate.*

Mia – *Fine. Keep it. Love you.*

Me – *Love you too.*

Taking a deep breath, I shuffle out of the car and head into the house alone with my stolen chocolates and plan to have my fill of them for supper while watching a tasteless comedy. Hopefully the combination will lift my gloomy spirits.

The sky begins to darken with the reality that I've spent another Valentine's alone. I fiddle with the end of the pink scarf I added to my usual outfit of white button-down and jeans with hopes of romance earlier today. Mia squelched that hope in one fell swoop, but I'm unwilling to take it off. Silly, right? My sticky notes peek from under the empty candy box, nudging me to go ahead and give Asher the gift I'm not so sure he'll appreciate.

After debating another thirty minutes or so, I peel my lonely, lazy self off the couch, gather the hearts and go adhere them to his door. It takes less time to cover the door in a misshaped heart of words than it did to write them. Satisfied with my job, I head back inside and begin cleaning up the living room where I spent the day sulking and consuming my weight in chocolate.

As I'm dumping the candy wrappers, large headlights shine through the house, alerting me that my neighbor has finally made it home. Giddiness ignites in me, sending my already elevated pulse to rev up a few notches. Skipping over to the door, I crack it open slightly to acquire a clear view to witness Asher finding his gift. He takes a few moments to climb out of his beast of a vehicle, and I'm getting right antsy with having to wait. When he emerges, his hands are filled with a white box and a couple of cloth grocery bags. The familiar heaviness of his steps sound on the porch before coming to a halt at his door. I have to open the door a little wider to see him.

"What's all this?" he asks without looking away from the hearts.

Of course, GI Joe would automatically sense someone stalking him. Knowing he's spotted me, I come out of hiding and join him by the door. "They're words that describe you."

Asher reads some of them out loud. "*Giving. Attentive. Compassionate. Hero.*" He reads one silently before looking over at me with an eyebrow arched highly. "Handsome?"

"You know you are."

He shakes his head and transfers the bags to his left hand and starts peeling the notes off his door.

"Why'd you do this?"

"It's my Valentine to you."

He grunts, not surprisingly, as I reach over and begin peeling them off and sticking them over his heart.

"You have a big heart, even though you keep it camouflaged from the world." One after the other, I place them on his black chef coat. "*Strong. Caring. Quiet. Chef. Soldier. Gentle. Tough. Entertaining...*" I keep on until he's covered with my gift. He stands stoically and allows me to continue, which is a gift in itself.

Some may view this as silly or cheesy, but it's not. *Significant* is the word playing through my mind as my eyes scan all of the words describing how incredible this man is and how important he has become to me in such a short time. My fingers trace the word *Friend* knowing that's what he's become to me whether he wanted to or not.

"Neena..." He shakes his head. "I don't know what to do with you."

"Start by being my Valentine," I whisper, keeping my eyes focused on the words covering his chest. I know I'm about to be rejected again.

"I don't do Valentine's."

And there it is. Even though I knew it was coming, the impact still stings.

Parker's wise words ring through my ear. *Give the guy some slack. You know it can be tough for soldiers to reenter civilian life.*

I nod with understanding and offer a small smile. "It's okay, Asher. Good night." Holding my head high with fabricated bravado, I head to my door.

"Wait. These are for you."

Curious, I turn back around, and he shoves the white box in my hand. Opening it up, I'm met with cinnamon warmth and beauty in the shape of... "Apple roses?"

"Apple puff pastry roses," he corrects. "With a cherry jam glaze.

I'm in awe of the beauty of the treat and completely blown away. Thinly sliced apples with the red skin glistening from the cherry glaze circles a layer of pastry, forming an elegant rose bud. Twelve in all.

"Oh, Asher. You made me a dozen roses." Overwhelmed with gratitude, I lunge forward and hug him before he can stop me. He doesn't return the embrace, but I'm okay with that. Leaning back, I give him a knowing grin. "I'm your Valentine, whether you want to admit it or not."

The big guy radiates that deep grumble before taking a step back. "I'll be over in a few to cook supper." He raises the bags slightly before stalking to his door.

Did he say supper? Hot dog! All that chocolate swimming in my stomach could really use something more substantial to join it. Asher Reid is so my Valentine!

"Don't forget your rearview mirror head gear," I holler out before he can close the door. "Because I'm totally checking you out tonight. Fair warning, sir."

Looking over his shoulder, he says straight-faced, "I think I can keep you straight without it."

I can't help but giggle at that. "We shall see," I tease with a wink.

Minutes later, the handsome chef has set up shop in my kitchen to cook me homemade pasta with a red sauce he prepared at work earlier. You can't get any more romantic than Italian cuisine. Am I right? The fact that he's still wearing the chef coat covered in my hearts turns my own heart into contented mush. The need to snag a picture of him cooking for me, covered in my gift, and send it to Mia is nagging me, but I know that little move would probably kill the night's mood, so I refrain and just keep watching him instead. I'm mindful to admire him from side views so that his back is never fully toward me. The crisp black coat against his light hair is such a handsome sight. Even though he is of a substantial stature, the man carries that strong bulk with exquisite grace. I could seriously watch him cook for the rest of my days. It's a confidently choreographed performance that could never become boring to me.

The aroma of tangy garlic and sweet tomatoes whirling around a medley of fresh herbs has my chocolate covered stomach growling all mean-like. I push all of my books to one end of the dining table and put together two place settings, with hopes that this unexpected change isn't too detrimental on this wooden table for it's never held such a responsibility as a meal.

Watching him gather a large serving bowl and two large spoons, I'm struck by an odd fact. Never has Asher actually eaten with me in all these months. It's just always him feeding me, so this is most certainly another rare gift. I want to celebrate it properly, so a few lit candles join the table as well.

With skill that awes me, Asher tosses the fresh linguine with the hardy sauce and carries it over. He serves us both generous proportions before bowing his head. I wait for him to speak his prayer, but realize it will be done as he does everything else — silently. Dropping my head, I offer mine to God silently as well, thanking Him for Asher and this unexpected albeit unusual friendship.

As we tuck into the heavenly fare, Asher studies my word wall. His eyes still and his brows furrow mid-bite. "Why is my name on your wall?"

My cheeks heat without my permission, not even thinking he would ever see my wall up close much less read it. "Do you know what your name means?" I ask, sidestepping his question.

"No."

"Asher means happy one. That's unique enough to make it on my word wall."

He shakes his head and takes another bite. I try not to stare, but it's such a rarity to see him do something as ordinary and mundane as eating. I'm quite engrossed to be honest.

"Do I have sauce on my face?" Asher takes his napkin and starts mopping it over his full lips.

Giggling, I shake my head.

"Then stop staring at me." Such a bossy grouch, this man. He motions toward the wall. "What's with this, anyway?"

I'm so over the moon that he asked me something personal, I have to giggle again like some silly young girl on her first real date with her longtime crush.

"Blame that on my dad. I inherited his love of words. Do you want to know about a secret he shared with me on how to steal properly?"

My dinner date sets his fork down. "I don't want to know."

Laughter bubbles out of me again. For someone

so down and out earlier, I'm too jubilant to maintain my composure now, making me feel a little bipolar.

Get a grip, Neena.

"My dad taught me the importance of stealing moments and opportunities to live," I correct his misunderstanding. "Life is but a vapor. God doesn't promise tomorrow, but He did give me the gift of life in the first place. In honor of His gift, I always try living to the fullest."

Asher looks at me thoughtfully as he picks his fork back up. "Life is most definitely a vapor." He allows some regret to seep into his words, making me want to pry him open even further. But I take his own word to heart, and *don't*.

He's given me enough gifts today that I will add to my precious plunder of moments and memories. For now, I serve us coffee to go along with his beautiful roses and spend the next longest stretch of time pronouncing and defining words he points out from my wall. He seems impressed when I explain the word paradisiacal and that his food inspired it. I remind him of using it to describe his cookies back at Christmas.

"No. Leave the dishes. I'll get them," I say, halting him from clearing the table after dessert concludes. Glancing at the clock, I'm shocked to find it closing in on midnight.

"I don't mind."

"Wow. You just used your ugly word positively. I'm impressed."

He rolls his eyes and goes to pick up his plate once more.

"No. Seriously, you cooked. I'll clean. Just leave it."

"If you're sure."

"Absolutely." I walk him to the door, but keep my hands to myself. "Thank you for being my Valentine, Asher."

"Happy Valentine's Day, Neena." With that, he reaches around and locks my doorknob before shutting it. Yet another silent giveaway that he truly cares.

Not being able to stand it any longer, I grab my phone and snap a picture of the scene of my date at the table—melted candles dripping happily, mostly empty plates and glasses, and linen napkins abandoned after properly doing their jobs. I caption it, *He was my Valentine after all* and hit SEND. My phone pings almost immediately with a new message, startling me. I figured Mia wouldn't even discover my text until tomorrow. She and Bode must be celebrating Valentine's late, too.

Mia – *Yay! I'm sorry for dragging you down earlier.*

Me – *No worries. I owe you a box of chocolates.*

Mia – *Word!*

Me – *No you did not just say WORD! You dork!*

Mia – *Straight up.*

Laughing, I put my phone down and get to work on cleaning up after my date.

Best. Valentine's. Day. Ever!

Chapter Fourteen

Have you ever made a bold decision only to have that nagging feeling it's going to sneak around and bite you unexpectedly on the butt? Well, here's hoping this won't be one of those instances. It might be deemed as meddling, but I pick up the phone and do it anyway.

"Hello, lovely," Luka answers on the third ring.

"Hey! I'm calling to find out when you're getting your cute hiney on a plane to Tennessee."

He chuckles. "I've been swamped between New York and LA."

"Stop playing around with those pretentious brats and come see me. I've found the next 'it' place in fine dining."

"Play pretty, love."

"I know. Just trying to bully you into coming here to check this awesome place out."

"Ah. Charlie Mike?"

"Yes."

"Is this place really that good that *the* NL Cameron is trying to persuade me into checking it out?"

I scan the menu I swiped on my last visit and confess, "I have to admit I'm heading to rehab soon I'm so addicted."

"Then I must bump it up on my list this instant."

Excited, I do a little happy dance around the kitchen. My elbow lands just right against the fridge handle, triggering my not-so-funny bone. The hateful pain races up my arm and slaps me in the face. Trying to rub the sting out, I nearly drop the phone.

"Neena, did I lose you?" I barely hear Luka ask.

Placing the phone back to my ear, I say, "I'm still here. This place is a must, trust me."

"Again, if NL says it, surely it's true. Just let me give my calendar a look…" I hear shuffling and then keys of a laptop clicking. "Humph."

That one word worries me. "What?"

"I'm actually available this weekend. That is if you'll be in town."

A smile spreads over my face as I step over to the

kitchen island and pull up my itinerary on the laptop. After rearranging a few things, my weekend becomes available, too. "My schedule just became all about you, my friend."

Luka chuckles. "Well, I do like the sound of that."

I close the lid on the laptop and lean against the counter. "Text me your flight plan and I'll pick you up at the airport."

"Sounds fabulous, dear. Can't wait."

"Me too!"

*****

Saturday finally shows up with Luka Ganty. The distinguished fifty-year-old can only be described as a silver fox. He mostly definitely gives George Clooney a run for his money on that title. And the man is in his element, scanning the scene here at Charlie Mike. I'm trying not to sway his opinion of the place in either direction, so I've mainly kept my mouth hinged shut on my opinion of anything.

"The atmosphere is very inviting. I like all of the military touches hidden about. Masculine, but not intimidating." He assesses the warmly toned space with approval while making notes.

I only nod, but what I really want to do is point out all of the little treasures I've discovered over the last several months while frequenting this amazing place. Instead, I busy myself with eating a majority of the creamy crab dip with the homemade chips.

Luka cuts his icy blue eyes at me. "Go ahead and moan, dear. It's that good." He chuckles as I do as I'm told.

"Sorry." I dab the corners of my mouth with my napkin.

He passes a hand through the air to bat away my apology. "What do you recommend on the menu?"

"Anything. Everything." Another moan slips out as I take another bite.

"Anything? Everything?"

"I should be ashamed to admit I've tried everything on the menu, but I'm not." I grin over at him, but he's shaking his head while looking over the choices.

"SOS?" he mumbles.

"Ooh! Get that! I'll get the chicken with succotash and share it with you." I hand Jessie, our waitress, my menu. She's been patiently waiting for our order.

"Anything else?" she asks.

"How about the catfish stew as well," Luka requests, finally relinquishing his menu.

"Good choice. I'll have it right out." Jessie gives me a knowing nod and I return it, before she hurries off. I hunted her down as soon as we arrived to let her know that Luka was an important guest. She's one of my favorite waitresses, so I always request her to be the one to put up with me and she kindly agrees to take me on.

I bring my attention back to my dinner date in his tailored gray suit and tease, "Hungry?"

"Sweetheart, I'm here to do my job and to do it thoroughly."

"Maybe I'm in the wrong profession. Do you have any openings?" I tease some more.

My friend chuckles as he jots a few more notes into his little journal. I keep quiet and allow him to do his job. I've been beyond blessed to meet some amazing people due to my journalism career, that's for sure.

Luka ends up doing his job thoroughly enough to clean all the dishes of any food, and that's a really good sign. I've accompanied him to restaurants where he only took his minimum two-bite test and pushed the dish away.

He excuses himself to go to the restroom while we wait on a medley of desserts, so I take this opportunity to flag Jessie down again.

"What's up, Neena?"

"Please ask Asher to come greet my friend. Tell him it's very important for him to be on his best behavior."

Her eyes widen. "You seriously want me to say that to my boss?" She shakes her head. "No way."

Silly girl. Silly staff for that matter. The whole bunch of them is scared of Asher for some reason. Yes, the man can be deathly intimidating, but that's beside the point.

"Fine. Just tell him it would mean a lot to me."

She lets out a sigh of relief. "I can say that. Okay."

"And hurry up with the desserts and coffee," I call out to her before she gets too far away. She offers a thumbs-up and keeps moving.

By the time Luka returns from what I'm guessing is a snoop job instead of a bathroom visit, the table boasts a beautiful array of petite desserts more fitting for the queen of England than mountain folk—pumpkin crème brulee glittering with burnt sugar, fresh fruit tartlets, mini chocolate hazelnut charlottes, and lemon scented cheesecake bites. The robust aroma of coffee mingling with the sweet fare sets my mouth to watering.

My sweet patience runs thin when we have to pause so Luka can snap a few pictures of the lovely spread before we dig in. Earlier, I made sure to sit in the chair that has a direct view of the kitchen door to keep an eye out for Asher. As I'm finishing off my cheesecake bite, he finally pushes through with his eyes landing immediately on me. There's almost a hint of happy peeking out from those camouflage eyes, but it quickly turns steely. He halts after only a few steps with his eyes sliding over to Luka, whom I'm just realizing is trying to feed me a bite of his crème brulee.

Asher does a sharp one eighty and disappears back into the kitchen. Great. Mr. Attitude has to show up on this day of all days. *Figures.* Shaking off my annoyance, I open my mouth and accept the spicy offering and savor the crisp crunch of smoky sugar.

"You were absolutely right about this place, Neena." Luka scrapes around the edges of the ramekin to get one last scoop of the crème brulee.

"Told you." I smile, grateful to give Asher this gift whether he wants it or not. Luka writing his review can make or break a restaurant. From his comments, Charlie Mike is about to land on the restaurant map in a mighty way.

After settling the bill, I reluctantly head back to the airport. I pull the car in the drop off lane and pull a pout.

"I just wish you could stay longer."

"Me too, dear, but you know how it is in this business." He gives me a kiss on the cheek and is gone.

The drive back home has me pondering on how to get Asher to loosen up. The man is just wound so tight all the time. There was no call for him acting like that at the restaurant. I'm just glad Luka is none the wiser on that little episode.

I plant myself on the porch after pulling on a coat to wait for my difficult neighbor to bring his grumpy butt home. The wait ends up short with him arriving home early. Guess it pays to be the boss.

He trudges up the steps around eight and comes to a halt once he spots me.

"You have fun on your date?"

Two new firsts are delivered at the same time in those six sharp words—jealousy and him taking the initiative to speak first. *Wow.*

"If you would have brought your moody self to the table as I requested, you would have found out that I was not on a date. The gentleman at the table was Luka Ganty."

He stares blankly. "And that's supposed to mean something to me?"

"It should mean something greatly to you. He's a world-renowned food critic." I cross my arms and glare at him.

Maybe something is finally registering, because Asher plops down in the rocker beside mine and releases a long sigh. "How was I to know that?"

"You're a restaurateur. This man should be on your immediate radar." I shake my head and watch absently as a few kids race by on their bikes. "You kids need to be home! It's getting late!" I yell. They throw their hands up in acknowledgement before turning back around.

"I've only been back in this country for a little over a year now. I don't know anything other than I want to cook and do it well," he says after we watched the kids scurry to their designated homes.

"Why didn't you come to the table as I requested?" I'm not letting him off the hook so easily.

Asher huffs, clearly becoming frustrated. "I didn't want to interrupt your date," he bites out.

"*No*. You cocked an attitude is what you did. Regardless of who accompanied me to your restaurant you should have been polite. You could have ruined your reputation tonight had you delivered that cold attitude to my table."

"The food was spot on, wasn't it?" A pucker forms between his thick brows.

"Yes." We sit in quiet for a few beats with our rockers rocking in a frustrated rhythm. "Tell me this... What if I had shown up at your door that first day with my delicious pie but with a poor attitude? Would you have wanted to accept my pie?" I let that hang in the chilly air between us for a few moments before continuing. "But put all of that aside. Luka is my friend and you should have shown him some respect based on that fact alone."

Asher says nothing—no surprise there—so I leave him on the porch to think about what he's done. This man has no social skills whatsoever. I kick off my boots by the door and retrieve my laptop. I've put my work on hold for that big lug on my porch this weekend, so now it's time to play catchup. Before I can pull up the interview email, Asher pushes through the door. Coming no farther than a step inside, he sighs heavily once again.

"Sorry," he mutters, studying his shoes. "Yes, I was jealous. It's just that you... me..." He shakes his head and swipes his hands down his face before motioning between us. "This is becoming too complicated. I don't do complicated... Not anymore."

My heart sinks. "Then un-complicate it."

"How?" That one word gives me hope that he's not ready to walk away from whatever this is between us just yet.

"Start by taking me to church in the morning."

His eyes sweep around the room, searching for an answer perhaps. "That sounds uncomplicated enough." He nods his head once, secures the lock on my door, and disappears.

I stare absently at the flashing cursor on the computer screen, knowing full well I won't be able to concentrate on the interview tonight. Powering the computer down, I leave the article for tomorrow night. My head droops until it lands on the granite countertop. I consider the complicated facets of Asher Reid as my overheated cheek takes in the coolness of the stone. He's making things difficult and not willing to open up, which keeps us both confused and frustrated. I wonder about the impact his military life had on him. Clearly it was extensive.

This thought has me rushing into my guestroom/office upstairs. After digging through my filing cabinet for the next longest, I finally unearth a file filled with some clues. Stretching out on the guest bed, I unfold heavily creased letters one by one and begin rereading them. I've read these words from those soldiers in that special ops unit so many times that each paper holding a military life testimony has become thinner and worn. Some are long and detailed and some short and to the point, but each one is beyond significant. After reading these letters that first time, I knew I had to meet their owners. And meet them I did on that secret military base in the middle of nowhere in a foreign land.

Their letters give away no specifics to their identity. They were only allowed to share their nicknames, but I'm thankful for their sincere words. Each one gave away their sacrifice and how they've coped with being in the battlefield. Settling in, I go back through and let their words give me some insight to how I can better understand Asher with hopes of being able to fit into his closed-off life.

Chapter Fifteen

Letters from the Special Ops Soldiers

Dear Sir,
During my first deployment, my eyes were opened wide to what kind of real evil the world holds. This evil had to have escaped the bowels of hell. When opportunity presented itself to help rid the world of this evil in a radical way, there was no hesitation to join this elite group of soldiers. Never did I realize just how much hell lurks right here on earth. I'm on a mission that will never be completed, but I've made an oath to my country to do my part to eliminate as much of it as possible.
This place isn't so bad. I have a stand-up group I call

my brothers. We've formed a bond no one in the civilian world can comprehend. We literally bleed for one another without so much as blinking an eye.

This place can even be better with a giant bag of peanut butter M&M's. Since you're one of the very few privy to knowing about us, surely you can manage us a few cases, right?

Sincerely,
Midnight

Dear Sir,

We all have scars. Some not so significant, easily forgotten. Others a little deeper, producing thick reminders. A few go all the way to the soul, and those seem to never heal completely, no matter how much time passes.

I try to keep my mind busy, always tearing things apart, and then putting them back together again. The crowd picks on me about it and it's why they call me Gadget. But we all seek some kind of refuge from our scars out here.

We were told not to ask you for anything, so I won't ask you for some Popular Mechanics magazines. Old or new doesn't matter. But I'm not asking for them!

Sincerely,
Gadget

Dear Sir,

I'm our unit's navigational specialist. I ride shotgun on all missions, upfront in all the action. It's my duty to navigate us in the right direction and back in one piece. That part I can handle. Losing members of my brotherhood, not so much.

I have nightmares. It's always the same one, just slight variations. A little kid wanders up to me asking for candy, knowing I have some tucked away in my cargo pockets for him. As I hand over the piece of candy, we both shatter and scatter into a million pieces.

This is actually a true story, just not mine.

Standing guard at a checkpoint not even fifty yards away, I watched this happen to my buddy. One second he's smiling down at a scrawny kid while handing over candy, then the next they both disappeared right before my eyes from a bomb hidden in the kid's coat. After I regained consciousness, the only thing remaining of them was now coated on me, head to foot.

I have to live with my nightmares in order to prevent others from having to live them. It's my cross to bear and I'm pretty certain I'll never be able to scrub all of the blood off my hands. I wouldn't mind trying one of those dream catchers out. You think they work?

Sincerely,
Compass

Dear Sir,

They call me Motor for obvious reasons. My old man owns a garage, so I knew how to do an oil change way before I mastered tying my shoes. I was already driving before I hit double digits in age, a benefit of living on quiet country roads. Everyone said it was my calling to take over my old man's business one day, but I felt a deeper calling.

I HATE when someone hurts. It causes me pain. In school I had a tendency of ending up in the principal's office for beating up the bullies. I've always wanted to protect the weak. So here I am, manning the wheel of my unit's Humvee while protecting a weak world from the nastiest bullies known to mankind.

You asked us to share our dreams. Mine are simple, a world without evil bullies…

And a world filled with the tastiest food ever prepared. Yes, I'm sick of MRE's. How about in exchange for this letter, you send us some apple turnovers. Man, I can almost taste them.

Sincerely,
Motor

Dear Sir,

I had me a girl back home. My high school sweetheart in fact. She wore my high school ring as a promise to marry me after we graduated. I could hardly wait to officially make her mine. It was all I could think about. When graduation was finally behind us, we began planning a fall wedding. That's what my girl wanted, and that's what she was going to get.

Then 9/11 happened, and as you know the world got turned upside down. I knew that very day I had to do my part to protect my country and my girl. She didn't feel the same. Said I would be no more than a murderer, just as guilty as those terrorists on those planes. I know better than that and even though we've not spoken since the day I enlisted, I'm fighting this fight to protect her. Our country's barriers are fragile, beyond what any civilian could ever comprehend, but that's all I'm allowed to say about that. Protecting my country's freedom was not just a choice made on that dark day, it was my destiny.

I wish I could ask you to check on my girl, but I can't. I'm not supposed to ask for anything period, but just wanted to let you know I <u>really</u>, <u>really</u>, <u>really</u> like Little Debbie cakes. That little lady knows how to make a cake...

Sincerely,
Nickel

Dear Sir,

I'm kinda big at six-nine and close to three hundred pounds. Not your typical soldier size, so that's why they call me Barge. They should call me Ghost, because I maneuver around the enemy line with more stealth than those puny punks that named me. All's good though, 'cause they're my family. You see, my parents died in a random drive-by shooting while they were at a grocery store back when I was a teenager. So when I enlisted, the military took me in as their long-lost son. I needed that, because I was lost and drowning in my pain.

I started out in the Army Special Forces. Overshot the scores needed in the General Technical and Combat Operation so big, them guys didn't blink before accepting me. The motto for SF's is "De oppresso liber." Don't ask me to pronounce it, but I can tell you it means "to free the oppressed."

That's what I want to do—fight for freedom and honor my parents while doing it. After they died, my college dreams died, too. My pastor encouraged me to join the Army, so I did. Only to be recruited out for this Special Division, so top secret, I'm still scratching my head on how a journalist is able to know of our existence much less request letters from us...

Oddly enough, the first time I picked up a gun, I found my calling as a sniper. I hated a gun, yet it became my specialty. I guess you can analyze that all you want.

I don't get it, but I do get that I'm severely in need of books. How about sending us some, sir? We see some dark stuff out here, but a book is a mental break from it. My Captain will probably mark this out after he checks this letter. Here's hoping he'll be kind and won't.

Sincerely,

Barge

A dozen or so more letters read closely the same. These guys surrender their lives to serve and sacrifice their entirety—no family, no creature comforts, nothing. Simple and not so simple things we all take for granted, these men gallantly live without. Their entire being is focused on these covert missions. These valiant soldiers live, eat, and breathe nothing but these top secret missions.

Surprisingly, their Captain must have taken pity and didn't mark out any of their requests. And such humble requests they were. How could I not fulfill each one? I went overboard with my dad's help and jumped through all kinds of security hoops to get it to them. By the time I arrived months later to meet them, the bounty of treats, books, a box filled with specially made dream catchers, and magazines had just arrived as well.

It was a small way I could say thank you, but my gifts seem so lacking compared to their own. I wasn't willing to lay my life down for them as they were for me and millions of other strangers.

That Bible verse, John 15:13, has resonated deeply with me since that eye-opening time of my life.

"Greater love hath no man than this, that a man lay down his life for his friends."

Our soldiers live this out daily, with us being completely oblivious to the impact of that oath.

Chapter Sixteen

An annoying pounding summons me from my slumber, but I rebel with not wanting to move. The demanding beat drifts until it fades enough for me to drift back to sleep. More pounding, a bit more harsh this time, ends my dozing. My tired body rolls over and the crinkling of paper registers. My eyes crack open and find the worn letter resting on the pillow with me as the late night comes back into focus. I've fallen asleep in the guest bed surrounded by soldier testimonies.

The knocking picks back up, so I dart out of the bed and rush downstairs to the front door and find my very own soldier waiting patiently—dressed in khakis and a dark-blue sweater. The man sure does know how to rock cable knit. The fabric stretches so nicely over his broad shoulders.

"You're late," Asher's cool words languidly sound, bringing a chilly morning breeze in with them. It effectively snaps me out of my ogling.

"Oh shoot. I'm sorry." I push the door open wider and gesture him in. "Come on in and get that coffee pot woke up while I run through the shower." I don't wait for his reply before hurrying back upstairs.

I'm ready in record time and hurry towards the robust aroma of coffee. My feet land on the bottom step and freeze. The scene in my humble kitchen renders me in awe with a warmth that is still confusing me… thrilling me… and if I'm honest, scaring me.

Observing this giant masculine man wiping my counters down while sipping a cup of coffee is detrimental to my heart—so severe I can barely swallow my emotions down. Asher Reid fits into my life in a way I bet he never wanted. From the look he gives me, I know his thoughts are on the same path. When his eyes flash towards the door, my body unfreezes, ready to block that particular path.

He offers me a cup of coffee instead of fleeing from me, thank the good Lord.

"Thank you."

He grunts—do I have to remind you of how nice that rugged sound is—and places the wet cloth by the sink. "I thought you like to wear dresses to church." His eyes peruse my normal daily outfit of jeans, white blouse, and boots.

"It's too cold for a dress today, but don't worry. My church family is cool like God. They accept me just as I am." Knowing we need to head out, I smile broadly before downing the coffee like a caffeine shot. "I'm ready."

Asher drives us to church in silence, so I decide not to push any words today and allow him to take the lead. If quiet is what he wants then that's what he'll get. My mind drifts back to those significant letters with a clearer knowledge about something rather important. This closed-off soldier is sacrificing a part of himself, by allowing me in. That is a gift I plan on praising my Lord and Savior for during this worship service today.

He parks, backing into the space closest to the parking lot exit before we head inside. I spot Mia and her fluffy headed dork… I mean husband right away about midway of the sanctuary. My normal spot is always by them, wherever they decide to sit. The cute little fact of them always choosing a different pew each service always brings a smile to my face. I truly love those two and want to be near them, but today I'm not taking lead, so there's no hesitation in following Asher to the back pew against the wall.

As soon as we settle down, it's time to stand back up for the opening worship song. The large screens up front flash the words of the inspiring song "Cast My Cares" by one of my all-time favorite bands, Finding Favour. This incredible band knows how to string words together to beckon praise right out of you for our mighty God.

Raising my hands to praise my Savior, I release the words wholeheartedly with no care of how I'm viewed. This is my personal time between me and God. With shivers racing up and down my spine I openly worship. A rich baritone joins the chorus of praise and summons tears to my eyes instantly. I dare not glance at him for this is his time with God as well, but Asher freely praising God is soul-touching. I drop a hand and subtly seek his. Tears release in a joy no words can describe as his warm hand willingly grasps mine as we unite in our worship.

Once the last note of the song fades, we are seated. My chest tightens even further with joy when I loosen my grip on Asher's hand, only to feel his tighten with not wanting to let go. And that right there builds a longing in me for the man to never let go. Again, I don't look over, just settle into his side and focus on Pastor Chase.

"Welcome to this fine Sunday morning. Spring is just around the corner, whether these mountains are ready or not." He pauses as the coat-clad congregation chuckles. It's March already, but the ground is still leaning toward frozen and the air crisp with chilly temperatures.

He pulls on his reading glasses and flips open his Bible. "The song we opened with couldn't be more fitting for the message God has laid on my heart to share with you today." He pauses to scan the vast group with a kind yet sad expression etching his face.

"Preach it," an elderly man encourages from the front of the church.

Clearing his throat, Chase begins, "We can all become heavy-laden with burdens of this life. Afflictions show up in the form of sickness, death of loved ones, careers crashing down, families breaking apart, war, infidelity... I could go on and on. We *all* face burdens, but I'm here to remind you today we are not alone in our sufferings. God's word is a promising testament to this. Let's begin in Matthew 11 verse 28."

Pages begin to flip as I realize I've forgotten my Bible at home. Asher produces a pocket-sized one and with one hand flips to the right section. I can't help but warm from the fact that he has no desire to release my hand.

"'Come to me, all you who are weary and burdened, and I will give you rest.'" He pulls his readers off and scans the group again. "I could say no more today, and Jesus's declaration should be clear enough for us all to grasp it." An amen-chorus rings out. "Oh but we're stubborn folk, though. We just want to take care of things on our own. And all that does is steal our focus off of God and plant it into our problems even more. Instead of finding a healthy root system of hope, we end up choking on the weeds of despair and disappointment." His strong voice rings out with earnest passion and the place comes alive with their exuberant agreement.

He continues by reading Psalm 55:22. "'Cast your cares on the Lord and he will sustain you; he will never let the righteous fall.'" He looks around again. "Yes, his people will suffer. Yes, our burdens are real. And it may seem the suffering wins and we fall, but do not forget the promises he has made right here." Chase holds his Bible high, the congregation cheers. "That's right! We already know the ending to our story on earth if we've accepted Jesus as our Lord and Savior!" He shouts, igniting the group. The spirit blankets over us and even pulls a strong assured amen from Asher.

The fired-up pastor flips to the very end of the Bible. "Revelations 21:4 says, 'He will wipe every tear from their eyes. There will be no more death or mourning or crying or pain, for the old orders of things has passed away.' Praise God, these burdens have an end!"

He runs his hands through his thinning blond hair and paces the stage. Quoting from memory, he shares, "1Peter 5:7 states, 'Cast all your anxiety on him because he cares.' As the song declared earlier, we are to cast our cares on Jesus. Give it over to Him today. Dwell in His words for encouragement. Root yourself in prayer, keeping your focus on Him and how we know our story will victoriously conclude, and you will find rest."

Later, as Chase concludes the message, "Cast My Cares" begins to play again and we all stand. The altar is filled before the chorus begins with people openly casting their burdens before God, begging Him to take them, to heal them, to grant them peace. I'm amongst them. Releasing Asher's hand, I head to the altar and direct my prayer solely for Asher, asking God to grant him peace from the burdens he carries. I also pray for God's guidance for my relationship with this man who has completely overwhelmed my heart. My hand clutches my chest, barely being able to contain my emotions.

This is the day the Lord has made and I've truly rejoiced and am glad in it.

*****

"Are you absolutely sure you want to immerse yourself in the kookiness of my family?" I glance over as Asher drives up the mountain and towards Mia and Bode's cabin, catching his shoulder shrug. "They don't know how to act any better than I do," I admit sternly.

His lip twitches, causing me to bite my own. "I've learned to survive your weirdness. I think I can handle theirs, too."

The man completely caught me off guard when Mia invited us to Sunday dinner after the service concluded, and he actually agreed—with no hesitation, mind you. He parks us in front of the cozy wood cabin and kills the engine.

"It's not too late. We can head home and you can cook for us." I bat my eyes and coyly tilt my head, hoping to convince him.

"Knock it off," he says in that bossiness he articulates so well. He gets out and walks over and actually drags me out of the Hummer. Not really. He simply opened the door and gave me that look that says *I'm not playing around with you*.

Bode is going to embarrass me, that's for certain. Gathering my nerve, I hop down and grab hold of his hand and lead him inside. The succulent aroma of pot roast wafts around the cabin, welcoming us right in.

Bode is right there, barefooted with his dress shirt already untucked. He pauses unbuttoning his shirt to shake Asher's hand. "Hey, man."

"Good grief, dork. Can't you keep clothes on properly? You're like a rebellious toddler, stripping down when momma isn't paying attention." I nod my head towards my sister.

Bode finishes unbuttoning the shirt to reveal his beyond tattered Tennessee tee underneath. He shrugs out of dress shirt and knocks me upside the head with it. "My house. My no dress clothes rules. You're one to talk." He motions towards my outfit and tsks. "You wear the same blame thing every day. What's the matter? Momma ain't around to dress you?" He smirks, thinking he's one-upped me. *Wrong*.

"Sorry, Asher, but Bode has a penchant for streaking." I turn my sharp gaze back to my goofy brother-in-law. "Please for the sake of us all, keep your pants on. No one here wants to see your tiny baby bits."

Asher coughs, but I'm not dumb. That was so a laugh. I give him a knowing look, but he quickly averts his eyes and retreats into the kitchen with Mia. I'm guessing that's more comfortable for him than me and my brother-in-law's lame squabbling.

Bode shoves me and says, "Are you trying to run the guy off? Good grief. It took you thirty-five years to finally snag one. Don't go ruining it."

"Nah." I knock off the kidding around and lower my voice before taking a step closer to him. "Hey, will you do me a favor and let Asher sit in your normal chair at the table?"

Bode looks at me curiously. "Sure, I guess. But why?"

"He's a war veteran, and has a thing for always having his back covered."

Bode nods in understanding. "Got it."

"And please don't mention anything about him being a soldier. It makes him uncomfortable. Just don't question him a lot, *period*. Maybe just eat and smile. Can you handle that?"

"Aww..." His big brown peeps go all doe-eyed. "You like him. I mean... really, *really* like him."

Oh, brother. Now the doofus is going to embarrass me for sure.

"Shut up." My two words come out on a hiss.

"Neena and Asher sitting in a tr—"

I deliver a warning punch to his gut, causing him to hush. "Please!" I whisper sharply, looking over to find Mia and Asher conversing over her mashed potatoes as if the subject is enthralling. Good. Ignoring Bode and me is always the best route to take in avoiding our nonsense.

Bode chuckles. "Don't worry. I'll behave. This is

the first real hope I've ever had that you may actually not end up an old maid living in my attic."

The second punch to his gut releases a sharp grunt from him. Good. Serves him right. I've had enough, so I head over to the table while Bode rushes upstairs, probably to finish undressing like a normal person would have done in the first place. I pause by his chair long enough to swipe his remote and hide it behind the family pictures lining the fireplace mantle.

Asher assists Mia in delivering a bounty of scrumptious looking dishes to the table. She still cooks in abundant quantities like she did when the kids lived at home. Fine by me. I reap the benefits of leftovers accompanying me home.

Bode joins us, wearing a hoodie and sweatpants, never one to put on airs. It's actually something I admire about him, but you'll never hear me admit that to him. He offers Asher his chair graciously before sitting at the other end. After we are all seated, Bode says a prayer as he always does, and then we dig in.

With our plates mounded high with potatoes, roast, green beans, and mac and cheese, we quietly eat for a spell. It's peaceful and not forced. Once we set a slower eating pace, we discuss the service and how amazing God's presence was today. Truly, it was euphoric.

Mia serves us thick slices of carrot cake with the most decadent cream cheese icing and coffee as the afternoon eases by with no rush.

"So your children are in college?" Asher asks, flooring me. He's never one to ask much about anything. Or maybe he doesn't care to ask me anything. *Is it just me?*

"Oh yes. Our daughter Kaisley is a junior at the University of Tennessee, majoring in Nursing. Our son Addison is a senior this year at Florida State with a Masters in Criminology. He takes a lot after my dad and Neena. He's always been a curious fellow, so being an investigator seems to be the perfect fit for him."

"Yeah. This one can be pretty nosy," Asher says, nodding toward me.

Bode snorts, so I kick him under the table for good measure. He cuts his dark eyes at me in warning. My eyes relay the same message back. *Keep it up, dork, and there will be more where that came from.*

"You've got your hands full with Neena. You sure you want to tangle with her?" Bode jerks his leg out of the way, causing me to land my next kick to the chair instead.

"Asher doesn't tangle with me," I sass. "He doesn't even like me." I shove another bite of cake in my mouth, hoping to stifle any more idiotic words from escaping.

Bode roars in laughter with my admittance. "Smart man." He cackles on and on like I'm the best entertainment ever. I bet he won't be laughing later when he can't find his precious remote.

"Bode," Mia says his name in a measured warning. She looks over at Asher, who seems deathly focused on his dessert. "These two together could worry a zombie to death. Pay them no mind." She begins clearing the table with Bode's assistance.

Asher leans over as they head into the kitchen. "I do like you."

I jolt back to eye him in astonishment. "You do?"

He nods his head. "A lot."

The smile on my face hurts from being so wide.

"Thank you for liking me."

His eyes twinkle in creamy golds today, but he only offers a grunt in response.

Bode rejoins us, delivering a fresh pot of coffee with Mia following.

"Bode, tell Asher about you perpetually living out your boyish childhood as a midlife crisis career alteration."

He rolls his eyes. "Really, Neena, it makes no sense stringing that many words together. You can be so verbose."

"Yay! You used a big word and even pronounced

it right!" I offer my brother-in-law a high-five and he accepts it just as enthusiastically.

"I've been waiting all week to slam that one on you." Bode's all smug about it.

We all laugh. Even Asher, yet he tries again to cover it with a cough.

"Well done, dork."

The rest of the afternoon dawdles by with Bode telling Asher all about The Lodge where he spends his days giving river tours, riding the white water rapids, or hiking a trail up the mountain. The man is in heaven doing this, and I really couldn't be happier for him. What's a life if you can't spend it doing what you're passionate about?

After being loaded down with leftovers, Asher and I head home. The ride is an amicable quiet and I'm actually fine with that. Even though it's chilly out, spring is peeking around the mountains in delicate new buds and green leaves, so I settle into the passenger seat and take it all in until we arrive home. He puts the SUV in park and just sits.

"You and Bode always carry on like that?" he asks.

"Yes. Sorry about that, but he is such a big brat. Mia can do nothing with him." I scoff and roll my eyes dramatically.

Asher sets a half-smile on those full lips before he

catches himself. Too late. I saw it! Before I think it through, I hop over the console and straddle his lap. He holds his hands out, not knowing where to place them. After some hesitation, he settles them on my hips.

With eyes wide, he asks, "What are you doing?"

"I could have sworn I saw a smile, and I refuse to move until it reappears."

His wide eyes narrow, trying to hold on to some sternness, but it's slipping. "You're so odd."

"Choose a better word than odd. I refuse to be called something meaning weird, peculiar, strange, and abnormal." I mock scold him and bam! Another smile! "There it is! Yes!" I cup his face in my hands and study all the changes the smile produced in his steely features. I'm shocked to feel him lean into my touch. "You're stunning when you smile." The words come out in a whispered awe.

He isn't mine to touch this way and I know I shouldn't, but when a softness appears at the edges of those tawny eyes, it compels me to continue this claim.

He rewards me with a more pronounced smile, transforming all of the sharp angles into an open softness. His lips pull back, revealing a mouthful of perfectly white, straight teeth. He takes on an air close to boyish or maybe youthful. Either way, he is absolutely stunning. Those camouflage eyes open generously, revealing every hue imaginable. The desire to set apart each color and analyze the world lived in them overtakes me.

"How long did it take?" I ask around a straining voice.

"How long did what take?"

"For the military to steal your smile?"

His beautiful smile falters before completely disappearing as he shakes his head. "The military didn't. The evil of the world did."

"Why not let the good of the world bring it back? Jesus wants us to have an abundant life, and I don't see how you can live abundantly sans smile."

He clears his throat as his watery gaze meets mine. "It's been a tough life."

I release his handsome face and wrap my arms around his neck and offer the only comfort I'm capable of, a hug. I hold him, burrowed in the side of his neck, breathing in his earthy scent that reminds me of a crisp fall day, until his strained breathing evens back out. No imagination of mine could probably come close to conjuring up the nightmares he's lived on the battle field. He offered the information a while back about him being wounded, so there's no doubt he's holding a burdening load of nightmares.

God wants us to give over our burdens, but that's easier said than done. I silently pray as I hold him with the verse, "Love thy neighbor," whispering through my thoughts. My promise to God during this prayer is that I will try my best to love this man who is so willingly letting me hold him, hoping I'm decreasing his burden by offering comfort.

Easing back after a while, I study him. His eyes have cleared the unshed tears away, but a faint blush gives away his emotions. "That's it, soldier. Operation Agelast is under way as of now!"

"Agelast?"

"It means a person who seldom laughs. You've sacrificed enough for this country. I'm not letting you sacrifice your smile, too."

I go to climb off his lap when my hand digs slightly into his side, causing him to flinch slightly. Ooohh... He's ticklish! Well, that's a good place as any to start. Catching him off guard, I set in to tickling a laugh out of him.

And it works! An amusing roar of joy bounces around the inside of this SUV, sounding like the most beautiful song I've ever heard. I savor the richness of it... for all of two seconds before his massive hands clamp down on my wrists, rendering me immobile.

"Who are you?" he asks between huffs, throwing the question I asked him during the snow back to me.

The ocher gold of his eyes liquefies and begins to whirl around his dilated pupils.

"Neena," I tease heavily before reaching forward and stealing a kiss. My lips meet a set of surprised lips that refuse to play along with me. I give him a chance to change his mind, but it's obvious this isn't a game he's willing to play. Awkwardness creeps over me at my folly, so I decide to ward off the tension by goofing off. I dote silly kisses all over his handsome face—cheeks, chin, nose, eyelids, and forehead, but Asher remains frozen like a statue.

Needing to escape my blunder, I open his door and hop out in lightning speed. Without looking back, I book it inside my house and lean against the closed door.

Dumb move, silly girl!

Whatever progress I've made with this man has probably just gotten shoved a million miles away. It's not slipped my annoyed attention that I've just ruined our first kiss in a big way. The sigh ricochets through my quiet house as I rest my head heavily on the door with mortification and frustration seeping over me.

His heavy steps sound outside, finding me holding my breath as they come to a halt right outside my door. This is something I've picked up about him. Asher only allows himself to be heard when he intends on addressing me. The rest of the time—too much of the time—he is one stealth sucker.

Before I can react by flipping the lock, the doorknob flicks abruptly. All of a sudden, my body is propelled forward as the door opens. Asher storms in, slamming the door, and then proceeds on pinning me to it with strong, steady hands bracing on either side of my head. He leans down so close his breath caresses my face, mingling with my own labored breath. I thought I had made the guy go running in the other direction and certainly not toward me. From the look in those molten eyes as they assess me, searching for an answer to an unspoken question, I'd say I was completely wrong.

"I don't... I... I can't." He huffs his frustration.

"Can't is just as ugly as don't."

"Either way, it's my reality." He says this as he takes a step closer to me, defying his own declaration.

"Then you should work on altering it." My words come out breathless from his nearness. I reach a hand out and rest it over his pounding heart, noticing it beating as vigorously as my own. My trembling body settles into the door and his touch. I dare not move, reveling in the feel of him being so willingly close.

"It's been a long time," he admits with his deep voice presenting huskily. His gaze never leaves mine as he slowly traces my bottom lip with his thumb.

Whatever this is between us, it's perfectly clear he

wants it as badly as I do. Trying to figure it out seems to be our hang-up. Honestly, I'm not certain of it myself. Confused, yes. Curious to see where we may go with it, absolutely.

"Whether this is your first kiss or your last, I just want to share it with you." I lightly tap my hand over his heart and whisper, "My only expectation is that you share it with me."

The apprehension relaxes a bit with his brow unfurrowing. Time ticks slowly by with him watching me, deciding on what, I don't know. But I patiently wait for him to figure it out.

At first, I expect him to leave as he always does, but time keeps treading with him staying firmly anchored before me. With absolute knowing he's not going to flee from this situation, my expectations settle on the idea that he is going to allow me a kiss, hopefully making up for my blundered one.

He approaches me cautiously before greeting my lips gently with his. I expect precision and demand as with anything else with this authoritative man, but I couldn't have been more wrong. Soft warmth touches me with the faint contact of his lips meeting me on his tender terms. These terms I could totally comply with for the rest of my days. There's nothing rough or demanding in his touch. A shy vulnerability reveals itself with his timid caresses, but I keep allowing him to take the lead. Sometimes it's best to just be still in a moment and let life lead it in the direction most fitting.

This kiss… My first real kiss. That's all I can say about it. Never have I felt this type of intense connection with such a delicate kiss. As Asher threads his fingers softly in my hair and deepens this kiss just barely, my soul opens wide and shows the exhilarating possibilities life kept hidden until this very moment of connection. Having this moment with him is exquisite and it beams with more possibilities. As flesh caresses flesh, the loneliness that has resided in me for far too long dissolves from his warmth.

The bond forming in our two hearts has slowly happened since we met last summer, instead of in an instant with a kiss sealing it. Yes, the altering rhythm of my heart is here and I can only hope it's permanent.

Asher may take a while to warm to an idea, but once the man is on board there's no holding back in his commitment to it. We live in this kiss, exploring it, for who knows how long. He continually grazes his soft lips to mine, feeling like we're making up for lost time. And maybe that's exactly what we are doing. We kiss until an ache forms in my neck from holding it back. Reluctantly, I'm the one to end it. Placing a kiss on the edge of his bottom lip, I unwillingly let go, but place my head on his chest to let him know I don't want this to end. Does it ever really have to?

Again, he seems to be on the same wave link as me, because his strong arms wrap around me with a clarity that he has no intentions of ever letting go. Maybe that's wishful thinking on my part, but there's no denying the connection I have with this man. It's been there from the very beginning and seems to only get stronger as time passes.

A heavy sigh expels through my thoroughly kissed lips. "Just think about all of the time we've been wasting."

He leans slightly away to meet my eyes. "My time only seemed to stop being wasted since I've met you."

His confession pulls a satisfied smile to my face. "Yeah, but we could have been kissing months ago. I feel cheated." I replace my smile with a fake pout.

Asher leans down and places a feather-light kiss on my protruding lips. "I guess we will just have to try making up for it."

"Sounds promising," I tease before reaching up to swipe another kiss.

Chapter Seventeen

Our kiss on Sunday really felt promising until Asher effectively closed himself back off. That man is not seen unless he wants to be seen. He keeps eluding me. Again, I've taken him and his background into consideration and have allowed him his space. He probably just needs to process what happened... Or that's what I've told myself until today. It's Friday and five void-filled days have passed, carrying my patience away with them. Operation Agelast commences today, whether Mr. Elusive is game or not.

I skip down the jungle hall at Sunshine Valley Pediatric with my boots clicking happily against the shiny floor, passing a group of giggling kids. The need to pull some more of those bright giggles out of them calls to me, so I perform a perfect cartwheel. My landing is practically flawless with my boots only sliding slightly on the linoleum floor. The little group claps exuberantly.

Striking my best Elvis pose with both hands pointing in their direction, I mutter, "Thank you. Thank you very much."

They roar in giggles, so I consider my goofing off job done and skip on into Mia's office. When she looks up from her desk, she literally clears the chair.

Clutching her chest, she squeaks out, "You scared the life out of me."

"Really? I was going for more on the lines of a laugh, not fear." I plop down in her guest chair.

"Why are you wearing a beehive of cotton candy on your head?" Mia eases around her desk to inspect the wig closer. She's like a child herself, having to poke at it. "Ooh... It even sparkles."

"I'm trying to find ways to make Asher laugh." I yank my head out of her reach before she sets the wig askew. "You ready to go?"

"We're going out to eat with you looking like that?" Mia's eyes widen with mock fear.

"What?" I clutch my chest dramatically. "Are you ashamed of your sister? That really hurts, ya know. I thought your love was unconditional." I pull a few sniffles out for affect.

Mia lets out an unladylike snort while grabbing her bag. Lacing her arm in mine, she pulls us out of the back exit. "Come on, Bozo. Let's go embarrass your neighbor."

I halt in my tracks, pulling Mia to a sudden stop right along with me. "You think I'll embarrass him? That's not what I'm going for at all."

Her eyes skim over my bright, glittery wig. "You can wear sunshades and we can sit out on the back patio. That should minimize the embarrassment."

"Oh, that's a great idea. It's really nice out today." Alluring warmth has finally showed up and chased the chill out of the mountain air.

We load up in my car and I rummage around in the console and unearth a pair of hideously large purple sunglasses. Why on earth did I ever buy these in the first place? After covering most of my face with the wild shades, I set us on a course towards Charlie Mike.

Mia leans up and turns the music down a bit. "This sure is a lot of trouble you're going through just to make him laugh." Her eyes keep darting to the pink wig.

I return my attention back to the road and pause at a red-light. "Asher is a remarkable man. A war veteran. He's earned a lifetime of laughs, and I feel quite honored to provide him with one or a million.

Preferably a million. He's that deserving."

"My Neena and her passionate convictions." She beams over at me with pride evident in her sincere smile.

A short ride to the restaurant is just enough time to work up my nerve to go through with this little stunt. The hostess gladly escorts us to a patio table overlooking the river. She's having the hardest time not staring at my pink bouffant.

"It's urgent that I speak with the chef this instant. Please don't make me wait."

Kaycee snickers. "Sure, Neena."

She turns to leave, but I stop her. "Don't tell him it's me who needs to see him!"

Kaycee laughs over her shoulder with Mia joining in. "Gotcha."

"You know you're visiting a restaurant way too often when they even recognize you underneath this craziness." Mia waves her hand in the direction of the wig.

"I'm not ashamed." I stick my tongue at her and adjust my oversized sunglasses.

Jessie comes over grinning and places glasses of tea before us.

"My favorite waitress!" I squeal.

Jessie shakes her head and chuckles. "And my favorite mischievous patron. The chef will be out momentarily." There's tease bouncing around in her formal statement.

Moments later Mia sits straighter in her chair. "Oh, here he comes." Then she roars in laughter.

"What's he doing?" I don't dare look to see for myself, but anticipation is about to get the best of me.

"He shook his head when he spotted you and hauled tail back inside."

"What?" Glancing over my shoulder, I catch a glimpse of his black chef coat before the door completely closes.

Jessie returns a few moments later with her grin still in place. "The chef sends his regards, but said he's too busy to put up with your mess today." Both women laugh, but I pout. "He said to inform you he will be preparing you a special meal, though."

"He did?"

"Yes, ma'am." Jessie gathers the menus and scurries back inside.

"I think you've met your match, Neena." Mia takes a sip of her tea, still regarding my wig.

I raise my tea glass in a toasting manner. "Here's hoping I have."

Mia clinks it. "I never thought the day would come, but I sure am glad it did."

"By the way, I wanted to tell you I have a new assignment coming up."

Mia's glass tilts, splashing a few drops of tea on the table. "You realize last time you did this, I ended up in the hospital."

There's no stifling my eye roll. "You cannot blame your appendicitis on my assignment."

"What if I put my foot down and don't let you go?"

"Mia," I say on a sigh.

"Where?" She crosses her arms and narrows her eyes.

"Uganda. I've been investigating human trafficking that's been going on over there."

"Can't you do all the investigating here?"

"You know I need to go. Don't worry. Parker is going with me."

"Hasn't he already moved back home?"

"Yes, but that's what airplanes are for, silly. We'll be fine. I'm not going into a warzone this time." I try to reassure her, but from her grim expression I'm failing.

Thankfully, dishes begin trickling out, ending the tense conversation. The meal is too delectable and beautiful not to focus completely on it. Much to our amusement, each course has a pink theme—pink tomato biscuits, pink beet salad, seared pink salmon with roasted purple potatoes, and pink raspberry custard.

"Tell me that man doesn't have a hidden sense of humor." I hold a spoonful of pink custard up to prove my point.

"I think all of this is really sweet and romantic even. You two would make such a sweet romance novel." Mia sighs before taking another bite.

I balk. "Don't go comparing us to your silly romances."

"What's so wrong with romance?" She glares in challenge.

"It's not real."

"Says the girl wandering around in her own romance story." Now she smirks.

What can I say to that? Nothing, so I *don't*. Ha! Asher would be so pleased.

"Neena, the way that man cared for you while you were sick is clearly one of the most romantic things I've ever witnessed. And at the house Sunday, he couldn't keep his eyes off of you. Nor could you keep yours off of him." She sighs dramatically, staring off into space. "The closed-off soldier finally opening his heart to the possibility of love with an unlikely heroine. It's an epic love story for sure."

"Shut up!" I throw my napkin at my cheesy sister. She bats it away with a girly giggle escaping her.

By the time I've scraped my little pot of custard clean, Asher still hasn't resurfaced.

Jessie reappears. "The chef said to let you ladies know lunch is on him today."

A free meal wasn't my initiative. Serving Asher a smile was my top priority. Deflated, I ask desperately, "Tell me this, did you happen to see him smile since I've arrived?"

"I think he did when... No, I'm absolutely sure I caught a hint of a smile when he handed me the pink salad course." She smiles warmly at my hair. "Seems he may favor the color pink." Jessie winks before leaving us to take care of other customers.

I clap my hands. "Success!"

Mia laughs along with me. "Let's go, Miss Romantic Goof."

*****

Back home, I work on typing up a quick post for my website about taking the time to be kind to others. This blog was a happy accident and has accrued quite a following along with several happy ad sponsors. It pays the bills without much effort. All I have to do is do what I love best—write!

I'm going back through some comments on last week's post when I hear a knock at the door. My eyes refocus on the window and find the day has darkened without my notice. I quickly close the laptop and go answer the door. I'm not disappointed at all as the door opens to reveal the most handsome man to ever put up with me.

The succulent aroma of food wafts from his glorious form like a beacon guiding my hungry soul closer. I motion for him to step inside. Instead, he leans on the doorframe while keeping a hand behind his back and watches me with that blank stare he has perfected.

"What was that all about today?" Asher asks, his voice stern.

"That was all about Operation Agelast," I answer with a shrug. His lips kick up slightly. "There it is! That beautiful smile. Oh how I've missed it all week long."

Asher tries to rebel with returning the smile deep within himself, but I do a little silly shimmy, making it impossible. He ends up chuckling. "I don't have time for your shenanigans while I'm at work." He's trying to be stern with narrowed eyes while fighting a losing battle with that beautiful smile of his.

"But you have time to whip up a pink four-course meal?" My eyebrows tick up accusingly.

At this comment, he produces a small bag and hands it over. I was so focused on his striking smile, I didn't even realize he had it hiding behind his back. A quick peek inside finds a lovely little pot of pink custard secured tightly in clear wrap.

"Aww. Thank you." Without thought, I lean up and press a kiss to his lips. This time he plays along and presses back. And that right there makes my world spin a little more harmoniously.

I go to take a step back, but find his arms surrounding me, pulling me closer yet. He deepens the kiss and my thoughts of the pink dessert scatter until they completely disappear. Kissing this man is becoming addictive way too quickly. It's not helping that his taste is of the very custard I'm holding. I like that he indulged in the treat as well, I just wish he would have waited and eaten with me. Something about sharing a meal with this man is so comforting. So right.

Asher slowly ends the kiss, leaving me hungry for more. Resting his forehead to mine, he whispers. "I think I'm in trouble."

I think that makes two of us.

"Why?" The single word comes out nervously.

"I like kissing you better than I like cooking."

My anxious body relaxes with his confession. "I really like the sound of that."

His grunt turns into a deep moan when I press closer and offer another languid kiss. We continue this new dance for minutes, hours, decades... All I know is I could get lost in it and never have a desire to return.

"I don't know what to do with you," he grumbles against my lips after a while.

"You and your propensity for using that ugly word need to be restructured." I don't allow him a rebuttal, pressing another kiss to his frowning lips until they meld back to mine tenderly. The man must have some awesome lip balm, because his lips are softer than mine. "All you need to worry about doing with me is getting to know me better," I say between kisses, "and making out with me more often," another kiss delivered, "and not shutting me out," a little longer kiss, "and feeding me." One last kiss is delivered before I untangle from his arms and go seek a spoon.

"Maybe that's all doable," he says from the door before flipping the lock and leaving me to enjoy my sweet treat.

Sadly, the custard isn't nearly as sweet as that man's lips.

Chapter Eighteen

April has shown up and stole my now popular chef from me. Luka's article hit the media, placing Charlie Mike on the map, just as expected. The problem with that is Asher stays way too busy nowadays. I selfishly regret aiding his restaurant now, because I really want him all to myself.

It's all my sore butt can do to climb out of my car on this fine Saturday afternoon, but I find it a little easier when I notice a fine set of jean-clad legs showing from the side of the Hummer.

"My eyes are playing tricks on me. Surely Chef Reid isn't home on a Saturday of all days! How will the famous restaurant survive without its star chef?"

Asher looks up from under the hood, giving me that blank look. I keep approaching until my body brushes against his and pucker my lips expectantly. The corner of his mouth quirks up before he rewards me with a sweet yet brief peck.

"I've taken the day off and want to spend it with you."

"Really?" I ask in unbelief.

He releases me and goes back to tinkering under the hood, so I hop up on the enormous bumper and watch.

"You stink," he mutters while adjusting some doohickey. I can't help but appreciate how the corded muscles in his forearms flex from his actions.

I pull my collar up and take a deep sniff. He's right. I stink. "I spent the morning on a horse."

Those assessing eyes slide in my direction. "Isn't that dangerous?"

His question sounds way too much like Mia for my likings. If the man knew half the stunts I've pulled, he'd think horseback riding was child's play.

"Only if you fall off. And I didn't, so I'm good."

"Why were you on a horse?" His asking another question beckons a grin right out of me. We sure have come a long way from where we began last summer.

"I'm doing a human interest piece on this camp for disabled children. It's a pretty neat place. All geared toward the children having a good time while their special needs are being met."

Asher grunts, replacing some cap. Grabbing a rag, he wipes his hands before securing me around the waist and setting me on the ground. He closes the hood and gathers a small bundle of tools and an empty oil jug.

"I want to spend the day with you," he repeats.

Not having to tell me again, I skip up the steps and head to my door. "Just let me go wash the stench off and I'll be all yours, big boy!"

Extra care is taken with washing my hair and body twice as well as carefully shaving my legs. To feel extra girly, I slather on my favorite gardenia body cream after toweling off. Next order of business is trying to tame my wild hair, so I man the blow dryer and get to work. After way too long, my arms give out so I click the dryer off and set it on the counter. Giving my light-brown tresses a good inspection, I find them to be a bit too poufy, but call it done anyway. I hurry into a fresh pair of jeans and a white bohemian blouse before heading downstairs.

It's a happy surprise when my eyes land on GI Joe sitting on my couch, legs spread wide with his arms resting on the back. The man makes my big couch look like a dwarf.

"Hey you!"

"Your door was wide open." Those hazel eyes glower. *Uh-oh.*

My head nods in agreement, trying to downplay it. "Okay. I must not have gotten it shut all the way."

"You come downstairs and find a man sitting on your couch uninvited and that doesn't bother you?" *Double uh-oh.* His tone could freeze water on contact.

"Well, I like said man most of the time." I smile warmly before adding, "Especially when he allows that morose façade to slip."

His edges stay steely instead of softening as I had hoped.

"I could have been a rapist, Neena." He actually growls in frustration. *Good grief!*

My hands settle on my hips. "Like a rapist would just hang out in my living room, giving me plenty of time to escape or call for help."

I'm about to lunge for the phone on the counter to make my point, but find myself pinned against the wall in just a blink of an eye.

"That fast, sweetheart," he says through gritted teeth. "That fast you could be in a world of trouble."

He's beyond serious and mad. He's also making a needed point, but I'm in the mood to make one myself.

Slipping my arms around his tense neck and then... *Look-a-there...* My legs wrap nicely around his lean waist. His eyes go from hard to liquid in a flash. He's freshly showered, so I can't resist leaning forward and stealing a deep inhale of his spicy fragrance that has become more inviting than my favorite season.

"I'll work on remembering to take care of my door, but you may have to keep reminding me until I get the hang of it." My voice comes out low and husky—a voice I've never heard come from my lips.

I'm expecting Asher to put me in my place and drop me on my backside. Instead, his expression grows into smoldering as he presses me closer to the wall. He bites his full bottom lip, forcing my eyes there. They are such a nice set of lips... Leaning in, I give them a tentative taste and simply get lost. There's still an edge of anger as he takes over the kiss aggressively. Oh, but it's just as appealing as his normal softer kisses.

Once we finally part, both with ragged breaths, Asher reaching behind him and grabs a piece of chalk from the bowl and scribbles on the wall. I look by my shoulder and see he has added the word, *overwhelming*. It's not an unusual enough word for me to add, but if he felt led...

"You are overwhelming," he rasps out.

He tries to set me down, but I cling tighter. "Is that a good thing or bad?"

Asher leans in and dances his lips along my neck, setting me on fire. "Both," he says against my skin.

Things are moving fast and close to going too far, so I unwrap my legs and drop my wobbly feet back to the floor. After taking a few deep breaths, I ask, "Do you want to go to a concert tonight?"

He takes his own deep breath. "I don't do concerts."

I start to tease, but abruptly swallow it back down. Of course, this soldier wouldn't be comfortable in that situation, surrounded by a mob of people. His reality will never be mine. I scoot around him and grab a bottle of water with hopes of cooling off.

"So let's do something you want to do. Surely you had something in mind when you took the day off." I take a deep pull from the bottle and then place it against my fevered neck.

Asher joins me by the fridge and swipes my half-emptied water bottle. He finishes it off and looks around the kitchen as if it's the answer. "I want to cook with you."

Oh no. I guess the kitchen does hold the answer.

I pull on my most steely façade and grumble, "I don't cook."

This earns me a deep belly laugh from him and, I swear to you, it's music to my ears. Now I have to cook!

"Fine." My arms sling up in surrender. "We'll cook. But I'm warning you, it won't be pretty."

"The entire experience will be pretty with you in it." He gifts me a gorgeous smile.

"Sweet talking! Since when did you pick that little characteristic up?"

"Always had it, sweetheart." Asher winks before heading to the door. "Come on," he calls over his shoulder, back to his bossy tenor.

My elusive, smooth-talking, Top Chef, GI Joe, sweetheart leads me next door where all of the makings for a private cooking lesson sit in wait on his kitchen island—chopping boards, scary looking knives, neatly stacked veggies, bowls, utensils... I spot my very own black chef coat resting on the back of the barstool along with his.

"Wow. You've got it all planned out already. I thought maybe we were going to just whip up something on the fly."

Asher helps me into my coat and even buttons it for me. "I don't do anything on the fly."

"I should have known." Spotting two identical pots on top of the stove, I pick one up and twirl it in my hand. "This is the cutest little pot."

Asher chuckles quietly, which is a perfect melody. The man really needs to share his laughs more often. He points to the pot. "That's a *skillet* and it's the perfect size for making omelets, which happens to be your first lesson."

The skillet twirling ceases and my nose scrunches up. "An omelet? Really? That doesn't sound like a fun date meal."

"An omelet is one of those dishes that if you can pull it off, then you can pull off cooking anything." He finishes buttoning his coat, taking on the air of teacher or boss or both. Either way, he is most definitely in his element, and I'm most definitely about to get schooled or charmed even further or both.

"We need to prep our vegetables first and then preheat our skillets." Asher begins maneuvering around the kitchen with precision as I bang around clumsily. He holds out a mean looking knife.

My head shakes vigorously as I take a step back. "No. I refuse to play with that. I need all of my fingers for typing."

He exhales sharply. "How are you ever going to learn, if you don't practice using one?"

I swipe a piece of cheese and pop it in my mouth and shrug. "I've got a master chef, who seems happy with feeding me most all of the time. I see no need in learning."

I'm about to eat another small wedge, but Asher plucks it out of my fingers and places it neatly back in its place on the counter. He holds the knife back out, clearly not taking *no* for an answer.

"Fine, bossy pants. You'll be the one who has to take me to the ER in a little while."

"No need. I know how to stitch up a wound."

I have no doubt this rugged soldier can do just that, but I really hope I don't have to find out. The knife trembles slightly in my hand as I watch him pick one up himself. He places an onion on his cutting board and severs it in half in one swift chop, then places half of it on the board in front of me.

We get through the dicing portion of the cooking lesson with me mangling my poor veggies, while Asher's are all in uniform pieces. Thank goodness, all of my fingers stay intact. The cracking of the eggs goes even rougher, but Asher patiently keeps dumping the egg mixture with shards of tiny shells, making me do it again until we achieve shell-free. A dozen eggs later we both have small bowls of perfectly whisked eggs.

"Now that that took way longer than it should." He levels me with a dubious look.

My hands go up in defense. "You were warned."

"How about you don't burn your pretty little self while I teach you to sauté."

"Well, since you said it so sweetly, I'll try my best." I bump my hip against his thigh playfully.

I manage not to burn myself, but end up slightly burning my omelet due to getting caught up in watching Asher cook. I declare that man cooking is an art form. We switch dishes, him stuck with my charred dish while I get his perfectly prepared omelet.

One bite in and he dumps the browned mess into the trash. "You're sharing that one with me." He dives in on the other side of the omelet, which sends us racing to see who can eat the most.

I win over the giant with no problem. Laughing at our silliness quickly leads to kissing until well after dark and I have to admit, it's the best date I've ever had.

*****

"Seriously, you cooked?" Mia huffs out from her treadmill. She's really got that baby rolling.

"If burning it counts." I keep strolling along at a languid pace on mine as I people watch. The gym is pretty lively for a Sunday afternoon. "This place is hilarious."

"What do you mean?"

"Look at those young guys over there." I point to the bank of weight machines where a motley crew of overly muscled Neanderthals holds their turf. "Every time they get close to the mirror, they flex while admiring their own selves." I laugh, watching one pretty boy do that very thing. "Isn't that something you do at home in private? It's pretty vain to do it in front of everybody. They can't even make it through one set without doing it."

Mia shrugs, her focus on her own workout.

"And look over there at the small group of guys and chicks. They've talked more than exercised. Is this modern day speed dating? Or the gym?" One woman in her perfect spandex attire is examining one guy's flexed bicep while another guy animatedly shows her matching friend how to squat properly. "Peacocking. All of them!" My hand flickers out in every direction.

Mia shrugs again. "I'm not here to watch people make fools of themselves. I'm here to exercise."

"Whatever. This is much more fun." I notice a few older ladies reading magazines while just sitting on stationary bikes and point. "Don't those machines work better if they actually pedal?"

"Says the girl at the gym not even breaking a sweat."

"Her sister forces her here against her will!" I scan around and feel my face snarl as my eyes land on a tattooed bad-boy. He runs his hand through his blond hair as he chuckles boisterously as a star-struck young woman ogles him. He's a celebrity motorcycle designer, but I don't see the lure of him, personally.

"There's Lee *Studly*."

Mia glances over at him as he picks up a massive set of dumbbells. He staggers a bit before catching himself. "Sutton is his last name," she mutters, turning her attention back forward.

"Close enough. He's not bothered you lately, has he?"

"No. He's been cordial, but the flirting has ceased, thank goodness." Mia manages to guzzle water and stay on pace. As she replaces the bottle back in the holder, she points. "Oh sugar. Look who just sauntered in." Her face beams.

I look over at the check-in desk and find Asher retrieving a towel. The sight of that man in mere workout gear of black track pants and muscle shirt makes my insides warm.

"Wonder if he'll ignore you today?"

"He better not."

He walks in our direction with his eyes focused forward.

"Hey, Asher," I call out as he gets within earshot.

As expected, his tawny eyes slide in my direction, but no words escape those stingy lips. Just looking at them makes me want to pull him in a corner and kiss them loose for the next hour or twenty. He does surprise me when he stops in front of my treadmill and eyes me curiously.

"Hey," Mia huffs out along with a quick wave.

He nods towards her, more in the way of a greeting than I received. I'm about to call him out on it, when he reaches over and dials my treadmill up to way past lightning speed. Thank goodness I have enough wits to set into running before the blame thing has a chance to sling me off the back of it.

"Asher!" I growl, punching the dial back down to turtle speed as a smile tugs one side of his mouth up mischievously before he walks away.

Mia's laughter rings out, drawing too many eyes in our direction.

"Not funny," I grouch, but end up laughing when I see Asher still smiling in my direction as he settles on a weight machine. His goofing off *and* smiling in public simply makes my day.

"Yep. You've most definitely met your match, little sister."

Mia continues to run nowhere while I go back to people watching. Well, more on the lines of Asher watching now. He's precise with his workout, as if he has a mental punch list and is completely zoned in on accomplishing it. There's no pause to flex in the mirror, nor is there a moment he spares any woman, even though a few have dared to approach him. Each time he finds me and they follow his gaze, making it clear he's not available. That little indicator makes me wonder if he considers us a package deal. I sure hope so, because it's exactly how I feel.

A loud commotion summons my attention away from my soldier and towards Lee Sutton. He's stumbling around and practically hanging onto some Barbie wannabe, who has replaced the star-struck female. Barbie seems not to mind his exuberant attention, but it's odd.

"There's something wrong with Lee," I comment while watching the hot mess. "I think he may be drunk."

Mia seems to notice it too, as she nods her head while taking in the scene he's causing. Some other guy snaps off something in his direction and Lee doesn't take too kindly to it. Next thing I know, Lee has shoved the guy pretty hard.

"This gym is better than any soap opera," I mutter, looking around for Asher and finding him over by the bench with his eyes trained on the squabble. He must sense me staring, because his attention shoots in my direction. I mouth, *come here*. I'm shocked when he actually listens.

By the time Asher's in front of me, Lee's rage has escalated and the other guy is cowering down and backing off. Lee starts collecting his stuff, making me nervous.

"You know that guy?" Asher asks, looking in

Lee's direction.

"Yes. I think he may be drunk and is about to make a poor choice."

Asher's camouflage eyes snap towards me. "I think he's already made a poor choice."

"True, but him driving is dangerous. Could you take him home?"

"I don't get involved with stupidity." He's all steely about it, and that's ticking me off something fierce.

"Allowing an intoxicated person on the roads is stupidity." I punch the stop button and climb off the treadmill. Before I take a step in Lee's direction, Asher's firm grasp halts me.

"What are you doing?" Mia asks as she stops her machine and joins us.

"I'm going to offer him a ride. The man has no business on the highways in that shape," I grind out between clenched teeth while trying unsuccessfully to extract my arm out of Asher's grip.

"No. I'll do it." Asher releases me along with a deep sigh and heads over, but boy does he not look happy about doing it. Mia and I trail behind in his irritated wake.

Asher approaches Lee cautiously. "Hey, buddy. Why don't I give you a lift home?"

Lee staggers back and tries focusing his drunken

eyes on Asher, who towers a few inches above him. Oddly enough, the two guys could pass for brothers with similar hair coloring and golden skin tone. Both also know how to wear a scowl incredibly well.

"How about minding your business," Lee slurs before making the mistake of shoving Asher.

My soldier doesn't move in the slightest from the forceful shove. Instead, in speed so fast, my eyes didn't actually register it, Asher has Lee pinned on the floor, with both of his hands secured behind his back.

"No need in causing a scene. I'm taking you home." Asher pockets Lee's keys that he's somehow managed to pilfer. *Wow. Just wow.*

"I'm fine," Lee snaps, but winces when Asher tightens his hold.

"No. You need to accept my kind gesture the easy way, which I strongly suggest you do. I don't have any patience and wouldn't think twice on making this the hard way. I have a feeling it would be more of what you deserve." Asher's voice is eerily calm and even though Lee is beyond drunk, he even seems to get that it wouldn't be wise to tangle with this giant of a man.

"Fine," Lee grumbles.

Asher pulls Lee to his feet. Making it look like the fairly large man is made out of feathers and cotton instead of thick muscle and bone.

"Thank you, Asher," I say, knowing they're about to leave.

"You owe me," Asher retorts in that bossy tone of his.

"I'll cook you an omelet for supper." I smile real sweet-like, even though it's probably not the best time to tease him.

"No dice." That blank stare waits for a better offer while his hand stays securely clamped on Lee's shoulder.

"Hey, Mia," Lee slurs, sending all kinds of toxic fumes in our direction. The man smells like a distillery.

"Hey," she says before scurrying quickly away. Smart girl. I'm glad she's finally realized Lee Sutton is nothing but trouble.

I move my attention back to Asher. "I can order a mean pizza."

"Thin crust with extra vegetables. In an hour," he orders before marching Lee on out the door.

Chapter Nineteen

The persistent clattering of dishes being scraped clean and hushed conversations mingle perfectly with the succulent aromas of scrumptious food, making me feel right at home. I pause here to snicker. That long thought would drive Bode crazy. *Too many words*, he would whine. Being wordy is my default setting and there's no way to reprogram it. Not that I'd want to, anyway.

Looking around the restaurant, I love that this place has become my second home in the last few weeks. I've spent the majority of my time here, considering it's about the only way I get to see my Top Chef Soldier. Charlie Mike has been jumping nonstop all spring. With summer on the horizon I can only imagine this place becoming even more hectic when vacationers discover it.

Charlie Mike seems to be Asher's safe haven, for which I'm grateful. And for this reason, I've claimed the back booth closest to the kitchen as my own just so I can be near him.

The chorus to "Sugar, Sugar" pulls me away from the computer screen I've been blankly staring at for the last five minutes while trying to decide if I want my chef to whip up a fruit dessert or chocolate. I've left him alone for the last hour, but my stomach and I are getting antsy.

Tapping the phone and placing it to my ear, I sing, "Hey sugar, sugar."

"When are you going to change that silly ringtone?" Mia asks, trying to sound annoyed and failing.

"Nothing silly about it. It's perfect for you, Miss *Oh Sugar.*" I reach over to the computer and click off the search page on Uganda and settle back on the cushiony booth bench, eyes steady on the kitchen door.

"Oh whatever. What are you doing?"

"Working."

"Where?"

My eyes scan the packed late lunch crowd, before going back to the kitchen door with hopes of catching a glimpse of my elusive friend. "Where do you think?"

"Asher should start charging you a booth fee." Mia laughs.

Evidently, she thinks that's funny. I don't. Ha! Again, my soldier would be so proud.

I ignore her jab and ask, "Did this call have a purpose?"

"I wanted to invite you and Asher to Sunday dinner. I'm trying that roast chicken recipe he gave me."

"If you can get Bode to behave, we should be able to handle that." We've eaten Sunday dinner with them for the last month now. I already like the idea of it becoming our norm. Bode has even taken Asher to the Lodge a few times afterwards to hang out, for which I'm thankful. I think both of them could use a good buddy.

"See you then. And try to behave yourself, too."

After we say our goodbyes, I shut the phone off and place it on the table. Each time I'm here, I take the time to play my own version of I Spy. Today, my eyes focus on something I've already spied, but it still captures my attention every time. The walls are painted a flat gray with green undertones, projecting an elegant masculinity. But if one is paying attention, their eyes will catch on the subtle semi-gloss design scattered on top of the walls. It took some closer investigating due to both paints being the exact same color, but once it clarified, I was completely struck in awe. Each military seal holds a carefully placed position on the walls of Charlie Mike.

Glancing behind me, my eyes focus between a set of windows overlooking the river where the Navy seal is subtly displayed—an eagle perched on an anchor with a ship in the background.

Just off to the left of those sets of windows, the Coast Guard seal is nestled—two anchors crossed with the shield in the center.

I look over towards the entrance where black leather couches line a wall for waiting. The wall above it holds the Army seal—cannons along with the U.S. and Army flags surround a Roman cuirass aka armor.

It's magical how not all of the seals reveal themselves at once. With the lighting and this angle, I'm unable to see the Air Force seal, but I know it's near the French doors leading out to the patio. Hidden on the wall at the moment, an eagle is perched on top of a shield and is surrounded by thirteen stars that represent the thirteen original colonies.

My eyes continue to peruse the dining area until landing near the kitchen door. Each time I glimpse this one, I wonder if this is the branch in which Asher served since it's close to his rightful place in the restaurant. The Marine Corps seal peeks out with an eagle sitting on a globe with an anchor in the background.

His military history is one subject completely off limits, but this restaurant clearly signifies the importance of that history to him. This place was put together with pride and respect.

My phone comes back to life with "Ramblin' Man," drawing me out of my I Spy game. I answer it immediately. "I miss you. Move that girl here, so I can have my best friend back," I sass.

Parker's light-hearted chuckle rings out from somewhere in Connecticut. "I miss you too, darling. Any progress on Uganda?"

"Ugh. No. You?"

"I may have another lead willing to talk, but it's not for certain yet. Mark number seven off the list. That's a no-go."

I leaf through the papers on the table until I unearth a list of potential informants. "This list we compiled is shrinking to hopelessness fast."

He sighs heavily into the phone. "Neena, do you think maybe that's our sign to leave this one alone?"

My back stiffens with stubbornness. "No, I think it's our sign to keep fighting. There's a reason why this task is greatly difficult. The evil of the world is working against us, because we're close to defeating it in one very important battle."

"The evil of the world outnumbers us significantly." His tone says he's already marked the entire list off and is ready to move on, but I'm not. "We're up against something neither one of us can conquer."

"If God is for us, then who can be against us?" I pick the pen up that is peeking at me from under the papers and doodle Romans 8:31 on top of the list while waiting for his response. Parker knows I don't back down easily.

Another sigh breaks the silence. "I'll keep at it, but if something doesn't pan out soon, we need to consider covering the story without the trip."

"Agreed." The word is delivered to appease him and he probably knows it.

"Enough of that. What have you been up to?" Parker asks after we talk through a few more leads and options.

The idea flits through my mind to lie, but that's not me, so I go ahead and tell the truth. "Spending most of my time with Asher." I glance around the room, noticing the late lunch crowd is beginning to trickle out, leaving a lull in the medley of chatter and dish clattering. "Parker, I think I'm in love with him."

He laughs. Of all things, Parker laughs at me. "Neena, darling, you declaring that out loud should clarify that you are. It's about time. Let me reiterate, Asher is one lucky son of a gun. Does he know how you feel or are you two still playing hard to get?"

"Oh, he knows. And I'm pretty sure we're past the hard-to-get phase." My thoughts happily tilt back to the sweet kissing sessions we've clocked in as of late.

"I'm happy for you," Parker says, sounding genuine.

"Thank you. How are you and Danielle doing?"

"We're great. Still getting to know each other again."

"Well, hurry it up and marry her so the two of you can move back here. Seriously, I miss you too much." I slump down in the booth, wishing Parker were here in person.

He chuckles. "Easy there. No need in slinging the 'm' word out there just yet."

"Why not? You're not getting any younger, ya know."

"You're a fine one to talk, old maid."

We bicker back and forth for a while about who's too old for what with us trying to one up the other. I remind him he refused to jump out of the plane with me, making me the younger-at-heart winner. Our conversation is refreshing and causes me to miss him even more. After going over a few ideas about the story, we bid our farewells.

"Call me as soon as you have any information." I close my notebook and stretch my back.

"Same here. Give Mia a hug for me."

"Yessir. Take care," I say before hanging up my almost dead phone.

More time ticks by with me consolidating some facts and questions on the evil of human trafficking. It's secretly hidden in the recesses of even the United States, which makes me sick to my stomach. After another phone call is made to an organization that sponsors baby girls, as they call them, who have been rescued from human trafficking, I've set up an interview and effectively drained all life from my phone. Tossing it in my bag, I email a few correspondents. Once some headway is done in that department, I take a break from the heart-wrenching nightmare and focus on next week's blog for a while.

Asher finally emerges from the kitchen as I close the laptop for the day, calling my work day done. That black chef coat gets me every time. The man totally dominates the look with enigmatic confidence. His eyes meet mine first before scanning the dining area, as always. After finding nothing amiss, he heads straight over to me, making me feel like the luckiest girl in the world to have even registered significantly to this man. I also like that he never sits across from me. Oh no. My man has to wedge in the booth right beside me. I begin to scoot over as has become the routine, but he surprises me when he grabs my hand and pulls me from the booth.

"What are you doing?" I ask as he walks us in a clipped pace down the hall toward his office.

"You've been distracting me all day, and I don't do distractions." His deep timbre rings out in that authoritative tenor as always and produces goose bumps along my skin as always.

"So what are you going to do, lock me up? You can just kick me out."

"I don't want you to leave." His assertive tone and declaration broadens my smile instantly.

"Good, because I'd miss you too much," I admit.

Asher yanks the office door open, ushers me in, and locks us in together. Those steely eyes soften as he scans over my face while his adept hands thread through my hair.

"I like this idea even better." My arms reach up and lace around his neck, effectively anchoring me to him.

And then his mouth descends on mine softly, nearing reverently. This giant man presenting the sweetest, gentlest kisses is my undoing each time.

Asher Reid does not kiss greedily or selfishly. No. This act of intimacy is on a level way beyond my understanding. The man is all about giving, and each caress from his lips is an extravagant offering that leaves me weak-kneed and in awe.

He pulls away long before I'm ready, causing me to whimper in protest. The deep grumble from his broad chest vibrates through mine as I cling to him for dear life.

"You're too distracting," he repeats in a labored voice, echoing my sentiments exactly.

"I'll go home." The words come out deflated as I loosen my hold on him, but his arms clamp firmer around me.

"I thought you wanted me to make you dessert," Asher murmurs while his lips coast the line of my neck.

My body shudders. "I was under the impression *this* was dessert."

"An indulgence indeed," he murmurs again, continuing to lavish kisses across my chin. "Maybe this will be enough to get me through dinner service." He releases me and takes a measured step back to readjust his coat and the buttons, which I managed to mostly undo in order to reach his T-shirt underneath.

Asher specially orders these baby-soft T-shirts from some big and tall company and they've become a security blanket to me. My fingers always seek the indulgent material. When I asked him why he prefers them, he muttered something about living with harshness for way too long. And that was all he would say about that...

My hands long to reach out and claim the shirt back, but all I can manage now is to lean on the door for support and watch. Of course, his eyes are steadily trained on me as well. I regard the slight flush of his cheeks. It's so attractive and is only brought forth by our kisses, and I adore the fact that it's something shared only with me by me. He has no control of it.

"What were you working on out there?" His head nods towards the direction of the dining area.

A smile curls my numb lips. I just love it when he asks me a question about me, which is something of a rarity. Asher has kept to his not-being-nosy stance, but his simple question gives away the fact he cares to know me better.

"Uganda. My inside resource fell through. Now I'm back to the drawing board."

The softness vanishes from his gaze and returns to steely. "I don't think that's a good idea."

"I know, but I do think it's important." We both cross our arms defiantly, although mine are nowhere near as impressive or as intimidating as his.

"I don't have time for this right now." Asher

gently but firmly moves me away from blocking the door and unlocks it. "Later." The one word comes out in a tone full of warning. He pauses to run his knuckles tenderly along my heated cheeks. "Dessert? Have you decided?"

I reach up and brush one more kiss to his stubborn lips before heading into the hallway. "Surprise me," I say, backing away.

He offers a tentative smile. "I can do that."

"Oh my love of words. A smile *and* a positive sentence. Maybe now I can make it through dinner service, too." I grin before turning around and skipping to the booth where my computer and notes scatter along the table to hold my claim on it.

Before the dinner crowd shows up, Asher presents me with a fruit napoleon drizzled with chocolate, effectively covering both types of dessert I wanted. Tell me he's not just the perfect catch...

*****

Summer will be coasting in soon, but I still have yet to resolve all of my New Year's resolutions. Asher, on the other hand, seems to be ticking his off in record speed. The man has commitment and determination down to an art form. He now easily offers me a smile each time we're near, and always when we are preferably alone. He's also stuck to the cooking lessons, but declared just last night to be done with the whole thing when I overdid cayenne pepper by mixing up the measurements and dumping a tablespoon into the sauce he was trying to teach me to prepare instead of a teaspoon. I received a text this morning saying I owe him some new taste buds from scalding his off. I sent him a simple, *ok hot lips*, with a smiley emoji sporting rosy cheeks. He kissed me after he dumped the sauce and sent my lips to tingling from the spice. Now he has another nickname added to the substantial list I have for him.

Mr. Elusive.
GI Joe.
Mr. Grouch.
Top Chef.
Mr. Bossy Pants.
My Valentine.
My Soldier.
Hot Lips.

This is one of those lists I'm hoping will be indefinite. Each new description is a new facet discovered, erasing a little more of the mystery of this man I'm hoping to get to know even better.

The strand of twinkling lights from New Year's is now draped above my bed, reminding me daily to get with it. I roll over and peep at them after my morning prayer. The tiny white papers draw my attention the most and I love that Asher wrote them in his precise handwriting just for me. He'll never know how much that meant to me.

My phone dings with an incoming message, so I reach over and retrieve it from the nightstand.

Asher – *What are you doing today, Miss Hot Lips?*

My laughter bounces around the quiet bedroom as I snuggle under the covers and reply. *OK. We can share the nickname. Today will be all about resolutions.* After hitting send, I go back to studying the little pieces of paper fluttering above my head until the phone receives another message.

Asher – *Get to it.*

Me – *Yes, sir! Sergeant is it?*

Asher – *How'd you know?*

Me – *Educated guess. You're too bossy not to be. Bossy is attractive on you tho ;-)*

Asher – *Stop flirting with me and get to it.*

Me – *You being bossy only makes me want to rebel. Sure could go for a spicy kiss…*

Asher – *Don't tempt me.*

Me – *Consider this tempting you.*

I send a kissing emoji to go with the message. The grin plastered on my face has no desire to ease as I leave the phone and teasing in the bedroom and go shower for the day awaits.

Once my day is clocked in at the office, I do something I never do and really *don't* care to, but Asher wrote it down, so I'm going to at least give it a go. With resolutions on my mind, I pull the car into the parking lot and find a spot near the front. I lean over the steering wheel and peer at the brick beast through the windshield, while trying to gather some bravado to get on with the task at hand. The building is intimidating and much larger than my normal quick-mart shopping. Yep, this will be interesting to say the least.

After finally exiting the car, I find a little lady heading in the same direction. She's not intimidating at all, dressed in a lime-green track suit and bright-white sneakers, so I decide to trail her. She has a list in hand and is scanning over it as we walk in sync towards the entrance. Maybe I should have put one of those together too.

"Good afternoon," I say softly as to not startle her.

The little lady glances at me with soft blue eyes. "Hello, dear." She goes back to the list, but I clear my throat to regain her attention.

"So, do you find grocery lists a must?"

"Oh yes, or I'd end up buying everything but what I needed."

We both chuckle lightly, but I'm not feeling it.

Shoot! I'm already botching Asher's grocery shopping resolution. We both head through the sliding doors and come to a halt at a decision. It's like the Three Bears of shopping carts—massive, regular, and mini. I ignore the first two options as the little lady claims a massive one.

"Aren't these just the most adorable carts *ever*?" I grasp a mini one and claim it for my mission. It looks like a doll baby cart and suddenly this shopping task is becoming fun. "Have these little cuties always existed?"

"For a while now," she answers, settling her enormous purse in the front of her cart—both items seem out of proportion to her tiny stature of no more than four-foot-something.

"This is so neat. And cleaning wipes, too!" I swipe two out of the container and hand one over to her. "This is so generous of the store to help us to stay sanitary."

"Do you grocery shop much?" she asks, wiping down her bar with the wipe.

"Never." I follow her inside the store and before we reach the first section, a young lady greets us with a sample of a new fruit smoothie. "This is so nice!"

The old lady laughs. "Sweetheart, you should get out more." She shuffles away from me, her little laughter chiming out. Yes, she's laughing at me, but I don't mind. I'm happy to be the reason to make people smile and laugh. There's just not enough of that in the world anymore.

After she disappears out of sight, I refocus ahead at the bounty of produce. The section is vast with more selections than necessary, in my opinion, and is enough to send me chasing after the little lady and begging for help. Taking a few deep inhales, I rein in my anxiety and head over to the bananas that aren't so daunting. I add two to my tiny cart and then proceed on adding two apples and two pears without any panic in sight. This isn't so bad now that I've calmed down. A little farther into the jungle of fruit and veggies, two gorgeous premade salads join the cart.

How funny is it that the healthy produce section leads me right into the sinful bakery section. The warm aromas of baked bread and treats drift through the air. Another alluring table is set up in a cozy corner of this section with an older gentleman smiling in my direction. I return his smile and push the cart over to him.

"Have one, young lady." He hands over the sample bite of a cheese Danish.

"Don't mind if I do." I pop the bite of flaky pastry and rich filling into my mouth and it practically melts on my tongue. *Oh. My.*

"Good, isn't it?"

"That was such a tease," I mumble, eyeing the platter of samples with longing.

His rusty chuckle bellows out. "You can have another one."

I eagerly accept the offer, but it still isn't enough.

"Ok, mister. You did your job. There's no choice but to buy them now. Where are they?"

He grins wide, seemingly proud. "At the bakery counter." He points me in the right direction.

Once two delicious pastries are added to the cart, the shopping trip keeps trucking along. The robust scent of coffee leads me down the aisle of my dreams. Choice after choice of gourmet coffee has me drooling. Coffee and Danish… Mmm… A good bit of time is taken with this selection until a pound of dark roast joins the party. I inspect the cart and only consider one item missing, so I wander around aimlessly until stumbling upon the cereal aisle. Oh, but this isn't the cereal I'm used to. There's more choices than one could ever imagine. I've narrowed it down to three choices when a familiar face comes into view right beside me, abruptly ending the fun party. Lee Sutton—clad in beat-up jeans and a leather jacket—with him carrying a shopping basket. It's a sight I never thought my eyes would witness.

"Hey there, sweetheart." His smile feels

inappropriate, causing me to look away.

"Hey, Lee," I mutter, eyeing the boxes intently.

He leans into my personal space and says, "Don't tell anyone, but I have a weakness for sugary cereal."

This makes me snort. "We have this in common." I take a small step away and pick up a box of sugary carbs to inspect it.

Lee doesn't take the hint and steps right back into my space. "You're just as pretty as your sister. Let me take you out." He edges even closer. Wow. He doesn't waste any time getting to the point.

"Look, buddy, I don't know who told you it's kosher to get all up in someone's personal space, but I'm here to tell you it's not." I take another step back, and thankfully he stays put this time.

Lee chuckles lightly, acting like I made a joke. Whatever. I toss the box into my tiny cart and set it in motion, but he has enough nerve to reach out and grab the end, effectively halting my getaway.

"Come on, Neena. No need in acting that way. Seriously, I'd love to take you out." His blue eyes bore into mine.

"I may not be married like my sister, but let me reassure you that I'm just as unavailable as *her*." I want to leave no doubt in his philandering head that Mia is off limits as well, but I'm pretty sure Bode already cleared up that point with him a while back.

Lee still doesn't release my cart, and I'm about to get annoyed.

"That your boyfriend at the gym the other day?" he asks, head tilted in what I'm sure is his signature wooing move.

"There's nothing boy about him." I cross my arms, and narrow my eyes.

"If you say so, sweetheart." Finally his hand releases my cart and grabs a brightly colored box of cereal and drops in his basket.

I get the cart turned around in hopes of fleeing the tense exchange just as Lee begins to speak again, but in a lower, less saucy tone.

"Tell him thanks for helping me out the other day. I've been going through some... *stuff* lately and he was pretty generous to listen to my crap. Dude even prayed for me." He scoffs at his own words in disbelief.

Well now, this has me swinging the cart back around. "Asher did that?"

Lee shrugs, eyes trained on the shelves of cereal now. He won't meet my gaze and looks a bit ashamed.

It's impossible to turn on the computer home page or glimpsing a gossip magazine cover in checkout lines without seeing the *stuff* this bad boy hasn't gotten himself into lately.

Motorcycle Bad Boy Caught in Bed with Celebrity Client's Wife.

Local Celebrity Arrested for DUI.

Lee Sutton Claim to Fame Failing.

And that's just recently. Seems the man is spiraling out of control.

"Now don't go looking down your cute little nose at me, judging me before giving me a chance." He cuts his eyes at me and glares.

I guess the man can read minds as well.

Straightening my back, I rebuke, "I'm not judging you, but I do pity you. Lee, there's much more to life than fickle fame and material possessions. When I look at you, I see a man lost and searching. I can promise you this—you won't find what you're looking for in the places you've been frequenting lately."

"Now you sound like your boyfriend," Lee grumbles and turns his glare to the basket in his hand.

"Well, I consider Asher's words very rare and precious. If he deemed fit to share them with you, then it's best that you listen." I glance down the aisle toward the front of the store and see an available checkout line calling my name, but God taps me on the shoulder. *You need to share me with him.*

I turn back and discover Lee already making his

way in the other direction, wanting to get as far away from this conversation as me, I'm sure. "Lee, wait a minute." He halts and glances over his shoulder. "How about that date?"

His eyebrows quirk up. "A real date?"

"Yes. With Asher and me."

He rolls his eyes and returns to walking away, shaking his head.

"You said not to judge. Now look at you doing just that," I say loud enough for him to hear, hoping no one else did.

Lee looks over his shoulder but keeps walking. "I'm not into threesomes with dudes."

My cheeks blaze as he grins, obviously receiving his desired effect for his inappropriate comment.

"Seems you don't have many true friends left in your corner lately. What's there to lose?"

"Where?" he asks, still walking away and close to making the turn completely off the aisle altogether.

"Church and lunch with us this Sunday."

"Babe, I don't do church."

"Good grief. Now you sound like Asher with that *don't* nonsense," I say rather loudly because now he's completely vanished from my sight.

No other comment comes from him, so that's that. I shrug the defeat off and head out, annoyed and a bit confused as to what that was all about. Why on earth would God want me to tangle with that man who has already ran amuck in my family's life? He caused enough stress in Bode and Mia's marriage, so I see nothing good coming out of inviting him in, but sometimes only God can see the big picture. Here's hoping my only duty was to reach out to the guy. And here's hoping even more that my part was completed in the grocery store.

The drive home finds me distracted with the odd encounter back at the store. Once I make it home, I absently gather my two canvas grocery bags and head to the door. As soon as my hand lands on the doorknob, the door slings open and an arm reaches out, suddenly snatching me inside before I can blink.

"I thought you were working on resolutions today," Asher says harshly, close to my ear as he pins me against the closed door. The house is dark with the curtains drawn and no lights on. *Guess he feels like making another one of his points...*

"I am," I screech out, my heartbeat hammering away in my ears.

"The door was unlocked."

"I'm sorry."

"Kiss me and I'll forgive you just this once."

Well, who am I to argue with Mr. Bossy Pants. I lean up and plant a soft caress against his lips. "There. All better?"

"No." He grunts. "What's poking me?"

"My resolution for the day." I wiggly the bags free from between us.

A slow smile eases over his handsome face as he regards the bags. "You went grocery shopping?"

"Sure did."

"And you bought something besides coffee and cereal?"

This man already knows me too well.

"Take a look for yourself." I hand the two bags over.

Asher presses a kiss to my forehead before sauntering over to the kitchen with the bags in tow. I watch on as he empties each bag and lines the contents along the counter in a neat row as if to inspect my bounty.

He glances over at me. "You bought everything in pairs except for the coffee."

My shoulder lifts in a shrug. "Yes. One for you and one for me."

"You bought me groceries?"

"Lands sake! Are you trying to reach a question-asking goal today?" My hands playfully land on my hips.

The timbre of his laugh reaches the depths of my soul. Before I can swoon, he picks me up and sets me on the counter beside the groceries.

"Now what are you doing?" I try to grumble but it comes out breathless.

"I don't want you to get a kink in that pretty neck while I kiss you." He leans in and touches his nose to mine, showing our heights more equally matched now.

"Just why do you want to kiss me?" My arms reach around and clasp behind his neck.

The gold flecks in his eyes dance with, I do believe, pure glee. "I always want to kiss you, but you buying me groceries... Neena, you don't know what that does to me... What *you* do to me." Asher secures my right hand and places it over his pounding heart. The vigorous beat matches my own and I have the sudden urge to cry. Why is that? When something makes you so happy you feel weepy?

"You do the exact same thing to me," I whisper. With our gazes locked on each other, I mimic him by placing his hand over my heart.

He shakes his head before leaning in and softly placing his lips to mine. The connection carries such a symphony of feelings that an ache blooms in my chest. I'm sure he's not ready for these words out loud even though I've shown them with my actions—*I love Asher Reid.*

Chapter Twenty

Church was a bust today, to say the least. It had nothing to do with God or Pastor Chase. It was all on me... And Asher... And Bode... And, truth be told, Lee Sutton. Now that I think about it, God may have been at fault a bit, too. It *was* Him who kept on and on all week until I agreed to hunt down Lee's email address to invite him once again to join me at church today. I was just trying to be obedient and all it got me was disappointment. Of course, Lee didn't respond to my email nor did he show up.

I spent the service positioned on the back pew between Asher and Bode, and never have I been in such an uncomfortable spot. Bode went to whining when I kept angling to look at the entrance, wanting to know who I was looking for. The thought of lying in church was way actually tempting, but staying true to myself, I admitted to inviting Lee to join us. That went over like a lead balloon.

I keep driving slowly through a nasty rainstorm on the way home, *alone*. After sitting through service with both guys hitting me with severe glares, I'm just peachy with having no company. With Mia out of town at some medical conference, no Sunday dinner plans were made, so the guys seemed to want to keep the mad-at-Neena united front and went to the gym together. We went a few rounds in the parking lot with me lecturing them on how everyone needs Jesus, even Lee Sutton, before they left. That only set Bode and Asher to boiling mad, so some space from them is probably for the best. Here's hoping they can work off their attitudes by the time they get home.

I hit the seventh red light of the day. My frustration lies more with the fact that Lee didn't even show up than the light, but I glare at it through the windshield like it's at fault for it all. Part of me knew he wouldn't show, but I prayed all the same that he would. And then I had to endure the wrath of not one angry man, but two. I'm not caring for them ganging up against me either. *Where's Mia when I need her?*

Finally, I pull the car into its designated spot in the driveway. The other spot is vacant, but maybe that's a good thing. Asher seething isn't a pleasant

Asher in the least. I cringe, knowing Bode is probably filling him in on all things Lee today, so there's no high hope of him arriving home in a better mood.

My phone starts twanging out Dixie Chicks' "Goodbye Earl." If Dad knew that was his ringtone, he'd get ahold of me. But honestly, how funny is it to have a song about committing murder as my murder-mystery-writing father's ringtone? It's hilarious, but I'm not feeling it at the moment.

"Hey, Dad," I answer.

"Hi, sweetheart. What are you doing this fine sunny Sunday?"

"Nothing sunny about it here. The sun has decided to hide behind rainclouds today. I met the youth for coffee and attended church afterwards."

Dad's warm chuckle resonates through the phone. "When are they going to finally kick you out of youth? I do believe you're close to twenty years past the age limit."

"Did you call just to pick on me?" I peer out of the windshield as the rain shower turns down to a mere trickle.

"Of course not." Dad laughs again. "I'm calling to make sure you're making the trip for Addison's graduation."

"You know it, but I'm not sure if Bode and I'll make it there in one piece with being stuck in the same vehicle for the trip's lengthy duration."

"Try to behave."

"Yes, sir." I adjust the phone and start gathering my Bible and bag. "How soon do you think you and Mom will move back here?" I'm so ready for my parents to be back in Tennessee.

"Not sure. I have a book tour this summer, so we're shooting for the fall."

"That long?" I whine.

"Sounds like someone is missing her mommy and daddy," Dad teases.

"Not at all," I sass back.

"At least you're spending a few days with us, right?"

"Yes, but I've got an interview in California. I'll need a ride to the airport on Friday."

"I should be able to handle that. Enjoy your Sunday and I'll see you next week."

"Okay, Dad. I love you."

"Love you too, sweetheart."

I toss the phone in the bag and slide out of the car just as the sun decides to grace me with its presence. That shiny spectacle summons the neighborhood to life all of a sudden as children begin emerging from their houses with boisterous laughter and hollering. I can't help but laugh as I watch on at the frenzy of the energetic youth. In no time, a ball has landed in my yard.

"Miss Neena, will ya toss that back?" Camden, a little cutie from next door, hollers.

After setting my belongings on the porch, I head into the soggy yard and toss the ball to him.

"Thanks!" he yells before running off across the street to join a herd of kids, who are all moving aggressively towards the next street over where the community playground resides.

"No problem." I offer a wave even though he's already out of sight. As I turn to go inside, my boot slips on the muddy grass, landing me on my back. The cool dampness seeps through my shirt, causing me to shriek. First instinct yells for me to get my butt up, but then it calms down and decides the heck with it.

Settling in the muddy yard, I let the world drift away as my fingers play along the drenched grass and soil. Even though my backside is soaked and chilly, the sun feels amazingly warm against my face. I close my eyes and bask in until nearly dozing off.

A shadow moves in front of the sun, but my eyes remain closed.

"What are you doing?"

My eyes pop open at the timbre of that deep authoritative voice, finding Asher's imposing form leaning over me. His church outfit has been replaced with workout clothes consisting of a gray T-shirt and dark shorts.

"I busted it."

"Are you hurt?"

"Nope."

"So then get up." Mr. Bossy Pants says this with that lip just a-twitching. It bugs me to see him holding his smile back from me. He's not been stingy with it in a while. I guess he's not quite over the Lee invite. *Men...*

"I don't care to," I mock him, deepening my voice.

Still no reaction, just the blank stare and a slight lip twitch.

My eyes drift back shut, not wanting to see that look on his face. "I'm already dirty, so I might as well live in the muddy moment for a spell," I mumble, inhaling the earthy fragrance surrounding me. "You're blocking my sunshine."

The shadow eases away, granting me access back to the sunny warmth. I settle back in and allow my thoughts to begin drifting away again. Everything relaxes and a pleasant lethargy blankets me...

"Why would you want to do that?" Asher speaks, startling me.

I open my eyes and find him standing beside me, still trying to figure me out, I suppose. I prop up on an elbow, feeling the mud soak through the fabric. "How often do you get to just wallow in the mud?"

Something flickers across his features, but he wipes it away so fast I'm unable to decipher it.

"I've had my share of mud wallowing on rainy battlefields."

His confession causes me to pause for a beat or two. I'll never grasp all he's had to live through. He won't openly share it with me, even though I've tried repeatedly. There's just no prying that box open. The need to protect him from those memories is so strong, it reverberates all the way to my bones, but I'm no fool. No matter how much gusto I give it, there's no way to do that. So I do the only thing I can do—I offer him another mud memory.

A lazy smile curls my lips. "I bet you've never wallowed in the mud with a *girl*." I wink and pat the saturated ground beside me. "I'll even dare to bet you've never had one kiss you while in the mud."

Asher doesn't move from his spot as he holds firm to that inscrutable look with arms crossed.

My hand pats the ground more forcefully, causing water to splash up. "Come on. Share this with me. Let's claim it as a good mud wallowing memory together."

He releases a long sigh as he eases down to the ground beside me. I entwine my muddy hand with his dry one. He doesn't flinch. Instead, he takes advantage of our tethered hands and pulls me close to his side.

"You are one odd woman, you know that, right?" His lips caress the side of my forehead affectionately, easing any sting of his declaration.

"What have I told you about calling me *odd*?" I poke him in the side, causing him to flinch away from the ticklish touch.

"How about rare? I've never met anyone like you."

"Rare? Now I sound like an undercooked steak. Buddy, your flattery skills need sharpening. I'd rather you call me unique." My muddy fingers dance up his side, beckoning a combination of a growl and laugh. He gathers my hands securely to prevent me from tickling him any further.

"That'll work, too." He squints those camouflage eyes in my direction.

"I suppose you want to collect that muddy kiss now?" I ask.

"You offered."

I lean over and place a soft kiss to his bottom lip and ease away, but before any progress is made in retreating, Asher rolls us and claims a more thorough kiss as he hovers over me. The sun has been blocked again, but this time I don't mind at all.

"Good grief!" Bode barks out. "You two trying to put on a show for the entire neighborhood? Take that mess behind closed doors!"

We glance over and find Mr. Mood Killer climbing out of his truck at the curb, wearing his own sweaty workout gear.

"Go away! You're not welcome here!" I yell back.

Bode grabs a pizza box and slams his door. "I was invited." He points toward Asher who is still hovering above me.

I look up and ask, "You did?"

Asher nods his head, wearing an amused expression. "I did." He looks back at Bode who is standing on the sidewalk glaring playfully at me. "Go on in. I'll be there in a minute."

Bode grumbles something under his breath and heads up the porch. "You're not invited, Neena," he says over his shoulder, sounding like an older bratty brother.

"What? Why not?" Neither one answers me. The two of them together... I'm just not sure how to feel about that, even though I initiated it in the first place. I fix my pouty face toward Asher. "You'll at least bring me a slice of pizza, won't you?"

He nods before going back to kissing me as if we were never interrupted. Each caress is as soft and languid as the Sunday afternoon we are living in.

Eventually he pulls away and helps me to my feet. A genuine smile lights his face now, and that totally cancels out the disappointing morning.

"Best mud wallowing ever," he says, drawing me in for a hug before leaving me standing in the muddy yard alone.

And I couldn't agree more. *Absolutely the best.*

*****

Skipping into Theo's office on Monday morning, I plop down in the chair in front of his desk and swipe the other half of his uneaten bagel.

"Please, help yourself," he mumbles sarcastically as his fingers type decisively along the keyboard.

"Don't mind if I do," I joke, taking another substantial bite.

I watch him as he continues to work. Theo reminds me of Sidney Poitier, with wisdom emitting from him even in his silence. He obtains respect from anyone lucky enough to cross his path without having to demand it. He's a man you want to mentor you. I'm blessed to have him as a boss and friend.

As the bagel completely disappears, Theo taps the mousepad and pulls his glasses off to look me.

"I'm heading to California this weekend to interview the founder of the home for human trafficking victims."

He laughs, surprising me.

"What's so funny about that?" *Nothing*.

"Not the interview, but you." Theo motions toward me. "You've sat still for almost six months. Longest in Neena history. I expected you to have gotten antsy way before now. What's wrong? Is my girl finally getting old?" He laces his fingers and leans on the desk, grinning with tease.

I scoff. "Not hardly."

"Then what is it..." He sits up all of a sudden with eyes wide. "Or better yet, *who* is it?"

"Umm..." My word stumbles about as I try to sidestep his accusation, but we both know he's nailed it on this one.

"You know I've had a hard time making progress with this story." I fidget in my seat.

"You've met someone," Theo declares, obviously not going to let this go.

"Yes, but that has nothing to do with me staying put for the last few months." My eyes narrow but relent and laugh with him. "Stop laughing at me!"

"You're laughing, too. This is a joyful laugh, not a mocking one. Good for you." He seems honestly pleased.

"Good. Now, let's go over what the interview should bring forth."

We settle in, both with notepads for brainstorming. Before noon, we've got it all hammered out.

"I'll be back first thing Monday morning." I stand up and head for the door.

"Phone me once your flight lands and I'll meet you here to go over the interview."

"Sounds like a plan. See you then." I wave before heading out towards the only place my car seems to want to go nowadays.

Charlie Mike is already slammed by the time I arrive. So busy in fact, my usual booth is preoccupied with a group of patrons.

Succulent aromas waft from the kitchen, drawing me in that direction. I crack open the door and get a glimpse of Asher tending to some steaks on the grill top. His eyes automatically meet mine in the mirror over the hood as though he could sense my presence. I offer a small wave with him returning it with a slight head nod.

"Lunch special?" he asks, turning his attention back to the grill.

Sad to say, I have the specials memorized. Monday is monster burgers. "Sure."

"We're packed, so you can hang out in my office." He glances back up.

"Okay." I leave him to it and help myself to a

glass of tea at the beverage station before making myself at home in his office.

Jessie delivers my burger and home fries along with a perceptive grin. I've learned in the last few months that the staff knows very little about their boss, and he is adamant on keeping it that way. It's obvious with me hanging around all the time that something is going on between us, but everyone pretends to pretend at not knowing. It's silly, yet they all seem sincerely happy for us.

The afternoon wears on with me polishing off lunch and typing up the interview questions on my laptop. I've moved on to answering emails by the time I'm graced with a visitor. The door clicks open and shut without much noise as Asher appears in front of his desk with arms crossed.

"You look like you belong there," he comments.

I close out the email folder before glancing up. "Feels like I do, too."

Bracing his hands on the desk, he leans over and offers me a sweet kiss. "Today has been crazy and it's been killing me knowing you're in here and I've not been able to be."

After another quick kiss, I stand and stretch out my stiff back. "Good news, you'll not have me in your hair for a few days." I ease around the desk and wrap my arms around his waist.

His posture goes rigid. "Why not?" he demands.

"I'm heading to Florida with the crowd for Addison's graduation tomorrow."

"Oh." His stance is still peculiar. "Bode mentioned that."

"You've got to be getting tired of me by now."

His arms tighten around me. "I like you here."

I sigh in contentment. "You won't hear me complain about that."

He presses a kiss to my forehead, and then eases back enough to look down at me. "When will you be back?"

"Well, after the graduation, I'm flying out of Florida for California. I have an interview scheduled, but I'll be back Monday around midday. I have a meeting with Theo as soon as I get back."

His gaze trails around the room. "Okay."

Monday is Memorial Day, so I figured he would be busy doing private military stuff. He shares nothing of that side of himself with me, so there was no question of him not wanting me around on such a significant day. I really didn't think he'd care if I was gone, but with his reaction, it's obvious I was mistaken.

"Do you need me home earlier than Monday?" I ask, hoping he'll let me in some.

"I don't." He releases me and heads for the door.

And the solid Asher Reid wall goes back up. *Great.*

"Would you like my flight itinerary?"

He pauses and turns around. "Is that any of my business?"

I search through his words to locate sarcasm or maybe attitude, but the only thing found is a genuine question mixed with what seems like a touch of disappointment.

Something has nagged me in the last several weeks and pops in my thoughts now. *Am I his first real relationship?* With at least fifteen years in service, time for a relationship may have never presented itself.

Clearing my throat, I turn his question back on him, giving him the option. "Do you want it to be your business?"

He considers it for a few beats as his eyes make another sweep around the room. They finally land on mine. "Yes."

The breath I was holding escapes. "Then it is. I'll text the information to you."

"Okay," he says, leaving me alone in his office once more.

Our skittish dance may have settled down a bit lately, but it still gets jumbled up with toes being stepped on and us going off in different directions.

One step forward, two steps stumbled back…

Chapter Twenty-One

The flight is relatively quiet as the plane heads east with the promise of delivering me home soon. After touring the home in California and meeting some of the victims of human trafficking, my heart weighs heavily. I cried myself to sleep last night with the echoes of extremely high statistics of victims, the stories of some of the girls being raped thousands of times, the cruel treatment of them by demons disguised as humans... My head shakes in bafflement as I scrub my hands along my tired face.

My conversation with God during those late hours of tossing and turning was closer to reprimands and questions. But then I thought of the people selflessly fighting against this evil, so I had to thank Him for them and the safe havens they are providing for victims.

A few victims that are of legal age graciously wrote me letters, expressing nightmares so compelling I would never be able to do them justice. I fish one out of my messenger bag and reread it.

I am wrong. I am bad. I have to earn love, approval, and affection. It is only appropriate if someone else initiates. I am inappropriate. I am a failure. I am a burden. I am a whore. I won't amount to anything. I will fail at my new life. I am failing. I deserve to be hurt. I deserve to be alone. I will always struggle. I will always be in lack. I am not enough. I have no value aside from what I do for others. I am a mistake. I have no value. It will never get easier and it will never get better.

These are lies I live with. My counselor has helped me realize they are lies. My head understands, but my heart does not.

Z

I slide it back in the folder and pull out another, more inspirational one. This young lady was a victim that found the strength to rise from her ashes. She is a mentor to other girls at the home now. I really connected with Scarlet and her story will forever be written on my heart.

When I first became free, I would shower so often because I wanted to scrub the horror off my skin. I was terrified to sleep because of what my brain might have me remember. Being sold by your mom, I believed it meant I was worthless and that I needed to earn love. That was my life from 6 until 23. I just wanted someone to love me but I believed I was unlovable and worthless.

But slowly, it began to change in my heart. Being sold has defined me. But now I want something different to define me. Being free is harder than I imagined because it is so different from what I knew. I have to keep choosing to be free - not from being trafficked, but because I have to believe in my own freedom.

I have an apartment now. I have my own place to call home. I have my own bedroom and no one knocks on my door at night. I don't take for granted that I have a keychain with actual keys that work to keep people in or out. It was one of the proudest moments for me, when I realized I had that kind of power now.

The hardest thing though is to begin to dream when I've settled for so much less and believed so many lies. But I'm starting to make a vision and dream for my life and finally believing that I will actually make it something beautiful.

I used to think that being sold was the most important piece about me. But, now, maybe it's that I'm choosing to stay free and find more areas of freedom for myself. I want my life to be beautiful and for whatever I really do to matter. But mostly, I want to find other girls in the darkness and give them a safe place and tell them they have the keys now, too.

Scarlet

The hurt threatens to bubble out so I forcefully swallow it down. Scarlet has no idea that she already matters beyond measure. I silently pray that God shines brightly in her life and rains blessings on her. I know nothing can erase what she endured. I can only hope she and the others can overcome it.

As I look out the window over the clouds, all I can see are those hollow eyes of some of the victims I've met. The director informed me that some are never able to overcome the abuse they endured and will eventually leave and spend their lives wasted and living on the streets, for it's the only way they can figure out how to keep the nightmares at bay. No imagination of mine could conjure up the scars they have to battle eternally. But the director also shared success stories of young women rising from their ashes to become ambassadors for the abused—using their stories to draw light to this crisis and mentoring other victims.

The seatbelt sign begins flashing along with the soft warning ding, bringing with it a sigh of relief. I clasp my belt into place with longing for home. Here's hoping to find Asher in a better mood than when I left him. I've not seen him since I left the restaurant the day I told him about the trip. He went all stealth on me after that, so there was no chance of tracking him down before the trip. After landing in California, I sent him a text to let him know I made it. All I got in reply was *ok*. Ugh. That brooding man eluding me again has me completely perplexed.

During the cab ride to the office, I send Asher another text to let him know I'm home and stopping by the office. By the time the driver parks at the front of the building, no reply has shown up. Giving up on receiving one, I pay the cab fare and head inside to meet with Theo.

"Hey, hey," I say, pushing through his door.

"Good to see you're back in one piece." He offers a pat on the back as we both take a seat in front of his desk.

"Always. Although I'm pretty sure I left pieces of my heart back with those girls." I study my hands, taking in a quivering breath in hopes of alleviating some of the ache.

The firm pat Theo offers my shoulder exudes reassuring comfort. "My girl is always going in with her heart wide open. You've got to figure out how to maintain these stories at arm's length, or you'll never make it in the long run of this career."

My head snaps up. "That is what defines me. It's who I am. There's no other way, Theo. If the world is hurting, then I'm hurting right along with them." He opens his mouth to rebuke, but I hold my hand up. "And when the world rejoices, I'm blessed to be able to rejoice right along with them."

"Okay. Let's just go ahead and declare an impasse for today and go over your notes. I've got a family cookout to go to. How about you?"

I hand over my notes and shrug my shoulders. "My plans are to go home and unpack."

"No get-together with your sister?" He asks absently as he skims the notes.

"No. They're still in Florida."

"Then come with me."

A pity-invite. No thanks. "Nah. Thanks anyway."

Mercifully, he lets it go and we manage to get a little work done. As I'm packing my messenger bag, there's a knock at the door. And that's peculiar in itself because no one bothers knocking around here.

"Come in," Theo says a few notches above his normal volume as he powers down the computer.

The door swings open, causing me to blink, then squint, then blink again. The image remains the same with Asher dressed in a dark suit standing in the doorway. He's so handsome and so *here* that I can hardly contain myself.

"Hello. May I help you?" Theo asks, ever so politely.

"I'm here to pick up Neena." Asher's eyes stay glued to me as he answers.

"Asher, this is my boss Theo." I wave in Theo's direction. "And Theo, this is my boyfriend Asher."

Asher accepts Theo's hand but eyes me hard with raised eyebrows.

Theo roars in laughter. "You have a boyfriend? From the look he's giving you, this is news to him, too."

My hands plant on my hips defensively. "He kisses me frequently, so that makes him my boyfriend."

Theo chuckles. "Depends on if you're kissing anyone else besides him." He nods his head toward Asher while giving me a pointed look.

Asher actually growls. "She better not be kissing anyone else." There goes that bossy tone.

Theo doubles over in raucous laughter while holding his side. "Young man, you just answered the question whether you wanted to or not. I hate to tell you this, but you're Neena's *boyfriend*."

My eyes narrow at my boss, who is just having himself a jolly good time at my expense. Theo wiggles his index finger in the air, summoning something else to say. Before he even speaks, my cheeks warm to an uncomfortable temperature, worrying about what he'll say next.

"I have to say..." Theo pauses to catch his breath. He's pure winded from laughing. "You're the very first boyfriend I've ever met." He reaches to shake Asher's hand again. "Congratulations... Or should I be offering you my condolences."

"That's it! I quit!" I storm out of the office, pulling Asher along with me.

Theo's hysterical laughter follows us all the way out the front door.

Asher loads my bags in the back of the Hummer as he cuts me a sidelong glance. "Did you really just quit?"

"Yes, I most certainly did. I shouldn't have to put up with such work conditions as that."

He keeps staring at me, so I wink.

"I officially quit until at least Thursday. We have a staff meeting then."

Asher's lip twitches. "One thing's for certain with you, woman, you're never boring."

"Why thank you, sir." I reach up and place a kiss on his cheek. "Thanks for giving me a lift home."

He closes the rear hatch and pulls me in for a hug, which I gladly melt into with relief. Seems whatever wall he had erected is now gone for the time being.

"I'm your boyfriend?" he murmurs into my hair.

"We've already answered that inside with the laughing hyena... That is if you want to be..."

"I don't know how to be a boyfriend," he admits with doubt blanketing his words.

"Showing up to take me home is in the right direction."

Asher eases back to look at me. "I didn't pick you up with the intentions of taking you home."

"No?"

"No. I want to take you on a date."

"That's very boyfriend-like of you." A smile stretches across my face, bringing forth one to Asher's face as well. "Oh how I've missed that smile." I want to ask him why it disappeared along with him before I left, but decide against ruining the moment.

"Let's go then." He walks me to the passenger side and helps me in before loading up.

We arrive to an abandoned Charlie Mike. Of course it would be closed in honor of Memorial Day. That reminds me...

"Nice suit."

Asher starts to climb out but pauses. "Thanks. I had a few observances to attend earlier."

That just makes me even more curious as to why he's not dressed in his uniform. I hold my questions back and follow him in the back entrance where the delicious scent of prepared food welcomes us.

"I stopped in earlier and cooked. Have a seat and I'll bring it out." He motions in the direction of my favorite booth before disappearing inside the kitchen.

Before I'm settled in place, he emerges, carrying two plates abundantly piled with succulent looking food. Gone is his dress coat and tie and the sleeves of his white button-down have been rolled to his elbows. No chef coat, though, and that's such a shame. He places the food before us and sits on the other side of the booth instead of his usual spot beside me. I guess the wall is still teetering.

We say our silent prayers before digging in.

"What have you prepared for us, chef?" I ask while slicing off a bite of pork.

"Pork loin with a pineapple horseradish glaze, greasy rice, and collard greens." He takes a bite of the collards first.

The tangy pork is so tender, I barely have to chew. "Mmm... This is delicious." I sample the collards and rice next. "This isn't on the menu, nor have you ever made it," I comment before taking another bite of pork. It's sweet with a heat gradually showing up. It's amazing.

"This was my buddy Jerome's recipe." He points to the pork loin with his fork. "And the sides were his favorites." Asher pauses to clear his throat. "I prepared it in remembrance of him today."

My fork halts in the mound of rice. "You lost him?" I ask on a whisper. He nods. "I'm so sorry, Asher." My free hand reaches over and clasps his.

He looks up and nods solemnly. As a civilian, there's no way of grasping what Memorial Day means to a soldier who has witnessed the very deaths we honor. They have to live with the memories each day and not just on a set day once a year.

"I would have come back yesterday. All you had to do was let me know you wanted me here for today. I would have gladly stood by your side at those services."

He nods again and clears his throat. "I know... We... My unit, we served our country in private and so we wanted to honor Jerome in private today. It's the way we've always done things."

"Oh. Okay." I already knew he wouldn't allow me in that part of his world, but it still stings the same. I start to move my hand back to my side of the table, but he catches it and holds on firmly.

"This morning was for just my brothers. But tonight... I really wanted to spend it alone with you. It's important to remember my past and my fallen brothers, but I'm just starting to realize I need to look forward. You help me remember that."

After the tension eases away, we resume eating in

silence. Or that is until my curiosity grows impatient and the pork disappears from my plate.

I gaze around the dining room, and ask, "Charlie Mike? What mission are you completing here?" My hand gestures to the pristine space that discreetly and reverently honors our military.

Asher sets his fork on his plate and wipes his mouth with the black cloth napkin. He then sets into taking a substantial sip of water, making me think he has no intention of answering me.

"Some ground missions can be mind-numbingly long, over twelve hours of being on watch. Me and Jerome liked to pass the time with coming up with recipes." He shrugs, not meeting my eyes. Then a hushed chuckle slips out as he shakes his head at a memory I'm so hoping he'll share with me.

"You have to share," I demand.

He finally lifts his gaze to mine with a faint smile playing along his lips. "The guys liked to call us Forest and Bubba." We both chuckle at that. "We were supposed to open this place together." He shrugs again. "I completed the mission."

Emotions bubble up my throat, constricting it as tears sting my eyes. "You completed it exceedingly well." I give him a minute—the gleam of unshed tears in his eyes evidence he needs it—before I continue. "The way you've dressed this fine establishment with such intricate subtlety is so awe-inspiring. A lot of thought and creativity was put into it." I glance over the brilliant walls that proudly hold the military seals.

Asher clears his throat and says, "Soldiers aren't in your face and parading around for everyone to target. Movies make us look that way, but we are to be behind the scenes, defending and protecting. I wanted this place to reflect that. To give off the vibe of security without being so visible."

"You absolutely nailed it. I also like how you've included all of the branches."

"Each one is just as significant as the other. All are needed. They all need to be honored."

"I couldn't agree more."

Our eyes meet and his reveal appreciation for me getting what he was trying to accomplish here. As I said, he has done it beyond well. This is nice and I'm about to open my mouth and chance ruining it, but there's no helping it.

"While we're being so forthcoming with each other… Do you want to explain to me why you shut me out over my trip last week?"

My question hardens his hazel eyes as I predicted it would, his inhale and exhale sharp with frustration.

"I don't do complicated. After retiring from service, I swore I would keep complicated away. Then you came along and ruined that plan entirely."

"Aww, way to make a girl feel special," I deadpan.

"I've grown attached to you." He shakes his head with a look of defeat, like growing close to me is unacceptable. "I tried so hard not to, but you've made it impossible."

My shoulders slump. Asher just keeps divvying out some lovely doozies. And I'm close to walking home. I begin to rise, but he throws his hands up in exasperation.

"See! This is complicated and I'm screwing it up."

"That still doesn't explain your reaction to the trip and the wall you erected as soon as I mentioned it."

He grunts, anger prevalent now. "I don't want to share you… I don't want you out of my sight… I don't see anyone or anything but you… I want to protect you, but the trip reminded me I can't control you or situations or life. I don't like how that makes me feel."

Whew. That was a whole lot of *don'ts*. I won't be pointing that out, though.

We sit in silence as I process all of those don'ts. Oh… It made him feel helpless and I make him feel vulnerable, something this soldier despises.

"It was for work. I'm back now." I stand and move over and insert myself on his lap. His shoulders relax as my hands thread through his blond locks.

The more length they obtain, the more of a soft wave appears in the texture. This simple change in his hair style reminds me of how far we've come in the last year. I have a feeling we have a lot farther to go.

He shakes his head after a while and huffs. "I've not even read one thing you've written. Some boyfriend I am."

"Asher, you've been understandably busy with this place." I wink, wanting to tease him a bit. "And you've only recently started liking me."

"I've never not liked you," he corrects, his features finally softening. "I should know more about you."

"That's an easy fix. All you have to do is ask me, and I'll tell you."

"Okay."

"I do have one more important question for you."

All the softness vanishes. "Neena, please, not tonight. You've asked enough." His brows pinch severely.

"But it's too important to wait."

He tries to push me off of his lap, but I cling to his neck for dear life.

"No," he growls out.

I lean close to his ear and murmur sweetly, "All I wanted to ask is if you would dance with me. That's all. Here. Now." My lips graze faint kisses along his earlobe until I feel him relax. "Please dance with me."

His arms encircle me, holding me close. "Okay."

"Thank you for answering." I place a kiss on his cheek and fish my phone out of my pocket. Scrolling through my music selection, I have my eyes set on one particular. "I've even found our song."

"We have a song?"

"Wait until you hear it. You'll agree it's perfect for us." After hitting the repeat button, I press play and set the phone on the table. "Come on, sir."

We scoot out of the booth and Asher gathers me in his arms. My head settles on his chest on instinct as I inhale the familiar comforting scent of all things Asher—crisp clean with the hint of spice. I feel him relax as our feet slowly circle.

As soon as Lee Brice croons the line, "I don't dance," Asher's chest rumbles in a deep chuckle. "You're right, sweetheart. It's perfect as our song." He presses a kiss to my forehead, melting me even more.

We continue dancing as Lee talks about love coming his way. Asher stiffens a bit at this declaration.

"Neena, do you... Do you love me?" For such a strong man full of assuredness, he is so timid when it comes to us.

I lift my head and meet his cautious eyes. "Asher,

I've loved you for quite some time."

"You do?"

"I really do." We complete another circle before I say, "Please don't tell me you *don't*."

His gaze flickers around the room before settling back on mine. "I've lived more life than I wanted. Seen things that should never exist." His fingers comb through my hair. "After the last mission... I shut down. Thought I had done all the living I wanted, so I just started going through the motions. But you keep reminding me there's still a lot of life to live. And more importantly, you make me want to live it."

He didn't answer, but I hear it in his words just the same. Probably even more. I rest my head back on his chest and let it go.

He leans down until his breath tickles my ear, and whispers, "I love you, Neena."

Even though my eyes are closed, tears find a path along my cheeks anyway.

The dance with this man may be a complicated one, choreographed with fumbling missteps and misguided directions into something we are both unfamiliar with, but there's no way I would miss this for anything in the world. It's worth every figurative sore foot.

T.I. LOWE

Chapter Twenty-Two

Nestled on the back pew of Valley Church, the melody of the congregation whispering greetings to one another emits the comforting feelings of being home. My hand placed firmly in Asher's massive grip, with my sister and her family taking up the entire pew, I'm most definitely in my happy place.

I glance to my left, just past my niece Kaisley and catch Addison's eyes watching me curiously. It's the first time he's seen me with Asher and I think the boy is in some kind of shock over it. He gives me a knowing grin, so I stick my tongue out at him. Addison is a fine one to try mocking me, with him being a newly engaged twenty-one-year old. His little sweetheart is sitting beside him, holding on to his hand for dear life. I look pointedly at their entwined hands and return his knowing look back to him. He in return sticks his tongue out. Ashley has one more year of college, so they've promised their parents to wait until she graduates. Thankfully, we all have at least a year to wrap our minds around this bizarre reality that our Addison is an actual adult. Never would I have thought my nephew would be heading down the aisle before me.

This thought has me stealing a quick glance at Asher. He catches my gaze and offers a slight smile, never one to offer a full one in public. We've come a long way, but I'm pretty sure we have a lot longer way to go before committing to something as permanent as marriage. I'm not even sure that's something he'll ever want.

"Let's begin praising our Lord this morning with a worship song," the song leader declares, pulling me out of my thoughts.

We all rise to our feet as the opening melody of Francesca Battistelli's beautiful song "Holy Spirit" echoes throughout the full sanctuary, sending glorious shivers along my neck. Unified voices surge into such a sweet chorus, singing out to our Lord and Savior. It's magnificent, but there's no describing what the deep baritone singing out beside me does to my heart. It causes me to ache as it soothes me at the same time, if that makes any sense at all.

As the song concludes and we settle back down on our pews, a slightly familiar man edges into the other back pew on the left. My heart squeezes with finding none other than Lee Sutton crouching low with a hat shrouding his eyes. It's obvious he's going for inconspicuous with a long sleeve Henley covering his colorful tattoos as well as the hat, but he's failing. From the surprised look on Mia's face and the indignation pinched on Bode's, I'm not the only one who has spotted the infamous motorcycle bad boy.

Thank you, Lord, for answered prayers.

It's been weeks, but I've not given up. Today is a divine appointment if there ever was one.

"Neena," Asher whispers harshly. Guess he's also spotted Lee.

I glance at him and shrug. I have no problem with Lee being here today, but I have a feeling I'm the only one on this pew to feel that way. He shakes his head before placing his attention toward Pastor Chase in the pulpit, so I do the same.

"What a great song to commence service on this fine summer morning. Turn in your Bibles to Acts 3:19." He pauses as pages begin to flip in a hushed ruffle. I already know what this verse is and silently say a prayer of thanks again to God, for I know He sent this to Chase specifically for Lee.

As the sound quietens, he reads, "'Repent, then,

and turn to God, so that your sins may be wiped out, that times of refreshing may come from the Lord.'" He pulls his glasses off and glances over the congregation slowly, exuding warmth and compassion with his wise eyes—never with judgement and condemnation. "This is the only verse God gave me today, but what a powerful one it is."

He paces in front of his podium and says, "How many of us have been on a road of life that seemed to be getting us nowhere fast?" Chase lets the question sink in as he turns to pace in the other direction. "I know I've been there. I felt there was no getting off that track, like I was stuck in the darkness of my sin, thinking I was too far gone."

An amen chorus echoes along the crowd. No doubt, we've all been there.

"But I'm here today to tell you, our Savior is faithful and just to forgive. All you have to do is... ask!" He declares the simplicity of this in an exuberant tone. Truly, it is so easy, but we want to complicate it as with everything else.

I let my own amen out, causing Asher to affectionately squeeze my hand with his thumb beginning to slowly draw circles on my wrist.

"You've got to repent." He points toward the direction across the stage and begins walking. "You're on the wrong path. What do you do? Keep going in that direction and become more lost?" He halts abruptly. "No! You turn yourself around." He turns and heads back. "That's all repenting is, turning away from sin and begin following God. Ask Him to forgive you. Let Him in so that you can receive a healing."

My eyes dart over to Lee, even though I beg them not to. Worship service is to be focused on my time with God, but I'm worried about this man. A lump forms in my throat with finding his head downcast and shoulders slumped, looking like the world weighs heavily on his shoulders.

"Sin is what chains us down with shame, doubt, and heavy consequences. Give it over to God. Let Him set you free of that burden today. It's time to say goodbye to the old you. Put that sin in its rightful place, the past, and move forward."

Shouts of amen and praise ring out boisterously as people begin moving to the altar even before Chase concludes. My skin prickles, rejoicing in my own freedom, and I pray that those seeking it are set free today as well.

Out of the corner of my eye, I catch Lee standing up and I'm ready to have a shouting spell. That is until he turns and stalks out the exit with me catching a glimpse of his flushed face with a deep scowl. My heart plummets, knowing he's running, but there's nothing I can do. It's his choice. I just hope this was a step in the right direction.

*****

The Sunday dinner crowd is vast today, so we've set up at the picnic table in Mia and Bode's backyard. The June sun is nice and warm, but the mountain breeze complements it nicely and keeps us all comfortable. A feast of fried chicken, potato salad, and all sorts of yummy choices keep the chatter of the group to a minimum, but it's not gotten past my attention that, every so often, various sets of eyes land on me—some in question and some in frustration. I focus on my chicken leg and ignore them all.

Addison leans over and whispers, "What did you do this time?"

I snort rather loudly and pluck another piece of chicken from the platter. "Isn't it always something?"

The eating continues with the three guys discussing a canoe trip. Surprisingly, Asher seems interested. He's taken a liking to Bode way too easily for my taste. Especially since it took him months to warm up to me.

"What do you think, Aunt Neena?" Kaisley asks.

I ease my focus off of Asher and place it on her. "What's that?"

She smiles. "Don't you want to spend another week at the outreach this summer with us?"

"Probably. I'll have to see what my schedule holds."

"Great. They've already asked if you're helping again."

"Really?"

"Yeah. The counselors said you were the most entertaining help they've ever had," Addison adds, making everyone laugh.

"You know me, never wanting to be the bore." I roll my eyes.

"That's the truth," Asher pipes in, causing everyone to laugh harder.

The false hope of getting away with the Lee Sutton situation evaporates as soon as Addison, Ashley, and Kaisley head out. Bode doesn't even wait for them to get out of the driveway before he starts in on me. No surprise. He despises Lee, and rightfully so, I guess.

"Mind telling me just what's going on with you and Lee?" Bode snaps at me as we head over to the front porch.

"Nothing is going on between us. I simply invited the man to church." I sling my arms up in exasperation and plop down in a rocking chair.

"Neena, you know he's bad news." Mia sits on

porch swing and begins worrying her hands together in her lap, the Lee Sutton conversation clearly upsetting her. "You're the one who told me to stay away from him. This makes no sense."

I won't voice the elephant on the porch, but this isn't about a guy trying his best to break up a marriage this time. This is much more and I have no idea how to explain it.

"The man is nothing but trouble. I can't believe you would even think about bringing him around," Bode grouches out as he sits down on the porch swing, jostling Mia beside him.

I look at Asher in the chair beside me, waiting for him to add his two cents. All he offers is that blank stare.

"Don't look at me that way." I turn back to the other two. "Shame on you all. Lee needs God just as much as the rest of us. He's hurting. I don't want to date him, nor do I want to cause my family any anguish over this, but he needs God. I've been led to invite him to church. Not on a date. Not into my life, and certainly not into yours."

The afternoon trickles by fruitlessly with us going back and forth with no resolution to be found. We offer one another somber goodbyes as the late day sun descends and head home. Asher's quiet on the drive home, not really that unusual, but he keeps glancing over at me with questions in his eyes.

"Go ahead. Say whatever it is you need to say." My wrist flicks out with little encouragement.

"Bode told me all about the history with Lee." His hands grip tighter on the steering wheel.

"I figured as much." I guess he knows all about Lee trying to seduce Mia into having an affair with him. The scoundrel even took it one malicious step further and openly rubbed it in Bode's face.

"Look at it like this…" Asher flicks on the blinker light and takes a right, seemingly using that time to build up to his argument. "You pretty much invited the enemy into your camp without warning your allies. That's reckless and puts people in danger."

"Well, when you put it like that…" I slouch down in the seat. He makes a good point, but then one pops in my head, too. "What if the enemy surrenders? Don't you have to offer him immunity or something?"

"From the look on that guy's face today, he wasn't surrendering." Asher turns the Hummer onto our street before glancing over at me again. "Lee looked like he was ready to rage a war when he stormed out of there."

"I ran into him at the grocery store that day I ventured out shopping. He told me you spoke to him about God, too. You feel the same way I do."

Asher parks in our driveway and shuts off the engine, but makes no move to get out. "Yes, he does, but now that I know the trouble he's stirred in your family..." He lets out a gruff sigh.

"I'm going to turn to Theo's favorite phrase he says to me, 'Let's go ahead and declare an impasse today,' because it looks like neither one of us is going to change our stance on this topic."

"I can only imagine how many times that man has had to declare that with you. You're one stubborn woman."

"I consider myself passionate. Big difference. I stand my ground on matters that mean the most, and a man's soul hanging in the throes of sin matters."

Asher opens his mouth for a rebuttal, but I hold my hand up and hurry out of the SUV after having my fill of the subject. He slowly follows behind me as I unlock my door—*yes, I remembered.*

"I admire your passion," he says before pulling me backwards in his embrace.

"And I love you." I spin around and reach up to place a kiss on his lips.

"Love you," Asher murmurs and then gives me another kiss.

A reminder flashes through my thoughts from out of nowhere. I pull away from his lips and ask, "How much do you love me?"

He eyes me carefully. "Depends."

"Well, don't you want to get to know my professional side? You did say that's something a boyfriend should know about. Am I right?"

He keeps eyeing me and repeats, "Depends."

Man, he's a tough sell. My fingers feather though his hair with hopes of softening him for my request. He leans into my touch, a very good sign.

"I have to attend a work banquet this week. The newspaper is celebrating its seventieth publishing anniversary. I'd like for my boyfriend to wear a sharp suit and be my date."

"I don't know," he mumbles as I massage his scalp.

My fingers stop. "Then I guess I'll just track down another date."

"I don't think so." His bossy tone finalizes it as I had hoped my jab would.

"Good. Make sure you line up things and let your other chef know to handle the kitchen Saturday evening."

Asher scrutinizes me with hooded eyes. "With all you've just demanded, I think it's only right we spend some time on your couch with you kissing me as your thank you."

Before I can agree or sass off about his request, Asher yanks me up and slings me over his shoulder, commendably stealing my breath. He stalks us straight over to the couch and thoroughly collects his thank you.

Chapter Twenty-Three

If purgatory were a real place, I'd consider myself smackdab in the middle of it at the moment.

"I'm not your Barbie doll," I snap at Mia as she tries adjusting the too-tight dress she's managed to help squeeze me into.

"You are for today, so stop with the whining." She takes a small step back in the cramped dressing room and studies me and the dress reflecting in the unflattering mirror.

"I'm over this already. None of them look good." I motion at the growing pile of gowns on the small bench.

"This is what you get for waiting until the day of to try finding a proper dress." She unzips the hideous pink frock, allowing me a breath of relief, and adds it to the pile.

"No. I was more than happy with wearing the new jeans and blouse I purchased last week. This is all on you." I point at her and glare.

"So you're willing to have Asher all debonair in a suit while you're on his arm in meager jeans and shirt?"

"Well, when you put it that way." I moan in frustration and rub my temples.

"That's what I thought." She escapes the dressing room to go on a hunt for more dresses.

Four more tries later, I've successfully, albeit bitterly, purchased a midnight blue gown and silver dress sandals.

"Now that wasn't so painful, was it?" She smirks to my glare as we head over to the salon to see if the stylist can manage taming my wild locks.

Too many hours later, after the hair taming took longer than expected, I'm now rushing around the bedroom to pull myself together before Asher arrives. Once the last sandal is secured to my ankle, I call it done and head downstairs.

As I reach the bottom step, my phone chimes in the small silver-beaded clutch Mia somehow snuck into my purchases. I fish the phone out and see my word of the day flashing across the screen.

Portentous - giving a sign or warning that something usually bad or unpleasant is going to happen.

My eyes lift from the screen and land on Asher's name on my word wall. *No. No. No.* That just won't do. I search for a spot farthest from his name, pluck a piece of chalk out of my dish, and scribble the word to the wall. I replace the chalk, take a step back with my eyes glued to the new addition, and try rubbing the worry tensing the back of my neck away.

I'm not a superstitious kind of girl, but there's no denying the prickling of uneasiness that is evoked by this word. Before I can dwell on it for too long, a knock hits the door. I turn my back to the offbeat worry and head towards the one something that I haven't been able to get enough of lately.

Opening the door does not disappoint. Mia's catchphrase echoes through my thoughts. *Oh sugar!*

A tailored black suit with a soft gray tie, oh my! How on earth can a suit jacket be broad enough in the shoulders yet tapered perfectly to rest along his lean hips? Undoubtedly, there is a secret boutique that caters to all of the wardrobe needs of superheroes.

"You are more handsome than you have any right to be."

Asher doesn't reply, just takes a step forward and slowly studies me, eyes traveling down and up and back down. The blank stare is accompanied by a faint flush to his cheeks, the only indicator that I affect him as much as he does me. His meticulous focus finally settles on my head. His lips twitch. "You brushed your hair."

"Yes, but I'm not a fan of it at all." This earns me a full grin. "Now you are just absolutely stunning." My hand reaches out to caress his upturned cheek that radiates warmth along my fingertips.

"You as well." He affectionately leans into my palm, making my heart swell. "You ready?"

"Yes. Just let me *lock* my door." I make a show of flipping the lock and securing the door closed, earning me a warm chuckle.

We arrive at the banquet hall on time, even though we indulged in a few kisses in the parking lot first. Music filters out and greets us at the entrance, beckoning us to follow its tune until we step inside the vast room brimming with guests.

Immediately, I sense Asher tense up with his grip on my hand tightening and his posture becoming severely straight. I glance up and see him surveying the space. I do the same in hopes of finding an area less congested near a wall. Thankfully, Theo and his wife are in such a spot to the right.

"Let's go sit with Theo." I begin pulling him in that direction without his reply, but I'm only able to go as fast as this massive man will allow. And at the moment, that's not very fast. Looking over my shoulder, I see he's still taking in the atmosphere, probably making note of all of the exits.

"Ah. Neena, I see you've brought your *boyfriend*," Theo comments, summoning the attention of way too many people. An assortment of eyes seeks me out in astonishment.

Asher visibly relaxes as soon as his back is to the wall, while I simultaneously stiffen. Theo is going to have himself some fun at my expense.

Portentous... This will most definitely be unpleasant. Thanks for the warning, dear phone.

Asher shakes Theo's hand and nods politely.

"Oh so that means she's still kissing you and only you." Theo chuckles with some of our audience joining in.

Asher seems proud. "That's correct," he answers firmly with a hint of amusement slipping through.

"Asher, I'd like for you to meet my wife, Carolyn, and I'm the only one she kisses."

Carolyn, a sophisticated lady who always stands tall, offers Asher a warm smile and her hand. "It's so nice to meet you, Asher."

He smiles politely before releasing her hand. "Likewise."

"I must say, that restaurant of yours is the best place to dine in town. You've done an exquisite job."

They chat about Asher's favorite subject while I turn my attention to Theo and his research assistant.

"Looks like Parker has secured a contact," Noah comments quietly, knowing this conversation doesn't need an audience.

"Really? He's not communicated this to me." I scan the crowd, wishing my friend were here tonight to celebrate with us. I tried last week to talk him into coming, but he was adamant on keeping his travel time available for Uganda.

"He sent me a one sentence email earlier today stating what I've just told you," Noah replies.

"We need to meet and go over the details once more." Theo's brows knit with concern. We all know this is a tricky one.

"Theo, we've gone over and over this. It's all set. My bag is even packed and waiting."

It's time for this show to get on the road. Human trafficking is like a dark plague spreading rapidly all over the world. Slavery is at an all-time record high and that's just not acceptable. Black markets lurk in each country, and the first one we've been able to get anywhere near is Uganda. So Uganda it is...

"These people are ruthless, Neena. Last month I did that interview with the prisoner out west, who is serving a life sentence. You know what that man said that has kept me sick to my stomach?" Noah's eyes darken.

I've briefly studied his notes and they're atrocious, but I say nothing and motion for him to continue.

"He said selling humans on the black market far exceeded any of his drug trafficking because you can sell the same human repeatedly." Noah shakes his head. "He was proud of it. Not even a hint of remorse."

We all stare off, repulsed by it all.

"Enough shoptalk, you three," Carolyn reprimands, causing us to un-huddle and rejoin the rest of the group.

Theo shrugs the despondency off immediately as though it was just a figment of our imagination and places a wide grin on his face. Uh-oh. Here he goes again.

Before he can start up, I interrupt. "Is that food I smell? I'm starving."

Theo gives me a sly look, letting whatever jab he wanted to deliver go. He motions to the table before us. "It's about time for service to begin. Shall we?"

I immediately block the two chairs close to the wall, earning me an appreciative look from my handsome GI Joe date. After he assists me in my chair and takes his own, Asher uses his foot to pull my chair against his, leaving no space between us. His strong thigh presses against mine protectively as an arm reaches around my shoulder.

Luckily, the meal is served with no hiccups and no more teasing from my mentor. Dessert is just too much—a giant vanilla cupcake with a silver fondant 75 resting in the mountain of fluffy buttercream. I dive into mine with abandon.

Asher chuckles from beside me and grazes his finger over the tip of my nose, coming away with a dollop of icing. "Saving some for later?"

He's about to lick it off, but I grab his hand and steal it back. Then he does something that completely catches me off guard due to it being a first—he leans over and kisses me. Just lip to lip with no lingering, but it's still a public kiss.

A low chorus of laughs brings my attention back to the table, finding everyone staring at Asher and me in fond amusement.

"This is just too much for me to take in. Does your Daddy know you've finally found yourself a boyfriend? Kissing him in front of an audience, no less?" Theo smiles and Carolyn tries to subtly swat him in the arm to hush him up.

"As a matter of fact, he does *and* approves."

"Richard and I will have to have a long talk. Speaking of that, when will he and your mom be back?"

I brush the linen napkin along my nose and mouth to catch any remaining icing. "Dad is on a book tour, but the plans are for them to be moved back here by the fall."

I glance up and find Asher with a brow hitched up in question. I'm about to explain, but Theo interrupts.

"Asher, what about you? Do your parents know you're hanging out with the likes of NL Cameron? The most noted journalist in this country?"

All at once, Asher stiffens and drops his hand away from my shoulder. He looks to me and then back to Theo, his features hardening with every passing second. They agonizingly tick by while I try to figure out what just happened.

Standing abruptly, Asher mutters, "Excuse me," before storming off.

"What did I say wrong?" Theo asks, looking as baffled as I feel.

"I have no idea." I excuse myself also and hurry to catch him.

My stomach flip-flops when I find him about to climb into his SUV. *To leave me here?*

"Asher!" I yell out, in a jog to catch him.

He turns around with a scowl so deep it causes me to halt in my steps, leaving several feet between us.

"What's wrong?" My voice quivers with uncertainty.

He slams the door, producing a loud bang, jolting me like a skittish cat. "You're NL Cameron?"

Didn't he already know? I've assumed all along he knew, but I guess he truly does keep to himself. My confusion is over how he's reacting to this. Why would it anger him?

"Yes," I admit with no hesitation.

He paces a tight circle before facing me again. "The same NL Cameron that somehow weaseled his way into my unit's mission? No one is supposed to know we exist!" His voice bites out each word through a stubbornly set jaw.

This pushes me back another step. *His unit?* "Clearly I'm no guy. But... Afghanistan? You weren't there... I would have remembered."

Swiftly, Asher unbuttons his coat and yanks up the hem of his shirt, revealing a spattering of white scars riddling his abdomen. "I was indisposed."

A gasp flees from me in shock, propelling me closer to him. "You're Motor? The hero who drove your men out of harm's way without clueing any of them in on the fact you were nearly bleeding out during the drive." My eyes scan the dark parking lot, finding us alone. Never would I have ever imagined coming face to face with this man, let alone having this private conversation out in the open in such a way. "By the time you reached safety, you were barely alive." I know this hero's story as well as my own. He passed out as soon as he put the Humvee in park. Only then did the others realize he was critically injured.

He pulls the suit coat off, harshly yanks the driver's door open, and slings it inside the vehicle. "I would have gladly died that day for my brothers."

"You saved them," I say, overwhelmed with emotions. My arms ache to gather around him for comfort, but that's not an option, so I stay put and watch cautiously.

"Not all of them," Asher whispers, his voice sounding gritty.

Then it clicks. If Asher is Motor, then Jerome had to be Barge. He refused to leave him even though he was already gone. That was when he was hit. Wounded, Asher carried his dead friend all the way back to the Humvee. "Oh Asher... I'm so sorry about Jerome."

"No! You don't get to talk about him." He points at me, seething in anger and hurt. "Don't."

Without another word, he hurries into the Hummer and abandons me in the parking lot with no way home and a confused amount of reality sinking my body to the pavement.

All this time... Motor, the one soldier who refused to meet me even after he fully recovered, living beside me *all this time* and managing to steal my heart.

Portentous... I didn't have a clue, did I?

Somehow, I had enough wits about me to grab my clutch on the way out of the door while in pursuit of my angered soldier. With trembling hands, I fish my phone out and call a cab. Then I send a text to Theo, explaining that Asher became ill and needed to go home. Not a total lie. He is ill in the most extreme meaning of thoroughly livid.

*****

As the cab delivers me home, anxiety gathers in the pit of my stomach with finding Asher's SUV in its spot. I pause on the porch, torn between letting him cool off and wanting to check on him. The decision nudges me to give him space and propels me on inside my house. Pausing at the door while scanning around, the space feels vacant as though all of the life the two of us have been building inside of these walls has vanished. Wanting to escape my despair, I hurry upstairs and change with hopes of shedding those desolate feelings.

After throwing on a pair of jeans and shirt, my

body gives out at the foot of the bed, demanding I sit. Second nature kicks in with me forming my interview questions, something I always do before confronting someone.

What angered you about discovering who I am?
Why does it matter that I found out?
Why wouldn't you allow me an interview?
Have you received help for PTSD?
What angered you?

Downstairs, the front door slams, signaling it's time for round two. I'm not confident on being prepared for it, so I stay in my spot for a while longer, contemplating all that has happened. My phone starts going off as I stand, but the need to unearth the cause of his wrath has me ignoring it and heading downstairs.

He's seated on the couch, as I had expected, but Asher cradling his head in his hands is unexpected. Gone is the tie and most of the buttons of his dress shirt have found their way loose. Unkempt is a new look on him, one that doesn't fit at all. The need to keep distance between us has me sitting close to the bottom step. He knows I'm here, so I sit and silently wait.

"Was this just a ploy to interview me? To expose me?" Asher asks, not looking up.

"How could you even think that? I exposed

nothing in that story…" Just now, I realize something. "You've not read it, have you?" His silence confirms he hasn't. "All I did was show you and your men the respect you rightfully deserve. I exposed nothing but your sacrifice for our freedom and how we as civilians take that very gift for granted."

I don't know what else to say, so I clamp my mouth shut. Silence falls thickly between us again.

"Do you have any idea how it came about me living beside you?" He asks without lifting his head.

"Fate?" It's completely baffled me in the last hour since finding this out.

Asher finally looks up, eyes red and swollen. My heart crumbles, not knowing why I caused such a brickhouse of a man to cry, but it's obvious I'm the source.

He shakes his head slowly. "No, sweetheart. Not even close. My captain… The one who drools over your old man's books… He set this up just like he had no right in allowing you near our unit." He lets out an indignant huff. "How in all of this time did it not come out who your dad is? Why have you kept it from me?" Vulnerability glistens in his damp eyes, thinking I've deceived him in some way.

Now my anger begins to simmer. "No. You don't get to turn that on me. I've offered myself up as an open book from the very start. It was you who never cared enough to turn one page to discover my story." As I sit here fuming, the impact of what he just said settles around me about as comfortable as walking through shards of glass.

Did my dad have something to do with this? I will definitely be finding that out.

"Your story?" he asks harshly, bringing my attention back to him. "I'm trapped in the nightmares of my own!" He's off the couch in a flash and is glowering down at me before I can blink. "You don't know what it's like."

My shaky legs propel me to stand. "Then tell me."

His head shakes in what appears to be disgust. "You can't imagine... Almost two decades of uncertainty. Doing all you can to complete the mission. To keep everyone alive in the process... Only to fail. I watched him die... Not the first I've witnessed, not by a longshot. I lived day in and day out around death and violence." His sentences come out disjointed while his head continues to shake in helplessness.

"Maybe you need to seek some help to deal with the trauma—"

"I don't have PTSD. I've gone through the gamut of testing. I'm just like every other soldier. We have no choice but to live with the nightmares we faced.

It's forever a part of us."

"I understand—"

"No, you don't! You will never understand what serving this country cost me." He clutches his stomach in both his hands. "Your life is all fun and games. You don't get it!"

Before I can rein it in, my hands lash out and shove him with all my might. He staggers a step back in surprise more than anything.

"No! *You* don't get it. I've done nothing but try to understand since I met you. I've tried and you pigheadedly wouldn't let me." I push him again for good measure. "As for you… Never have you tried to get *me*!" I take a step back and yank the hem of my shirt up, revealing the top of my own war wound. "I didn't receive mine on a battlefield, but it's cost me dearly." I release the hem, allowing it to conceal the evidence as I bat an angry tear away, but his eyes stay pinned to my abdominal area. A few beats pass before he lifts his confused gaze. Sniffling, I continue, "At the age of seventeen I had the great big world in my sights, just ready for me to go out and claim my rightful place."

"Neena," his gruff voice begins, but I push forward while ignoring his pleading gaze and my phone belting out 'Ramblin' Man' upstairs.

"Who understands cancer and its selfish claim?

Not me. Not even a little. The disease robbed me of some of my most sought after dreams. I don't feel like a whole woman." A bitter laugh pushes through my lips, as I demand my eyes to stay locked with his glare. "Women are created to create life, but my body never will. That's why I've never even dated, knowing I had nothing to offer a man."

Asher steps closer and reaches for me, but I jerk away from his touch. "Neena—"

"That's how I felt until I met you." I motion between us. "We're both incomplete... I thought God placed you in my life, so that we could mend together and be imperfectly complete."

My phone has kept an irritating marathon of ringing during this entire argument. Not being able to ignore it any longer, I leave Asher stunned quiet and dash back to my room. That persistent ringing can only mean one thing—it's time to go.

"Parker," I answer, rushing around the room and gathering my boots.

"I've already emailed your flight plans. Be to the airport within the next hour. Sooner if you can. I'll meet up with you on the connecting flight." His voice is rushed, sounding like he's scrambling around as frantically as I am.

"Okay," I mutter, shoving my feet into the boots. Luckily, my clothes are already packed and ready by the door. Grabbing the suitcase up, I rush downstairs to gather my laptop.

Asher continues to stand at the bottom of the stairs. I shoulder my way past him to the dining table and start shoving everything into the messenger bag.

"Where are you going?"

Yanking the bag over my shoulder along with my purse, I beeline to the door. "I'm not at liberty to say," I snap off. There's no time to waste going another round with him.

After slinging everything in the trunk of the car, I pause at the driver's door and look back at him. He stands on the porch with a grimace heavy on his face, fists balled tightly by his side.

"I've watched on as you've continuously torn down walls, only to resurrect new ones in the rubble. I realize you've spent over half of your life fighting the enemy, but you need to *realize* I'm not the enemy. I'm not against you. I'm for you. Whatever crass notion you've manipulated in your head about me is completely delusional." I inhale a shaky breath with hopes of holding back the tears. "This back and forth… It's exhausted me."

He says nothing, staying true to form, so I do the one thing Asher Reid has been demanding I do ever since the day we met.

I leave him alone.

Chapter Twenty-Four

As soon as the plane touches down for the connector flight, my jumbled-up brain finally registers that I've not called Mia. Rushing through the terminal, I dial her number.

"Hey you," she answers on the first ring. She sounds so chipper. If only I could steal some of her joy at the moment for myself.

Well, I'm pretty sure I'm about to unintentionally steal it, but not for myself...

"Hey. Just wanted to let you know I'm headed out and should be back in maybe a week or so."

"Where?"

"We've already discussed this. Extensively."

Her sigh is audible through the phone, so heavy it still registers over the busy goings on of the airport.

"Neena, I was hoping I had talked you out of it."

"You should know better than that by now." Glancing around, I spot Parker in the waiting area. "Look, I don't have time for this. Just remember what I said about tracking my location every day."

"You're worrying me. Never have you asked me to do that."

"It's just precautionary. As soon as we hang up, test it and then text me if it worked." This trip has too many uncontrollable variables. Precaution is all I can do, not leaving more than I have to up to chance.

"Where are you?"

"Track the phone for the answer."

I wave to catch Parker's attention, sending my messenger bag plummeting down my arm. I readjust it and hurry in his direction as he stands.

"Mia, one more thing... If Lee shows up for church, will you promise that you and Bode will be cordial?"

"There's no chance in him showing up."

"Way to think positive," I snap.

"No, that's reality. It's all over the headlines today that he wrecked his bike last night. Another DUI. They're all predicting jail time."

My stomach flips, causing my steps to falter. What is it with all the people I've been reaching out to lately? My intentions seem to be going in the totally opposite direction. Asher's stoic face flashes before my eyes, and I have to blink him away quickly. I cannot do this right now.

"I have no words."

"That's a new one. Are you okay?" Concern riddles her words.

"Yeah. Sure. Gotta go. Remember to track me now and once a day. Love you." I don't wait for her reply before ending the call.

Parker finishes eliminating the distance between us and offers me a quick hug. "You ready for this?"

I shove a smile on my face, but from the cautious look on his face he's not buying it. "Absolutely."

"Neena, what's wrong?"

"No time for a soap opera show." I turn on my heel and head to the terminal for the next leg of the trip with hopes of leaving my broken heart behind to worry about mending later.

One misconception people have about me is that I'm a fly-by-the-seat-of-my-pants girl. I don't even mind their fallacy of my character. It keeps life more interesting that way. But nothing I do is done without complete care in planning. I'm meticulous on mapping out even the most minuscule of detail. Parker grants my request not to talk about what's bothering me. Instead, we focus our time on the flight to go over the details again.

*****

Over a year's worth of research and planning has been invested in the preparation of this moment. The main focus of my investigation has centered on the dark side of life in this country, so never did I expect to step off the plane and into paradise. It's breathtaking.

"Seriously?" I mumble as my confused gaze tries taking in the tropical forest surrounding the small airport. Everywhere my gaze settles, vibrant green foliage waves in the breeze.

"Wow," Parker says from behind me. "Most definitely the Pearl of Africa."

We both take our time scanning the beauty of Uganda. I thought we were heading straight into the bowels of hell. Gazing around, I could not have been more wrong... Well, that's what the façade tells me, but I know what's lurking around the dark edges of this lush area. That idea has me coming up short. Isn't that exactly what my home country is doing as well? Hiding right under the pristine façade of the United States of America lurks the exact same horror. People are delusional to think the U.S. is immune to such horrific abuse as human trafficking.

A warm, reassuring arm drapes over my

shoulder, snapping me out of my thoughts. I glance up and meet Parker's stormy eyes and easy smile.

"No worries, darling. I've planned our entire vacation, so we'll get to explore this paradise." He winks, readjusting his backpack on his shoulder, and ushers me forward. He easily slips into character, our charade as a couple already planned out.

My eyes avert from his and land on a small welcoming group. They offer thickly accented welcomes as they relieve us of our bags, and then a thin, willowy man escorts us to a late model Range Rover that waits on the other side of the airport building.

We bump along a red clay road with thick ruts carved out from the weather and over usage in the air conditioning-less vehicle until we reach a thick wrought iron gate. The vehicle slowly heads up an incline until a large immaculate hut comes into view at the end of the driveway. Several smaller huts seem to stem out from the larger one with winding pebble paths tethering them together. Gas lanterns flank each path and are just starting to glow in the early evening. Just past the half circle of huts, a view of a lush valley cascades as far as my eyes can see. It's absolutely breathtaking.

"Welcome to Paradise," the driver offers as he shuts the engine off and climbs out.

Parker and I exchange a concerned look before he opens his door and scoots out as well. The heat has pressed down on me and has my clothes clinging to my skin. Between that and feeling downright bruised from the ride from the airport, it's all I can do to climb out of the stifling vehicle. Parker notices me struggling, and offers a firm yank to dislodge me from the sticky backseat.

The larger hut turns out to be the resort's check-in reception area. We are greeted by a short, round woman with midnight skin who shows us to our hut.

"Dis is you," she says in a rich vernacular, offering Parker the key after unlocking the door. "Don't spend entire stay inside. Lots to see out here, too." She motions around and offers us a deep laugh. Her wrap dress is pulled tight around her thick middle and offers a jiggly show as she laughs. Still chuckling, she waddles back down the pebble path, her sandals flapping happily along until the night hides her from our sight.

Parker gives me a knowing smirk and I, in return, stick my tongue out at him before pushing past him. Having to share a room with him should cause unease, but we have been a working team for so long that the awkwardness vanished long ago. We are here on a mission, and I don't think I would be comfortable being separated from him. He's also been my confidant for so long that I yearn to confide in him about my argument with Asher, needing to talk about it, but knowing now is not the time. I'm sure he'll be as surprised as Asher and I were to find out our shared history. It's hard to push the pain aside, but as soon as my eyes land on the handwritten notes from the girls back in the U.S. that I tucked into my suitcase as a reminder, I regain my focus. This is for the victims here as well as all over the world.

Silently praying, I begin unpacking my belongings in the honey-hued wicker wardrobe as Parker noses around the small space that reminds me of a safari explorer's tent—maps, a mosquito net draping over the bed, binoculars... All tools for a challenging journey into the unknown. It's going to take God's divine power to get us through this dark journey. The tingling up my spine warns of an unknown storm coming our way.

Please, God. Please send us in the right direction.

*****

Two days dawdle by with nothing but time being wasted as we aimlessly roam this foreign country. The first day was spent looking the happy couple part with us going on one of those safari excursions, and then yesterday trudged by with us exploring the busy

African town. We've decided to try that again today.

The open-air market is filled with jovial dialects in several foreign languages that tangle around English as we weave in and out of the booths. The sun baked down relentlessly the two days before, but the clouds have showed up today, making this outdoor activity manageable even though it's not productive.

I've grumbled this all morning, but mutter again in annoyance, "This is such a waste of time. How on earth are we to find anything out in this mass of chaos?"

Parker hands over his money to a little wrinkled-up man for the bunch of bananas before breaking one off and handing it over to me. With his hand on my shoulder, he leads us over to a small tent where a man bangs rhythmically on a pair of worn djembe drums. It's quite loud, so I know why Parker ushered us over here. We listen on for a while along with a small group of spectators.

Parker takes a bite of his banana. After swallowing, he leans close to my ear and says, "The contact knows we're here. I'm guessing he'll seek us out. We've just got to sit tight in the meantime."

Giving up a few hours later, we take a taxi back to the resort. And by taxi, I mean a tin can minivan that whines with every gear change. No matter, these little vehicles seem to soar over the rutted roads and have delivered us to our destinations remarkably fast in the last few days.

While Parker showers off the dust and disappointment of another futile day, I stretch out on the bed and call Mia.

"Hey!" she answers on the first ring.

"Hey. Just wanted to check in." I toy absently with the delicate, gauzy fabric of the netting hovering over the sides of the bed.

"You sound defeated." Her voice is reserved, but there's a flicker of hope edging through. No doubt, she's hoping I'm ready to give up and go home.

"Just a little frustrated. Parker and I thought we were coming in here like gangbusters but it's not been that easy." My sigh is so heavy that the netting ripples from its force.

"Then come on home."

"Not yet." The shower shuts off, so I scoot off the bed and gather a change of clothes.

"Oh, by the way, Asher showed up this morning at the Lodge and demanded that Bode to tell him where you are at."

The phone almost slips from where I'm cradling it between my ear and shoulder. "What?"

"Yep. GI Joe got all up in his face, too."

"What did Bode tell him?"

"He told him you were somewhere in Uganda,

but didn't know the specifics."

"Well, tell Bode to take the brute out on the rapids and dump him somewhere. Maybe that'll cool him down a bit."

"Did something happen between the two of you?"

"Just Asher being Asher. Jerk," I mutter, turning around and finding Parker eyeing me. "Look, I need to go. I love you." I hit end and toss the phone on top of the dresser. My hopes of hiding in the bathroom are dashed as soon as Parker grabs my shoulder and veers over to the table.

"Sit down." Parker points to the chair and takes the one opposite of it. "You've been distracted since we arrived here. It's time we talk about it."

He's right. The way things were left unsettled with Asher has been eating at me. Maybe I owed him some type of apology.

"You remember the soldier severely injured in Afghanistan, the one they called Motor?"

My friend seems taken aback by the direction of the conversation. "Yes?" he mumbles hesitantly, scratching his scruffy jaw.

"Well, Motor has actually been living next door to me for the past year."

Shock and then, to my annoyance, amusement flash across his face. "No way! Asher is Motor? Only you, Neena. Only you!" He barks out in laughter.

I reach over and pop him good and hard in the arm. "It's not funny. He thinks I deceived him somehow just so I could get an exclusive interview or some absurdness as that."

"Oh, he's mad. He thinks you were responsible for him moving in next door?" Parker settles back down and slumps in his chair. "That is absurd."

"Sadly, I think my dad and his captain did set it up. That's way too coincidental. I've not had a chance to talk to Dad, because all of this oh so dramatically unfolded mere moments before you called." I don't know if the stifling heat is intensifying or I'm just that upset, but I lean over and switch on the ceiling fan with hopes of stirring some of the thick air away. "As soon as we get back, Dad and I will be having a long chat."

"It'll all work out."

It's all I can do to sniff back the threatening tears. "He was so livid. So hurt. He thinks I betrayed him."

Parker reaches over and squeezes my hand into his. "If Asher is looking for you, then maybe he's had enough time to cool off. Seriously, Neena, that man loves you. He'll get over it."

I regather my change of clothing, offer him a frail smile with a head nod, and head for the bathroom to try to regather myself.

Chapter Twenty-Five

Back in Tennessee, the nights are perfumed with the sweet mountain breeze while the crickets graciously serenade anyone who cares to listen. Nothing feels like home here in this strange land, that's for sure. The breeze here is thick with musky earth scents and the sounds of giant animal moans rumble in the distance. Even though the night is warm, a shiver skirts along my back from those dangerous murmurings and causes me to pick up my pace. The glow of the gas lanterns along the path does very little to offer me any comfort. I just hope Parker hurries up with booking a few more nights. Being alone here is unsettling. Flicking the key between my fingers, I'm now wishing I had patiently waited with him. I reach the hut door and really wish we had left a light on earlier to greet us on our return.

As I push open the door and step into the pitch-black space, an aggressive hand snakes around my neck, effectively stealing my ability to scream. The door slams and locks before I'm being dragged further inside. I feel something sharp push against the side of my neck. My pulse frantically pushes back.

"Stupid 'merican woman. So stupid coming here. How you know?" A man's raspy voice hisses out in broken English. His vice grip lets up slightly on my neck.

Shocked and scared, I remain mute until my head is yanked back harshly.

"I... I can't really say." Barely swallowing, I continue, "God sent me and all I know is this is where I'm supposed to be."

"Don't bring your god into dis!"

"But He's in everything." If I'm going to die, I'm going to do it standing firm on my faith.

He pushes a huff of sour breath my way and it assaults me even though he's standing behind me. Between that and his body stench, I'm unable to hold back the gag. The blade bites a little into my skin with warning, so I try tamping it down.

"You no idea what people you messing with. Your country cry out over ISIS and Taliban. You know nothing yet. They worse. Walk away while you can."

As his shaky grip tightens around my neck once again, it hits me all of a sudden. *This is our informant.* Of course, I should have known better than to think he would simply meet us for a nice dinner and discuss his ties to human trafficking.

"Please. I need your help," I say in only a squeak.

His hand loosens just enough to allow my lungs to grasp a pull of air. My eyes un-blur and finally adjust to the dark, but there's still no security to be found.

"I'm good as dead. They know of my betrayal in contacting you. They let me loose in the jungle to give me a day's head start—a game for them. I've been hoping big lion would find me and put me out of my misery. I welcome death now. I can't live with what I've done." A sob escapes him and his entire body trembles from behind me.

"God will forgive you if you ask. He's a God of forgiveness," I whisper, hoping to soothe him.

"I deserve no forgiveness. I deserve death." His breaths become labored and his hands begin to shake severely. One slip and my neck will be severed.

With my panic escalating, I can find no comfort to offer him. This is all slipping through my fingers, so I beg, "Please. Where are they?"

"Hidden in plain sight."

"Where?" I strangle out, feeling his fingers bruising my skin.

"You and your companion been right on top of it last few days and you fools didn't see."

The doorknob jiggles. "Neena, it's me."

My head jerks toward the sound of Parker's voice. A mistake that delivers an instant sting as the blade slices into the side of my neck.

Ignoring both the pain and Parker, I continue, "The market? We've been looking there."

"Not close enough. They've already spotted you, pretty 'merican woman. Not good." His tone holds such bitterness.

"Neena! What's going on in there?" The door protests against Parkers heavy knocks.

The intrusive hands disappear, propelling me forward onto the floor. I stumble back to my feet and rush over to the door, fumbling with the lock until it clicks free. Before my hand makes it to the knob, Parker yanks the door open and rushes in.

Flipping the lights on, his eyes grow severely wide as they zone in on my neck. "You're bleeding!"

My trembling hand begins to reach up to the wound, but he snatches me close to his body and scans the small space. A few things are knocked over by the open window from the wake of the man's quick escape.

"He's gone. It's okay," I mutter.

Parker pulls back and leans down to inspect my neck. The muscle in his jaw ticks as his fingers brush along the wound. "It's not very deep. There's a first aid kit in the bathroom. Let's get it cleaned up." He ushers me into the small space and sits me on top of the vanity.

I numbly watch on as he digs the kit out and produces a bottle of antiseptic and cotton balls. He presses the liquid fire to my neck, causing my body to buck.

"This is stupid. We shouldn't be here. It's time to go home." His head continuously shakes as he keeps his eyes on the cut.

"No," I croak out as he administers more antiseptic. "*Oww*! I think it's clean."

"We're in a foreign country in the middle of nowhere... I'm not so sure."

And I guess he's not. Before the sting of the round fades, he delivers more.

"Enough," I hiss, grabbing the cotton ball out of his grasp and slinging it into the wastebasket.

"Did you get a look at the thief?" he asks while rummaging through the kit.

"What?"

"The guy who attacked you. Did you see what he

stole?" Parker presses a square bandage to the side of my neck. "Hold this while I tape it."

I do as he says. "That was your informant."

His stormy eyes meet mine. "That makes no sense. Why would he hurt you?"

"He's terrified for his life. They found out about his contact with you and now he's hiding out in the jungle." I struggle to swallow from my throat beginning to swell. I grab a pack of acetaminophen and hop down. "You startled him. I don't think he meant to hurt me."

Parker is right on my heels as I head to the small fridge for a bottle of water. "He didn't mean to crush your throat?" His tone is thick with angry sarcasm.

I give up on that and try redirecting our conversation. "The black market is actually hidden *in* the market." I let that resonate with him while downing the two pills. My throat constricts and almost refuses their passage, but another gulp of water helps to push them on down.

We both plop down in a chair. The adrenaline coursing through my veins feels close to petering out, leaving my limbs quite heavy.

"Neena, we're getting in over our heads." Looking as defeated as I feel, Parker drops his forehead into his hands.

"I've not come all this way to go back

emptyhanded."

He doesn't acknowledge my declaration. Instead, he rises and begins checking the door locks and securing the windows. His actions are obviously fruitless. The man hiding in here earlier is proof of that, but I decide voicing this won't help the situation. After he finishes, Parker begins to pace. An eerie déjà vu chills me—we've already lived this moment just last fall in Texas.

Ungluing myself from the chair, I walk over and halt him by grabbing his arm. "Parker, I completely understand if you want to head back. Truly. You shouldn't have to be in another situation like this."

His brows furrow deeply over his gray eyes. "We're a team. That won't be happening unless you go with me."

"I can't go just yet."

He releases a deep sigh and settles on the edge of the bed. "So that's all the informant told you?"

"Basically." I sit beside him and gently rub my neck, thinking it's best to keep the tidbit about them spotting me to myself for the time being.

"What's the plan?" Parker asks.

"I guess we go shopping again."

*****

And shopping is exactly what we do for another few days. Needless to say, the crowd is going to have enough African souvenirs to show off back home. Parker is growing antsy, thinking we are snooping out the operations, but I'm actually hoping to offer myself as bait. The informant's statement was confirmed yesterday when I spotted the sharks circling. We are watched carefully throughout the day, but the figures stay shrouded in the shadows.

Dawn hasn't made a peep yet, but I sneak into the bathroom while Parker continues to snore. It's time for me to make my move, so I pull up Theo's contact and send him a text.

Me – *Need you to track my phone every hour starting today until I say otherwise.*

That means he will have to do this throughout the night as well, but there's no doubt Theo won't do it. He's on phone duty with Mia, but I don't want to alarm her with this request. It takes several minutes for him to reply.

Theo – *Why?*

Me – *I have a feeling.*

Theo – *You having a feeling gives me a bad feeling.*

Me – *Don't forget. Every hour.*

Theo – *Your boyfriend came by looking for you.*

My stomach tightens in discomfort. I don't have time for this. There's no room to focus on Asher right now, so my fingers quickly type a reply.

Me – *I don't have a boyfriend. Phone. Every hour. T2UL.*

He texts something else, but I delete it along with all of my other texts and contacts list before placing the phone on mute. Taking it a step farther, I turn off the vibration option as well with hopes of keeping my phone concealed for as long as possible.

For the next hour, I go over all of the facts gathered about this group and try forming several different plans. Mainly, I plan on putting a little space between Parker and me today, hoping this will lead to some move on the shadow's part.

After dressing, I shove my phone deep into the inner side of my boot and go wake up Parker with thoughts of the early bird getting the worm.

The day heats up as all of the other days have done since our arrival. Thankfully, the rain has only shown up occasionally. The bruises on my neck have faded but the tiny cut still remains, so my sweaty hair stays down to hide it, making me miserable. I continue to wander away from Parker throughout the morning, wanting to look naive. He's already reprimanded me a few times. The shadows showed up as soon as we hit the first vendor and have tagged along. Nothing new, but this afternoon as we rummage around a table filled with hand-carved wood statues my hackles are raised. This is the farthest we've ventured into the market so far, and this part seems a little seedy. There's more trees in this area, too, and closes us off in sort of a semicircle.

Glancing around, my eyes land on double the earlier shadows. Taking a steady breath, I casually lean my head on Parker's shoulder and whisper in his ear, "We've found it."

He keeps flipping thru a stack of wood plaques, but his back stiffens. "How so?"

"We've been followed since we got here today, but just now the group has doubled." I run my palm along his back, hoping we convey a distracted couple.

"And why are you just telling me this?"

"Because now it matters."

"Neena," he says as a warning.

By the edge of the tent, the old man running the table suddenly drops an arm load of statues. Without hesitance, Parker steps over to help pick them up.

In a rushed blur, a hand clamps over my mouth and drags me away. Eyes wide, I watch as a thick group descends towards the table, instantly eliminating any sight of Parker.

One minute I'm standing in the blazing sun.

The next, I'm in the deep shadow of a thick jungle, being submerged into a horrific nightmare.

Chapter Twenty-Six

A stale stench is the first thing to register as the world begins to seep back in. Several attempts fail before my eyes cooperate with opening, but all I want to do is close them back with hopes this makeshift prison will disappear. The ache in my back escalates, so I cautiously roll to my side, but recoil when my face lands on the surface of the moldy mattress I'm lying on. It's so thin I might as well be on the concrete floor.

"Hey," a small voice calls out.

I blink a few times before searching the dimly lit room. It's nothing more than a square cinderblock building with filthy pallets lining the floor. Most of them hold bodies that are curled up on their sides.

"Hey," the small voice registers again.

Scanning around, I finally spot a young girl two

beds over. After the beating that was delivered to my body, all I can manage is a small wave, and that even hurts. A small sob slips through my clenched teeth as the nightmare flashes right along with the pain.

I was brought to some type of compound with several block buildings. As soon as the shadows got me here they dragged me into one of the larger buildings and on into a private room where a buyer was already waiting. I'm not sure what I expected, but it most certainly was not a man in an expensive suit with a proper haircut. It became clear that evil can be disguised in all forms.

"I never buy without a test drive." His hand flicked out toward me as he smirked darkly.

Defenseless, I had no choice but to stand there and allow them to strip me. My only relief was that the phone remained lodged inside my boot.

The look of revulsion registered on the buyer's face as his eyes landed on my long vertical scar.

"I made it clear she had to be untouched! Clean!" He stormed out with a few of the shadows following him. Never had I been so thankful for cancer in all of my life.

"You stupid woman," one of the shadows spat out before delivering a punch to my abdomen that sent me to my knees.

"Don't kill her yet. We can sell her for other uses," another shadow said, yanking me back to my feet.

That's all my foggy memory can recall before my body was engulfed in pain. They beat every inch of me but my face.

I vaguely recall someone in this room helping me into my ripped tank top and jeans—the only two articles of clothing I was allowed back. Even though the humid air trapped in here with us feels close to boiling, my exposed feet long for my boots. They've been a part of my uniform for so long. Without them, I don't feel strong enough to get through this.

"Hey," the little voice pulls me back and is closer now.

Looking over, I find her curled on her side on the mattress beside me. I glance around with caution, hoping she won't get in trouble for moving. She brushes her blonde hair away from her face, revealing a unique birthmark on her cheek. The heart-shaped stain is oddly familiar... My mind races through its file bank until it registers.

Emergency news reports flashing that angelic face with the heart on her cheek, along with headlines stating, EIGHT-YEAR OLD ANNALISE WATTERS ABDUCTED.

Painful shivers race along my back with knowing I am lying beside the very same child who was abducted while on a weekend family vacation in Europe a few months back. This poor child has been living in a hell right here on earth, but seems stronger than I am at the moment. Her little hand reaches over and entwines with mine. There's no holding back my whimper.

"Shh, love." Her English accent confirms it.

It's her.

Annalise is here.

Alive.

Slightly malnourished.

But alive.

The little mother hen soothes me until I regain my composure. By this point, she's wedged her tiny frame on my bed with me.

"How did you get here?" I whisper.

"I vomit every time. They say it's not good for business and don't know what to do with me." A darkness creeps in her eyes, clarifying that *every time* means when she is raped. My empty stomach convulses at this thought.

Annalise is by far the youngest in this group at the moment. By my estimations, the rest of the girls range from teen to young adult. I'm pretty sure I'm the oldest here.

Before I can question her further, the door rattles as it's being unlocked. Annalise scurries back to her bed just as a shadow drags in a screaming teenage girl, naked with blood trickling down her body. He backhands the distraught girl so harshly it sends her to the floor. He yells obscenities at her and tosses a few pieces of clothing beside her. After taking a look around, the shadow slinks away.

As the locks click back into place, two young women slowly rise from their beds and help the poor girl dress before placing her on a vacant bed.

Her screams echo in confusion and grief and fear until her voice completely gives out.

Living nightmares…

The day moves along with steady activity. This

place is a revolving door with girls being taken away, only to be replaced with others. I was dragged to my feet at one point, but another shadow reminded the one pinching my arm in his grasp that I was *unclean*. He shoved me back down onto my sour confines and that's where my tender body has been ever since. They don't even look at Annalise. For that, I'm thankful. I imagine a client wouldn't take too kindly to being thrown up on. Thank God for that, too.

Not able to do anything but stay hunkered in this spot, I flip between praying and observing, filing away as much information as possible. One observation is this place seems to be maybe a type of quick sale setup or a halfway house to some other demented location. It's a rapid turnover, with only a few original girls remaining. Another sad observation, the younger girls aren't held here for very long before they are being dragged back out the door.

From the looks of it, there's only a fleeting timeframe for Parker to find me with that window already rapidly closing.

After only being given a murky cup of water, we are told to go to sleep. Stupid request when it's clearly evident that's the only thing any of us are capable of doing. My body has been anchored in this spot all day. Not even once has the urge to urinate shown up, an indicator of dehydration, but the shadows seem to have no concern about it.

Repetitious prayers continue…

Please, God. Please have mercy on us. Please rescue us.

Grant Parker the needed clarity on how to find us. Please let my phone be a guide. Please, God...
Until sleep overtakes me.

Chapter Twenty-Seven

A cacophony of mayhem presses against my dreams. *Tata tat tat.... Tata tat tat.... Tata tat tat...* Distant at first, but quickly growing in ferocity. The orchestrated beats erupt into rapid-fire succession, completely eliminating the thin haze between sleep and reality. As urgent voices lash out in a mix of languages, my eyes finally open wide in alarm. My first instinct is to get up, but with a swift look around, I notice no one is moving from their beds. However, everyone is looking around, not able to see anything in the recesses of this prison.

Tata tat tat tat tat tat... The hasty beats finally register as machine gunfire.

"I'm scared," Annalise whispers as she wedges herself close to my side.

My arm pulls her in closer with wanting to offer protection against whatever conflict is progressing just outside. A barrage of bullets rings out, some ricocheting off the blocks of this building, mingling with shouts and more harsh language.

All at once, silence blankets us. It's as if the conflict never existed. The only evident noise is our heavy breathing. A few more moments pass before everyone drops their heads back down. The peace is short-lived and is completely destroyed when the boom of a severe explosion rocks the building.

I'm not sure if it's my body or Annalise's that is trembling—probably both. All I know to do is hold tight to her. Something strikes the door suddenly, causing my body to clear the mattress as a jolt of fear races through me. Everyone pops into a sitting position as the door is struck again. This time the force splinters a section away. Another strike, the door is disintegrated, revealing several figures dressed in fatigues wearing helmets with tinted face shields. They look more on the lines of massive robots with no human features revealed.

Rushing through the door while slinging their weapons across their backs, the soldiers begin picking up girls and running back out. Nothing is said, they are on a mission and all we can do is hope it's for our betterment. One soldier passes several girls as he heads straight to the back where a few of us are hunkered down. I offer Annalise first, thinking my turn will come, but he surprises me when he shuffles the little girl onto his left hip and picks me up with his right arm. Once we make it to the door, he hands Annalise over to another soldier. It's then that I realize no identification can be found on their uniforms—not even a patch with a flag to indicate the country they are representing.

We emerge with thick plumes of smoke surrounding us from a building burning rapidly towards the right, causing my lungs to expel a wheezing cough and set my eyes on fire. The wind shifts direction, and the smoke alleviates and reveals the sun. The harsh light hurts my eyes, but I'm unable to close them when I notice bodies deathly still and scattered along the ground—some displaying their lethal wounds while others don't.

"Close your eyes," the deep voice behind the shield orders. His hand secures my face into the crook of his neck as he begins to run, which is where I remain until we reach a Humvee. He climbs in the back with me cradled in his arms like I've become an extension of him.

"The other girls," I mutter, noticing more military vehicles lined up with this one.

"They're coming."

Another guy hurries into the front seat after he places a few more girls inside the vehicle and immediately takes off.

"I thought you were the driver."

His arms tighten around me. "Not today." He takes a ragged breath. "I don't think I can let you go."

It's only a short drive to where a C-17 sits idling. Through all of this bizarreness, I recall touring one of these cargo planes at an Airforce base during a visit. The driver doesn't even pause, but drives right up the open ramp and into the plane. Once the vehicle comes to a halt, the men rush out. They all hurry on to tasks needing to be done, but there's no chaos. It's all in a focus-driven manner.

Asher places me on his vacated seat and is about to dash off, but turns toward me before he gets too far. Feeling exposed, I cross my arms and hunch my shoulders to conceal where the wide rip in my tank top exposes my chest.

After taking a few steps back to the open vehicle door to block me from view, he pulls his helmet off, revealing a flushed face, and glances over his shoulder. "Gadget!"

"Yes, sir?" He doesn't wait for Asher's reply and is over to us in a flash. I catch a glimpse of his smaller frame just before Asher's massive frame angles in a way to block me from his sight.

"I need your undershirt," Asher answers.

The guy says nothing, but in the next instant Asher is pushing the tan shirt over my head and helping to pull my arms through the sleeves. It's still quite big on me, but does its job of covering up my body.

Kneeling down, Asher says, "We're setting up gurneys."

I glance through the window and see that a soldier is already placing Annalise on one. He has his helmet off as well as his jacket, making him look less intimidating. I want to go over to her, but feel close to collapsing. "Please tell them to take special care of Annalise. She… She gets sick easily."

"The little girl who was with you?"

"Yes."

Asher hurries over and speaks quickly to the soldier. He then bends down and says something to her as he points in my direction. I offer a weak smile and wave when she sees me. She nods her head and looks back to him. He says something else before hurrying back over.

Leaning into the vehicle, he asks, "Has she been given any type of drugs?"

"Not since I've been there."

He stands and directs his answer to the soldier caring for her. "She's good to go." He leans back down to me. "We're going to give her something to help her rest. One of the beds will be ready for you soon."

"I... I would rather sit please. I need... I need to sit."

His brows furrow, but he carries me over to the bank of chairs built into the side of the plane and places me on one. His hands deftly secure the harness over my shoulders and lap. Once that task is done, he sits back on his heels and looks me over again.

"Any wounds?"

I shake my head. "Just some bruises."

"Some?" Now he shakes his head, picking up my arm to glare pointedly at the dark patches. He moves on to examine my exposed feet that are caked with dark clay.

"They took my boots," I mumble.

His grunt is forceful, sounding close to pained. Saying nothing, he storms off, but is back before I can blink with two bottles of water and some cloths. Unscrewing the cap of one, he hands it over to me. I drink it greedily while watching him saturate the cloths with the other bottle of water.

Emotions threaten to overtake me as this man kneels before me and begins to wash my feet. Watching him do such a humble task, the memory of him brushing my hair while I was sick reflects through my thoughts.

From the very beginning I correctly saw him—Asher Reed is a superhero. More importantly, today the realization that he is *my* superhero clarifies. For someone of his stature, Sergeant of a Special Forces group, this amazing man seems to have no hesitance when it comes to offering comfort in the gentlest forms.

He is precise with this task, glancing up every so often to gage my wellbeing. After most of the clay is removed, he dries my feet.

"I'll be right over there." He points to where soldiers are already settling girls onto the gurneys with a few administering IV's, but I can tell he's hesitant to leave me.

"Go," I whisper.

With a firm nod, he strides over and starts unfolding more beds. Within the next fifteen minutes, the other side of the plane has become a makeshift hospital right before my eyes, with a total of fifteen patients strapped down and attended to.

More soldiers arrive, some helping bolt down the vehicles, while others stow their weapons. The plane engines begin to rise in volume as the men start strapping themselves into chairs. Asher takes the one to my left while a familiar face sits to my right as the plane ascends. We remain quiet until the plane levels out. Several men unstrap from their seats and beeline over to the girls and go back to attending to them.

Captain Shiloh pats me on the shoulder. "Young lady, do you realize you just took down one of the largest black markets in the world?" There's too much undeserved pride in his voice.

"No, sir. I didn't. You and your men did. You rescued me... and fifteen others..." My voice chokes off as everything hits me all at once. Abruptly, my bravado shatters, leaving me falling into millions of helpless pieces.

Questions begin whirling around my dizzy head.

What just happened?

How did I survive?

What... How...

A vicious tremor slams into my body as my vision dims around the edges.

"Ma'am?" The captain's voice is oddly distant. "Ma'am!"

Jumbled voices barely break though the roar attacking my ears as my eyesight blurs until fleeing away completely. A tingle nips at my fingertips before traveling up my arms, causing everything to go numbly cold.

"She's going into shock!"

Time caves in and swallows me.

UNTIL I DON'T

*****

The escape back from the thick fog takes a great deal of effort. Failing several times, I give in to it and remain in the darkness—push, stumble back... push, stumble back...

Slowly, very slowly, the edges of darkness pull away with the world welcoming me back as the sound of the plane's hum mingles with the chatter and activity surrounding me. I open my eyes and find myself staring at the rounded ceiling of the plane. Something grasps my face. As I try to pull it away, an odd pinch registers from moving my hand, drawing my focus to discovering an IV attached. Then, a set of sad hazel eyes catch my attention from beside me. Even odder is the fact that he's sharing the cramped gurney with me. I glance around, but no one seems to notice or care that this soldier is doing this. Lying on his side, he watches me carefully.

We do nothing but stare at each other for a while. I hold tightly to his gaze as my lifeline while breathing in and out with the aid of the oxygen mask. In... Out... Eventually, all of the cobwebs scoot away, leaving me feeling whole again—or close enough. With my untethered hand, I pull the mask down to my chin.

"I think I'm okay now," I whisper, trying to

smooth my voice out. From the narrowing of his eyes, Asher isn't buying it.

He says nothing, just reaches over and replaces the mask over my nose and mouth. My hand goes to remove it again, but he catches it and entwines our fingers before resting them both on my stomach.

"Rest," he quietly bosses, and this time I actually listen.

The nightmare nudges me, but I focus on the rescue and the comfort of knowing the girls are safe. Between the rescue and boarding the plane, I vaguely remember being told about another group of girls being rescued before us, who were being kept in a warehouse on the compound property. So I settle my thoughts there and keep my eyes locked onto my hero's, thanking God for the rescue and sending this man to do it. Eventually, exhaustion begins weighing me back down, so I give up and allow sleep to overtake me once again.

Chapter Twenty-Eight

Drifting in the land of nod for some unknown time, the rhythmic beeping of a machine and familiar voices whispering begin to release me from this desolate state. My heavy lids unhinge and reveal a jarring view.

Stooping beside my bed, a mess of a man stares at me at close range to my face, causing his annoying face to blur a bit. I jolt my head back so my eyes can focus on him. My hand itches to pop him for startling me, but I offer a glare instead.

"Wow, Neena. They must have given you some really good stuff. You've been snoring louder than a chainsaw at full throttle." He laughs at himself, like he's the funniest thing.

Clearing my throat, I say, "Wow, Bode. Looks like

the psych ward needs to readmit you. Are you off the meds again, wild man? Seriously, would it hurt you to buy a razor and get a haircut already?"

My hoarse words are nothing more than a taunt. His brown curls are a mess and his beard is a bit disheveled, looking like he's been sleeping sitting up, but I know I'm the reason behind this look. His tired, brown eyes squint with mischief at the moment, so I know he's about to deliver another jab. Bring it on! I need this right now. I need to feel normal and this silly squabbling with him feels close to that.

"Now, little sister, do we really want to get on the subject of rat's nest... I mean *hair*? Seriously, buy a flipping brush *already*."

"Your precious TV remote is toast next time." My eyes narrow even more while delivering this threat.

A subdued round of laughter pulls me away from bantering with my brother-in-law. I roll over onto my back and find myself surrounded by family members—Dad, Mom, Mia, and Parker. My eyes settle on my friend for a beat, scanning him over and finding him whole. The tightening in my chest alleviates a little more now that I know he's physically okay.

"Ah, our girl is going to be just fine if she's already bickering with Bode," Dad comments while patting my foot.

I scan the room until my eyes land on a set of hazel ones that are steadily watching me. Propped against the wall, still wearing fatigues along with a few days' worth of scruff shadowing his jaw, my superhero faintly lifts the corner of his mouth. This gift from him beckons my own lips to pull up in a smile.

"Neena, did you hear me?" Mom's southern drawl reels me back to the group.

"Sorry, what was that?" My achy body protests, but I scoot up onto the pillows in more of a seated position, being mindful of the IV still latched onto the top of my hand.

"We're just so proud of you." She sniffs, her blue eyes brimming with tears.

I move over and pat the spot beside me. Mom moves to sit there and gently lifts my tethered hand and places it on top of hers.

"Why?" I ask her.

Mom shakes her head. "Why? Because my daughter goes gallivanting all over this world on a mission to save it. Your heart is one of a kind, young lady."

"Thank you."

The sweet moment is shattered when my silent sister erupts in a tizzy.

Launching herself across my legs, Mia lets out a

jagged sob. "Neena... Never, never, never again." Her sobs hiccup between each word. "I can't let you do this dangerous stuff anymore!"

Feeling right lousy for making her this upset, I work my fingers through her soft hair to offer her comfort. "I'm fine... I'm okay."

She glances up abruptly, her nose and eyes red. "Well, I'm not!"

Bode eases over and rubs her back. "Come on, Babe. Neena has been through enough for now. We can get ahold of her real good in a few weeks." He offers me a wink as he pulls Mia to her feet and into his arms.

"Sweetheart, are you sure you're okay?" Mom eyes me, wanting the truth. I nod my head. "You sure?" she asks again, obviously not believing me.

"I will be," I whisper.

"The doctor said you refused a rape test... Neena, are you sure you're okay?" she whispers back.

Glancing around the room, it's clear every ear has heard her comment and is eagerly awaiting the answer. Taking a deep breath, I feel it necessary to offer them some reassurance, even at the cost of my privacy.

My eyes focus on the soft blanket draped over me as I say, "They... They were going to... but one glimpse at the scar on my abdomen changed their minds. Funny... I'm probably the first virgin in history to be deemed unclean." I release a humorless laugh.

Next thing I know, Mia is back clinging to my legs and sobbing.

The family keeps on debating whether I'm okay or not for a while, but I zone it out and keep alternating between staring at Parker and Asher—both wearing a mask of disquiet on their tired, handsome faces. A nurse comes in to check my vitals but is back out of the door quickly. Her uniform reminds me I'm in a military hospital in Missouri. I think it's Missouri...

I'm not sure how much time slips by, but the pressure in my chest begins to rise as well as the shrilling in my eardrums.

Dad walks over and clamps Asher on the shoulder. "Thank you, young man, for rescuing my daughter. Your captain was absolutely right about you."

I focus on him and his comment, feeling the heaviness ebb just a bit.

"Speaking of that," I start, causing Dad to turn back in my direction. "You owe him an apology as well." Both Dad and Asher look shocked by my stern declaration.

"Why's that?" Dad asks.

"You know as well as I do. I think his captain owes him one, too."

"Neena," Asher warns, but I continue on.

"You were both in cahoots with Asher becoming my neighbor."

Bode chooses to bark out in laughter at this and Dad actually looks a little ashamed, which confirms my accusation.

"We just thought—"

"Actually, sir, I owe you a great deal of gratitude for the both of you being in *cahoots* with me becoming your daughter's neighbor. It's the best deceptive ploy my captain has ever planned and executed. Thank you for aiding him." Asher shakes Dad's hand firmly.

"Richard, you looking to switch your murder mystery genre for *romance*?" All eyes dart to Bode, finding him waggling his eyebrows at Dad.

Dad's relieved face turns steely as he says to Bode, "Don't ever forget what I told you on your wedding day, son." He pauses for effect. "At *least* a dozen ways."

"A dozen ways to what?" Mom asks what we all want to know.

"To murder someone and dispose the body without leaving trace evidence." Bode rambles this off, sounding like he's heard Dad threaten this more than once.

"Oh, Dad, your book tour," I mutter with the thought just hitting me.

"I cancelled the remaining stops."

"I'm so sorry."

"Nonsense. What you did is heroic. Me signing a book is insignificant in comparison. Here's where I need to be. Besides, your mother and I are ready to be back in Tennessee. We need to be here to keep you straight since your sister is failing at it miserably."

His ill-timed joke pulls another gut-wrenching sob from Mia. "Dad!" She screeches, looking at him in pure horror.

"That wasn't funny, Dad," I reprimand.

"Sorry," he says around a laugh that he's sharing with Bode and Bode only.

Everyone else has a stony expression edging onto their weary faces.

With this matter settled, the conversation moves on. A nasally Mia talks about the rescue and how little Annalise is back with her family. Mom discusses some of the news stories about a special ops group taking down a deadly black market in Africa. Dad talks about the poor girls and how abused and malnourished some were. With each passing piece of this conversation, the pressure rebuilds in my chest. Tingles prick my arms as my heartrate rises. The hasty beeping of the machine finally stills the room.

Asher pushes off the wall and is by my side in a flash.

"Get this off of me." I motion to the two wires stuck to my chest that are snaking out from the top of my hospital gown, wanting a nurse to remove it, but he surprises me by turning the monitor off and freeing the round stickers from my chest. I don't know if this is against the rules, but right now I really don't care.

Mom asks that dreaded question once more, "Neena, are you okay?"

No!

I'm not fine!

I'm about to break!

"Umm… could I talk to Parker alone? Please?" The words barely choke out of me as my vision distorts.

They all cast concerned looks my way, but quickly exit. Parker steps over and sits in the spot on the bed Mom just vacated. I glance over and see Asher pushing the door closed.

"Asher—"

"I'm not leaving." The three words leave no room for argument. He resumes his post by the wall, watching me guardedly.

Turning my eyes back to Parker, all I have to do is reach my arms out. He knows and wraps his arms firmly around me, tucking me in his safe embrace, allowing me to break. His body holds a reserved tremble, showing just enough of our shared hurt but not enough that I can't just let it out and be vulnerable in this moment. This is how we cope with the nightmares we have willingly launched ourselves into over the years. The role has been reversed in some instances, with me allowing him to break.

I allow the evil of human trafficking, the angry encounter with the informant, my abduction, being stripped and then beaten, opening my eyes in that desolate room for the first time, sweet, little Annalise, those terrified girls with bruises so deep they will never heal... I allow all of it to rip through my overwhelmed body and release in fierce sobs while clinging to Parker's shirt.

Once I calm down some, he leans close to my ear. "They arrested a total of thirty men and women at the compound. At least that many more are being investigated. I'm talking key players. So far, twelve more black markets have been infiltrated overseas, as well as two here in the U.S. that had direct ties to the one in Uganda. Over a hundred women and children have already been rescued in the last few days..."

Parker knows the facts are what I need right now, the reassurance we did what we set out to do. By the time he rattles off more information, mainly about the girls being dispersed to hospitals and Annalise being back with her family, my sobs have subsided.

"The informant turned himself in. In exchange for more information, he will be served a lesser sentence. He helped us find you."

"He did?"

"Yeah. He also said something about needing to know more about your God and His forgiveness... Only you, Neena Cameron, would be witnessing to someone while they pushed a knife in your neck."

A sharp intake of breath pulls my eyes over to Asher, reminding me he doesn't know everything that happened over there. From the fire ignited in his eyes, I'd say maybe it's best he doesn't know all of it.

Looking back to Parker, I say, "Thank you for having my back."

His expression falters to what looks like shame. "I didn't." Now he looks disgusted. "I can't believe I let you slip through my fingers that day. Turned my back for a second and you were gone." A quick huff escapes his gritted teeth.

"That's nonsense and you know it. I'm to blame. I intentionally wandered off from you that day, trying to draw their attention."

Another frustrating huff sounds near the wall, but I ignore it.

"You never make it easy on me." Parker leans away and gives me a sly smirk that goes nowhere near his stormy eyes.

"I think it's time I leave you alone for a while. Get your butt home to Connecticut, marry Danielle, have some beautiful babies to cherish." I pull him in for a hug before pushing him off the bed.

Standing by the bed, Parker opens his mouth to say something, but seems to think better of it. He glances over to Asher before returning his attention to me. "All you have to do is call when you're ready to write the article. I'll be there."

"I know," I acknowledge barely over a whisper, knowing this time I'm going to actually leave him alone and handle it myself. No matter how harsh the realization disappoints my heart and stings my eyes, it's time I let Parker Davidson go.

Parker places a soft kiss against my forehead, nods to Asher, and heads out.

As soon as the door closes, Asher pushes off the wall and eliminates the space between us in only a few long strides. He doesn't stop until he picks me up and cradles me in his arms. He takes my spot on the bed and just holds me, and I can't think of anything I need more right now than him and his strength.

"I'm so sorry. So sorry," he murmurs into the side of my neck. His lips press against the very spot where the knife penetrated, making it clear the mark is still visible. I've not heard him sound this shaken since our falling-out.

"Me too."

He leans back, the camouflage completely removed from his gaze to reveal a deluge of emotions. "It's all on me, sweetheart." The look he gives me leaves no room for argument.

I nod my head. He seems to accept this answer and places his head against the side of mine.

"Parker's name isn't in any of the bylines for your articles," he says out of the blue.

"No. His name is always listed along the pictures he's taken." I nestle closer to his chest, so the lullaby of his heart can reach me.

"But he said he would help you write the article when you're ready."

"Some of our reports are hard to deal with, and over the years he's always shown up with food and moral support. This way I don't have to relive whatever we unearthed by myself."

Asher grunts his response, just as what he's actually saying registers to me.

"How do you know what's listed or not listed on my bylines?" I glance up curiously.

"Theo gave me copies of your articles. I read the one from last November... I had no idea what you and Parker had just gone through." He groans in frustration. "And the article about my unit... Neena, you did nothing but honor us. With you gone, I had time to think over the last year and how you've been so supportive of me. And all I've done is be a certified jerk to you and your friends. I'm really ashamed of how I treated you."

This is the longest set of words Asher Reid has ever strung together in my presence and I'm left without one word to offer in return.

"I love you," he says after a brief silence.

Well, I know how to respond to those words. "I love you, too."

More time slips by until Asher's eyes grow heavy and his head wanders back against the pillow. Who knows how long it's been since he's actually slept. Mom peeks her head in the door at some point, sees Asher holding me as he sleeps, and quietly recloses it to allow us privacy.

Later, I'm not sure how much later, I grow antsy. Testing to see how deeply he's sleeping, I whisper, "Asher?"

"Yes," he responds immediately, completely alert.

"I want to go home."

He pulls a phone I've never seen from his pocket, hits a button and begins speaking. "I need the plane ready to take Miss Cameron and her family home, ASAP." He listens and then hangs up before retrieving the phone by the bed. "This is Sergeant

Reid. I need Miss Cameron's discharge papers."

Asher takes care of things as he does everything else, with precision and no time wasted. He stands up and places me on the bed before gathering a few things from a supply cabinet. The next thing I know he's removing my IV.

Watching him carefully, I mutter, "Umm... Should you be doing that?"

"I'm the one who put it in," he says as he eases the needle out of my skin.

"How do you know how to do that?"

He places a bandage on top of my hand, and then a kiss, causing my eyes to water up from his tenderness. "Everyone in my unit has to be medically trained to an extent. Just basic stuff, but we need to be prepared in case situations arise."

Our private bubble is interrupted by a nurse, a familiar-looking soldier entering the room, followed by my family. They all look worn out.

Clearly, we need to go home.

Chapter Twenty-Nine

A truce was finally presented between me and Mr. Superhero. It looked like our days of butting heads would finally be behind us.

It lasted until the plane touched down on Tennessee soil.

"I don't like it," Asher gritted out in a sneer once we reached home.

"Don't I know it," I sassed back before slamming the door in his face and locking it before he could reopen it.

It's been close to a week since I demanded he give me time to myself. I also reminded him about last November when I needed some space, but Asher was still not pleased. It's how I've always dealt with things. Maybe it's time to change that, he argued. He's probably right, and I've been considering all of this while burrowed away these last few days. He has respected my wishes, but the food is delivered each day, reminding me even though I may need to be alone, I'm not alone. He has no idea how much that means to me.

The exterior bruises have mostly healed and the cut on my neck only holds a pink reminder of its existence. But the interior bruises riddled deeply into my memories and soul will take longer.

During this time of much-needed isolation, I've worked on overcoming what happened in Uganda with lots of prayer and lots of rest. The only contact with the outside world has been via email and texts. Parker sent pictures that he managed to snag after we were all evacuated out of the compound. After looking at them, I recoiled back into a dark hole and haven't been able to write one word for the article. It's due to go to press next week, but there's no forcing my mind to get with it.

A knock at the door releases me from the stare-down I'm in the midst of having with my blank word document. It's been taunting me on the computer screen for the last several hours. Glancing at the clock, the time shows the delivery guy to be a little earlier than normal. Tossing my wrinkled robe on over my ratty pajamas, I head over and open the door. What I find is outright nerve-racking and causes my reflex to slam the door, but a giant foot halts the process when its owner wedges it in the way.

"Asher said for you to get dressed and allow us to take you out to eat," the familiar man says with just as much authority as Mr. Boss normally applies.

I glance at the whole lot of them, five burly men in all, and shake my head. "I'm good. You guys go have a good time." I push on the door with all my might, but another guy, a slightly smaller framed one who I'm pretty sure gave up his shirt to me, easily pushes the door open with the palm of his hand. With no helmet to obscure him, I realize he has red hair and a dusting of freckles along the bridge of his nose.

"He said not to take no for an answer," Gadget says, an eyebrow raised in challenge. "I'm Garrett by the way." He strolls right past me like he was invited in.

Ugh. These guys mean business. Asher mentioned in a text that a few of his buddies would be staying with him for a couple of weeks. I've heard them come and go, but this is the first time I've laid eyes on them in civilian clothing. Nevertheless, they are just as intimidating now as they were wearing fatigues and sporting mean-looking weapons. Without waiting for permission, they file in and overwhelm my small living space with their imposing forms.

The guy with black hair, who seems close to Asher's size, steps closer as he eyes me. "And I'm Nick." He points to the guy in glasses without looking away from me. "Wes." He then points to the black man with stunning blue eyes. "And Devon."

"It's nice to meet you," I say awkwardly, wrapping the robe closer around me.

"Asher also said to make sure you brushed your hair first." Nick smirks as his dark eyes roam over my frizzy hair.

Nick's comment somehow snaps me out of my haze. Hands on hips, I sass, "And what exactly is wrong with my hair? I just fixed it, I'll have you know." I would run my hand through the frizz, but I'm pretty sure my hand would get caught in the snares of some aggressive knots. My hand safely flips the ends instead. "It takes effort to look this good."

This earns me a lip twitch from each of the giants invading my house, which is very reminiscent of their Sergeant.

"Did the big lug offer special training for that lip twitch maneuver?"

A few coughs ring out to cover laughs.

"No, but our Sergeant did train us in following through with orders. So we can do this the easy way, little lady, or the hard way," Devon threatens while going as far as cracking his neck.

All five men cross their arms and fix their best steely gazes in my direction. Good grief. They are most definitely not playing around. Visions of me being hogtied and hauled out of here against my will have me shuffling toward the stairs immediately.

Throwing my hands in the air, I huff out, "Fine!" before deliberately stomping upstairs. Their chuckles reach me before I slam the bedroom door.

By the time I've washed, dressed, and managed to tame my hair into silky waves, I reemerge to a sparkling clean living room and kitchen. I feel a little embarrassed I let the place go since returning home, yet awestruck that they would willingly clean it up for me. Stunned, I look around and find all five men squeezed into my dining room, studying my word wall.

"What's up with this?" Wes asks without looking away from the sea of words.

"If I find a unique word, I write it on the wall so as not to forget it."

Garrett grins widely and points at Asher's name.

"Do you realize his name means *happy one*?" I ask from behind them as their focus continues to peruse the wall.

This remark delivers a round of laughter from the

entire group.

"What's this one mean?" Wes points to the word bifurcate.

"It means to divide, branch off, fork."

"Gobbledygook?" Devon laughs out.

"Nonsense, just as it sounds when saying it." I smile.

The word lesson continues for a few more rounds with this unlikely group of students, until Nick glances back at me and releases a low, exaggerated whistle.

"*Dang...* Motor has snagged himself one fine-looking lady." Everyone nods in agreement with Nick's assertion.

I smooth the front of my white, gauzy top and fix them with a pointed look. "We've met what, three times now? And you're just realizing this fact?"

Lip twitches are quickly replaced with a round of deep chuckles.

The somber interviews in a desert after losing one of their brothers, and then the rescue mission in a jungle full of wickedness, and them storming in while I projected the wild woman façade are the only times I've interacted with these men. Yet, they feel like a part of my family with deeply rooted bonds. I guess the shared history of such catastrophic circumstances can have that effect.

Garrett steps over to me and offers his arm. "We're doing this the easy way and just walking out of here, right, pretty lady?"

"Do I have any other choice?" I weave my arm around his elbow.

"Asher warned you're a feisty one, but I think us guys could handle hauling you out of here if need be."

"No need for that this time. I'm starving, so let's go."

Fifteen minutes later, we are pulling up to Charlie Mikes. The only vehicles in the parking lot are Asher's Hummer and Nick's giant Yukon.

"Where's the normal crowd of customers?" I mumble as we unload.

Devon picks me up off the backseat and sets me down without permission before closing the door. It's clear when these men see a task needing to be performed, they just instinctively take care of it. "Thought you knew this place is closed on Sundays."

I run my hands through my hair while trying to mentally pull up a calendar. It's a bit unnerving to not be able to locate the date, much less what day of the week I'm currently residing in.

"It's Sunday?" I ask absently as the guys guide me to the back entrance, treating me like I'm incapable of handling it by my own wits. They probably think I've lost all sense of direction along with my grasp of time.

"All day long," Wes answers. He pulls the door open and we enter the empty dining area with most of the lights off. The familiar crowd may be nonexistent today, but the succulent aromas wafting from the kitchen are present and welcoming.

As my stomach takes to growling in approval, I notice two tables near the kitchen door have been pushed together and set with silverware and dishes. A few frosty pitchers of tea and hearty baskets of cornbread take up the long center.

Garrett pulls a chair out and motions for me to have a seat. The rest of the guys claim a chair, leaving the one to my right vacant. The conversation is centered on some baseball game. I tune it out and think about wandering into the kitchen. Just as Wes begins filling our glasses, Asher pushes through the kitchen door with a massive platter of BBQ ribs. The sight of him sporting his black chef's coat turns my growling stomach silent, realizing just how much I've missed him in the last several weeks.

His camouflage eyes seem to not be in a sharing mood, only holding that blank stare as he places the platter down. He slides his gaze from me over to Nick and nods his head toward the kitchen. Nick is up and following him after the silent command, only to return moments later with other platters. Both men place the food on the table and settle into their seats with Asher taking the vacant spot beside me.

The guys go to town piling their plates a mile-high while chattering away. Asher glances around at them before focusing on me. His eyes scan my face, my neck, my exposed arms, and then back to my face. He brushes the tips of his fingers under my shadowy eyes and then to the hollow of my cheeks. The bruises may have faded, but the impact is still lingering slightly, I suppose.

"You've not been eating the food I've sent?" he quietly asks, brows pinching together in concern. He cups my cheek, and I automatically lean into the comfort of his palm.

"Mostly," I try reassuring him. "I've not had much of an appetite though." My throat thickens as my vulnerability surfaces, but I manage to swallow it down along with my unshed tears and offer him a weak smile.

"I should have kicked your door down and force-fed you." His posture stiffens all of sudden before cutting his eyes to the group gathered around the table. It's then that I realize they have fallen silent and are curiously watching us. "What?" he growls out sharply.

The guys seem to think it's in their best interest

not to answer, but Asher's stern glare won't relent—his understated authority over them evident.

The guys cautiously look to one another for direction. A few offer a half-shrug or a subtle head shake.

Garrett takes a deep breath and holds up a finger, requesting a moment to gather his thoughts, before saying, "The nuance of your approach is just so laden with garish veneration, it stunned us."

Asher drops his hand from my cheek and full-on regards the group. "*What?*" This time the word is filled with confused curiosity.

They are surprised at how openly he adores me, but I keep that to myself and listen as they continue to spew unusual words. I'm impressed they actually absorbed so much earlier even if they aren't quite using them properly.

"Clearly, you've eradicated your inhibitions about falling in love." Wes points to me. "Neena has become your cynosure."

Cynosure – something that strongly attracts attention.

"Neena, you're one impressive lagniappe. Asher is completely enamored by you," Devon adds, botching his use of the word.

Lagniappe – special gift, benefit used as a marketing tool.

The guys crack up at this with me joining in. I

decide not correct Devon since he managed to pronounce it correctly.

Asher snorts. "Guess you girls enjoyed Neena's word wall."

"My favorite word of them all had to be the strange five-letter word that means *happy one*," Nick taunts with the guys roaring in laughter.

I lean my head against Asher's thick shoulder and admit, "It's my most favorite word of them all, too."

Asher drops a quick kiss on top of my head. "Food's getting cold. Let's say grace and eat."

All heads bow as he gives thanks for the food and for each one present at the table. The rest of the late afternoon is spent grazing over the delicious fare provided by my Top Chef while the guys share stories with intentions of trying to embarrass one another. Before we conclude, I've discovered Nick is Nickel, Compass is Wes, and Midnight is Devon. Everyone thanks me for the gifts I sent to them. Asher even thanks me for his apple turnovers, which was the one request mentioned in his letter.

I stay behind with Asher to help clean up while the guys head out to go bowling. We were invited but declined. He busies himself with cleaning the grill top and counters while I tackle the dishes. My hands are deep in bubbly dishwater when I feel Asher's arms wrap around me. He places a caress to the side of my neck.

"Let's head home."

"But I have a few more pots." I begin to scrub the bottom of a stubborn one, but Asher pulls the scrubber out of my hand and offers me a towel. He's Mr. Bossy Pants in full force today.

*****

Once we reach my door, I pause before unlocking it. "Thank you for... everything." I ease onto my tiptoes and place a timid kiss to his lips. He says nothing—shocker—so I unlock the door and step in. I'm about to shut the door when I realize he's making his way inside also.

"Umm... What exactly does Parker do while you write your articles?" Asher asks as he unbuttons and removes his chef coat.

His question comes out of left field, confusing me a bit. He kicks his shoes off, making it clear he plans on staying a while. I follow suit and remove my boots.

"He usually just hangs out near me. Sometimes he does some of his own work on his laptop." I shrug, looking around the clean room.

Asher motions toward the couch. "So all you need is for me to just quietly sit beside you."

It's then that I understand exactly what his intentions are and I can't help but smile. "You're an expert at quietly sitting, but why do you want to do that?"

"I know you and Parker have been a team for a long time. Same as with me and my guys. But I think it's time you and I become a team." He says nothing more, just takes a seat on the couch and patiently waits for me to join him.

After I gather my emotions, I gather my laptop and notebook. Settling on the couch, I reopen the blank document. My fingers hover over the keys, but continue to be lost on which key to press first.

Asher seems to pick up on my hesitation and shifts closer. "What's the problem?"

I sneak a side-glance at him before directing my focus back to the laptop. "I don't know how to begin..."

He remains quiet for a while before saying, "What drew your interest to this in the first place?"

Good question. I collect my thoughts, thinking all the way back to almost two years ago. "I have a little blog—"

"Little? Sweetheart, you have close to a million followers."

Astonished, I look back at him. "How do you know that?"

"You're worth knowing. I've been working on doing just that."

"Oh…" I let that admission sink in.

"So… The blog had a part in this?" He points to my notebook with *human trafficking* scribbled on the cover.

"One of my followers sent me a private email. She told me about her adopted daughter. The little girl was only six at the time and had been sold by her birth mom. We exchanged several emails after this. She even shared a few photos of the little girl posing with her and her husband. They looked like an ordinary picture-perfect family. No outward sign was evident of what that little girl suffered. At first I was grateful that she had a happy ending, but then something started eating at me. I couldn't sleep, nor could I focus on anything else. I prayed, knowing God was trying to tell me something. It became blatantly clear that light had to be shed on the hushed crime of human trafficking. It's as though the world doesn't want to admit such a wicked evil exists, but it's at the expense of millions of innocent victims."

The blush of my cheeks creeps down my neck with my emotions becoming riled up.

"There's your beginning."

I glance over, blinking the tears back. Asher nods to the keyboard for me to get on with it, so I do. My fingers rapidly fly over the keyboard for the next few hours, only to pause when I need to talk something out with him. He even gives me a perspective from the soldier's view of what transpired in Uganda.

Close to one in the morning, I email the rough draft to Theo. Feeling the weight lift from my shoulders, I stand and stretch out my stiff back.

"Do you remember what the letter I wrote you said?"

I look over at him and watch as he stands. "I have it memorized," I admit.

Dear Sir,

They call me Motor for obvious reasons. My old man owns a garage, so I knew how to do an oil change way before I mastered tying my shoes. I was already driving before I hit double digits in age, a benefit of living on quiet country roads. Everyone said it was my calling to take over my old man's business one day, but I felt a deeper calling.

I HATE when someone hurts. It causes me pain. In school I had a tendency of ending up in the principal's office for beating up the bullies. I've always wanted to protect the weak. So here I am, manning the wheel of my unit's Humvee while protecting a weak world from the nastiest bullies known to mankind.

You asked us to share our dreams. Mine are simple, a world without evil bullies...

And a world filled with the tastiest food ever prepared. Yes, I'm sick of MRE's. How about in exchange for this letter, you send us some apple turnovers. Man, I can almost taste them.

Sincerely,

Motor

He truly meant it when he admitted to hating when someone hurts. I've seen my own hurt cause him pain. Needing to be closer, I take a step and wrap my arms around his waist while settling my ear against his chest to listen to his steady heartbeat.

"So you remember the part about me confessing my dreams?"

"Yes. 'A world without bullies.'" I quote, but then quietly laugh at remembering the next part. "'And a world filled with the tastiest food.' You have most certainly filled *my* world with the tastiest food."

His protective hands rub along my back. "I've got a new dream."

"Yeah? What's your new dream?" My shoulders tense up, worrying he's going to say he's rejoining the military or something.

"A life with you. Neena, I don't think I can ever let you go again."

I lift my head from his chest and gaze up into his sincere eyes. "Then don't."

Epilogue - *Asher*

Don't. It's the first word that flinted through my mind the moment my eyes landed on this exasperating woman. Neena Cameron infiltrated my life, taking me on like I was her covert duty to complete. And man did she commit to the mission at hand. *Relentless*—another word that pushes *don't* to the side. She's relentless. And she gave me no other choice but to relent.

The sun glances off her light-brown hair as I watch her smooth a ruffle on her lacy dress. The color is a creamy white, making her look angelic, even with the dusty cowgirl boots adorning her feet. She fidgets with a lock of her wavy hair, causing the daisy tucked behind her ear to sit lopsided. I reach out and set it right before placing my hand back to my side. It's killing me not to smile at her, but I stubbornly hold it back, knowing now's not the time. I have to stay strong. She's gave me no choice in anything when it comes right down to it, and so I have no other choice but to do what I'm about to do.

"Are you ready, Sergeant Reid?"

I stand a bit taller in my dress blues, hoping to garner some courage, and nod my head. I gather Neena's tiny hands in mine, knowing that's where they belong.

"I, Asher Reid, don't want to survive another day without you. I don't want to welcome another sunrise or celebrate another sunset without you as my wife. I don't need any other blessing but you. I don't see any other desirable choice but to love, honor, and cherish you unconditionally for the rest of my days."

Her sassy eyes sparkle and I catch the corner of her lip twitch. I want to call her out on it, but, again, now's not the time. There will be plenty of time later when we ditch all of these people gathered here in this apple orchard—the very same one where Neena picked those apples for the pie she gave me the first time we met—to witness me finally claiming this amazing woman as my wife.

"You only managed to work four don'ts into your wedding vows." She doesn't hold back the smirk.

The pastor clears his throat, so Neena grows serious, or so I hope.

"I, Neena Cameron soon-to-be-Reid, admit I've called you many names since we've met. I even made a list, but I am most honored to add husband to the list today and know beyond knowing it will be my most beloved name for you." She looks toward the guests sitting on old church pews under the shade of apple trees. "Asher means happy one, and truly today, I declare that I'm the happy one to be blessed with this man to be a part of my life." When she meets my gaze again, the blue of her beautiful eyes shimmers. "You're my partner and I am proud to have you protectively by my side. I don't want a day to go by that you don't see firsthand how much I love you, honor you, and cherish you for the rest of the days God grants me on this earth."

She only hit two with the word don't. I win!

There's no waiting for Chase to conclude before I pull Neena into my arms and kiss my wife for the first time, knowing I don't ever have to let her go.

Sacrifice - the surrender or destruction of something prized or desirable for the sake of something considered as having a higher or more pressing claim.

Our troops, brave and unyielding, surrender their lives daily for the sake of our freedom. Have you ever stopped to think about exactly what that sacrifice holds in its gallant grips?

These brave men and women sacrifice:

Family life.

Simple dreams we take for granted such as love, friendships, hobbies.

Health.

Their lives.

John 15:13 sums it up best. "Greater love hath no man than this, that a man lay down his life for his friends."

Do we count ourselves as friends to this courageous group? Faces we've never glimpsed, voices that have never reached our ears... Out there, sacrificing for us.

NL Cameron
aka T.I. Lowe

Also…

Even though this is a work of fiction, Human Trafficking is not. It's a living breathing nightmare that has claimed millions of victims. The letters I shared in Chapter 21 are from an actual victim whom I've become email pen pals with over the last two years. Her story devastated me and I know God sent her to help me share the truth about this vicious crime. Please pray that God continues to heal "Scarlet" and the millions of others.

If you'd like to learn more on Human Trafficking and how to help, check out Courage World @ https://courageworldwide.org/

Until I Don't Playlist

"There Will be a Day" Jeremy Camp
"God Made Girls" Raelynn
"I Don't Dance" Lee Brice
"Greater" MercyMe
"Never Say Never" The Fray
"Cast My Cares" Finding Favour
"Rollercoaster" Bleachers
"It's Not Over Yet" for King & Country
"Limitless" Colton Dixon

ABOUT THE AUTHOR

If T.I. isn't writing a book, she's reading one. She's proud to be a part of a tiny town in South Carolina where she is surrounded by loved ones and country fields.

For a complete list of Lowe's published books, biography, upcoming events, and other information, visit www.tilowe.com and be sure to check out her blog, COFFEE CUP, while you're there!

She loves to connect with her reading friends.

ti.lowe@yahoo.com

www.facebook.com/T.I.Lowe

Made in the USA
Middletown, DE
06 June 2024

55423262R00257